A TEMPORARY RESIDENCE

OTHER BOOKS BY HELEN HUDSON

Tell the Time to None
Meyer Meyer
Farnsbee South
The Listener
Criminal Trespass

A
Temporary
Residence

HELEN HUDSON

G. P. PUTNAM'S SONS / NEW YORK

Published by G. P. Putnam's Sons,
200 Madison Avenue, New York, NY 10016
Published simultaneously in Canada by
General Publishing Co. Limited, Toronto

The text of this book is set in Garamond.

Library of Congress Cataloging-in-Publication Data

Hudson, Helen.
A temporary residence.

1. Japanese Americans—Evacuation and relocation,
1942–1945—Fiction.   I. Title.
PS3558.U29T4   1987   813'.54   87-10856
ISBN 0-399-13312-7

Printed in the United States of America
1   2   3   4   5   6   7   8   9   10

The Mt. Hope Assembly Center never existed. But there were many camps just like it in the United States during World War II. In creating Mt. Hope, I leaned heavily on a great number of sources. Among them, the following were especially helpful for my purposes: *Farewell to Manzanar* by Jeanne Wakatsuki Houston (Houghton Mifflin, 1973); *The Governing of Men* by Alexander Leighton (Princeton University Press, 1945); *The Great Betrayal* by Audrie Girdner and Anne Loftis (Macmillan, 1969); *Journey to Topaz* by Yoshiko Ushida (Scribner's, 1971); *The Kikuchi Diary* by John Modell (University of Chicago Press, 1973); and the Human Relations Area Files in New Haven, Connecticut.

In addition, I would like to thank Yoshitaka Nishizawa for his generous advice with certain aspects of the work.

—HELEN HUDSON

To the victims—particularly Estelle Ishigo

With special thanks to my son, Thomas Lane

A TEMPORARY RESIDENCE

"Welcome to Mt. Hope," the old sign read: "The World's Most Beautiful Racetrack, Playground of Millionaires, Sport of Kings." The new sign was shorter, welcoming a different clientele. It read simply, "Welcome to the Mt. Hope Assembly Center." But it was a hot, dry, dusty welcome. For Mt. Hope was not a playground anymore. The whole area had been bulldozed so that no trees, no shade remained. Only the racetrack was still there, still tearing its way through the center. But around it the grandstand was empty. The luxurious restaurants and bars and the noisy betting booths had been converted into living quarters, like the stables beyond, from which the horses had only lately been removed. Even the ramps were still there.

The parking lots, once crowded with Lincolns and Duesenbergs and Rolls-Royces, were now filled with newly built barracks, blunt, crude buildings covered with tar paper. They were drawn up stiffly into blocks of fourteen, each with its own mess hall and latrine and wash house and recreation hall. But many were unfinished, their roofs forming funnels for the wind. They stretched across the asphalt and spread out into the fields. Only the administration building just inside the gate, and the staff and military quarters just outside, were finished. Solid buildings, they stood up squarely to the wind and the sun and the sand. Off season, the heat was oppressive, but the administration building and staff houses controlled their own climate. The air-conditioning moaned like a disappointed crowd.

The entire area was enclosed in a barbed-wire fence. Beyond it, a narrow road led up to the gate—and back. Otherwise there was nothing but desert, scruffy as an old goat. The fence was broken intermittently by high towers complete with soldiers and searchlights and machine guns—waiting for the desert to rear up and attack?

Clouds of dust appeared above the road. Over the gate, an enormous American flag waved frantically, waving a violent welcome to a long line of rickety buses. Beneath it, a tiny band of soldiers stared at the road and waited nervously. The wind rose, tall as a man, and screwed sand into their faces.

In the distance, Mt. Hope crouched on the horizon and stared at the camp with a hole where its head should be.

ONE

THEY streamed into the mess hall, masses and masses of small, quiet people with black hair and black eyes, the men in colored shirts and the women in dark dresses; neat, smooth-faced women with hats and gloves. They included all ages and all classes. Some were highly educated, some illiterate. Some had once been rich, others had always been poor. Some spoke only Japanese, some only English. Some spoke one dialect, some another. They came, originally, from different regions and different climates. They practiced different religions—Shintoism, variations of Buddhism, and different sects of Christianity. They did not even look alike, except to the Caucasians, whose round fish-eyes were unable to perceive distinctions; who had no idea that every ripple in the lake, every wave in the sea, every petal on the flower was different.

Now they waited patiently to be interrogated and fingerprinted, to have their bags and their bodies searched, to be examined and inoculated with huge doses of serum, enough to immunize the horses they had displaced; to report case histories and to be given numbers and badges and assigned to quarters—one room to a family. If there were fewer than five in the family, they would share their space with strangers. They stood in long queues, their arms sagging from the weight of babies and bundles and the hours piling up.

A large American flag stood in one corner of the hall and large American soldiers lined the walls. Everytime the door opened to let in more people, a vicious wind came with them, swirling sand into their faces, scattering papers, waving the flag. Work stopped while papers were gathered up and sorted. The queues bent and curled back around themselves, trapping the people inside.

Cots had been placed at the back of the hall for the faint and the sick. Most of them were occupied. One old woman lay on a stretcher, making strange sounds as if she had swallowed an egg beater. Near her, on an enormous suitcase, a plump, middle-aged woman in a purple kimono fanned herself with a huge silk fan decorated with gold and lacquer. Her face was white with rice powder and her black wig stood up high and stiff with pomade. She was shouting angrily at her daughters-in-law, two slim young women in blue-flowered *yukata* who rubbed her wrists and wiped her brow and fanned her steadily, their faces shining with perspiration.

Near the door, two little Japanese nuns with their hands up their sleeves waited for the busload of orphans to arrive. A young man with a violin under his chin swayed to music no one else could hear. An old man stood all alone, holding an open book close to his face as if trying to feel the print with his eyeballs.

In the center of the hall, teenaged boys and girls in trousers and saddle shoes, carrying guitars and baseball bats, laughed and teased each other in English. They were Nisei, born in America, who dressed and sounded and acted like Americans.

Near them, a group of old men, known as Issei, stood with their backs to them in silence. They had been born in Japan and had come to this country as young men. They had worked hard. They had laid down roads and railroads and scooped out mines. They had farmed and fished and planted and harvested. But they had never been allowed to become citizens or own land; and they had never been able to marry. They had earned a meager living and now even that had been taken from them. They had not much living left. They would spend it in a racetrack, like horses. The gates of the camp had closed behind them. They would die here and be buried beyond the barbed-wire fence in a barren field with that sawed-off mountain sending its harsh breath across their graves, scattering their dust.

The two groups, the young Nisei and the old Issei, stood close together but kept their backs to each other. They did not even speak the same language.

The old woman on the stretcher was making whirring noises now, as if her insides were being beaten to a froth.

Mr. Ishii, in his World War I uniform, held his grandson, Ken-chan, close to his chest and stared stonily at the American flag in the corner. Once he had followed that flag with a gun in his hand expecting to kill or be killed. Now he was being "processed"—like cheese. It was a shame not to be endured. In Japan he would not have endured it. But here he could do nothing because of the boy in his arms; nothing except to wear that outdated uniform to shame the *hakujin*. But they had no shame, those people with their big noses sticking out into other people's faces and other people's business; with their loud voices and coarse manners—boasting and shouting and interrupting; people with too little hair on their heads and too much everywhere else. No wonder they had that offensive animal smell, *bata-kusai*, like rancid butter. They paid no attention to his uniform, only to his face, which they considered all wrong. But it was the uniform that was wrong. It was much too tight across the shoulders; because of the boy in his arms?

The Matsuis, mother and daughter, stood huddled together. They were both named Emiko and known as Emmy and Miko. But Danny Matsui, husband and father, was missing. He had been arrested two weeks after Pearl Harbor.

Little Miko was holding on to her mother's wrist with both hands, looking desperately around the room, looking for her father. But all she could see were buttons and belts and dangling pocketbooks. She had never seen so many people in one place before. They were like a high wall that kept pushing against her, trying to push her—where? She thought of the children in school, calling her "dirty Jap," telling her to go back to Japan. She thought of that long, hot, stuffy, crowded bus ride that went on and on and on with not enough to eat and nothing to drink and a seat that bounced and rattled and rocked and poked sharp points into her day and night. So many days and nights that Daddy would never be able to find them. She tugged at her mother's arm. "Let's go home," she whispered. "I don't like it in Japan."

A very young white woman with long pale hair was leaning against the wall beside her young Japanese husband. They were both handsome, though their hair and their skin and their features had taken slightly different turns. But they were exactly the same height, leaning together in perfect parity against the wall of a Japanese internment camp. Nina Curry looked about to cry.

Sam Curry put his arm around her. "It will be all right, darling," he said. "It's only for a little while. Remember what the evacuation notice said: 'a *temporary* residence.'" He bent down and took a pad and charcoal from his bag. "Try drawing it," he said. "It will help."

But *he* was the artist, she thought, a sculptor who carved huge statues of displaced persons—displaced from myth and literature and legend and the Old Testament. At home, when he wasn't chiseling or chipping or peeling potatoes, he had sketched constantly. "What about you?" she said. "*You're* the artist."

"Not my medium, remember?" He grinned and put his hands back into his pockets. He used to keep bits of clay and burnt matches and peanut shells in his pockets; never his hands. How long, she wondered, before he would be allowed to hold a mallet again.

She stood fingering the charcoal. "It's not my medium either," she said. "I always flunked art. My stars and stripes never had enough character and my tulips always had too much." But Sam was asleep with his head against the wall.

Near the door, Channing Haydon, the camp director, stood and watched them: the old and the young, the hopeful and the depressed, and that pale young white woman looking as if she'd been nailed to the wall. He was an observer by nature and profession, a social psychologist whom the war had yanked out of a corner of Harvard Yard so still he could almost hear the ivy creeping toward his window, and dropped into the director's chair of a Japanese internment camp. Haydon, who came from a long line of senators and ambassadors and cabinet members, had been recruited by the attorney general himself, a friend of the family. "An opportunity to observe an unusual experiment in human engineering," he had written. "The transplanting and governing of masses of people in an orderly and humane manner."

Haydon was observing it now with a dry throat and clammy hands, amazed at how clean and tidy the evacuees looked in spite of the excessive heat and that long trip in ancient, overstuffed buses. They even seemed to give off a faint odor of musk, as if they had just stepped out of one of their long ritual baths. He had been reading about the Japanese. He had never known any except for Mr. Sasaki, a visiting scholar at Harvard when Haydon was a student, who spent his days and nights translating the works of Thomas Jefferson and who bowed to Haydon whenever they met on the steps of Lowell House. Haydon began to search for him now, but all he could see were masses of small dark men in hats who all looked alike, and, except for the hats, all looked like Mr. Sasaki.

Haydon's throat grew drier and his hands clammier as he watched more and more people piling in, as he tried to imagine Mr. Sasaki at Mt. Hope, jammed into a stable or forced to sleep on the floor of a mess hall. For nothing at the Center was ready, not even the living quarters. The barracks were unfinished and the stables still looked like stables and smelled like stables, with the partitions neck-high—for horses, not people—while the wind blew dust in steadily through the holes in the walls and the floor and the roof. There were not enough mess halls or laundries or latrines. The plumbing was faulty, the refrigeration erratic and the water supply low. There was virtually no medical staff and almost no medicine. There were not enough beds and not even enough mattresses. The list went on and on. Thanks to the Wartime Civil Control Authority and the Army and the War Relocation Authority and the Bureau of Indian Affairs and the Office of Emergency Management—for all of them had a hand in the running of the centers.

Yet the staff quarters were finished, beautifully finished, solid, comfortable houses, complete with heat and air-conditioning and efficient plumbing, with the curtains all up and the carpets all down. Haydon's office was bigger than the space allotted to a family of nine. His desk alone was twice the width of a cot. There had not even been enough trucks to deliver the luggage of the evacuees. It had simply been dumped in the middle of the fields among the cactus and the snakes, for the evacuees to find and lug to their quarters themselves. It was not the welcome Haydon had intended.

At a long table at the back of the hall, behind piles of printed forms and instructions, Tony Takahashi sat ready to translate on request. He was small and thin, with an enormous smile that shattered his face like a stone in a pond. He had been among the first volunteers to arrive weeks before to help set up the camp. He was known as a Kibei, a person born in the United States who had been partly educated in Japan. He spoke English and Japanese fluently, understood both cultures, and was, he knew, distrusted by both. But he was useful. He had a desk in the administration building next to Haydon's.

He had never seen so many Japanese in one place at one time before. He hated the idea of asking so many personal questions—of people more than twice his age. Just translating the personal history form seemed unforgivably rude. To hand out *The Assembly Center Handbook* seemed deceitful. He picked it up and began to read it for the fourth time:

WELCOME TO MT. HOPE ASSEMBLY CENTER

This is an assembly center, not a racetrack or a concentration camp.
We eat in dining rooms not mess halls.
We have safety councils not internal police.
The people here are residents not evacuees.
We speak of mental climate not morale.
Evacuees will live lives as normal as can be arranged under the circumstances.
They will have the freedom of the grounds.
Food will be on a par with Army rations.
Wages at the Centers will conform to the going wage in the surrounding areas.
There will be special recreation centers for both adults and youngsters.
There will be special facilities for mothers with young babies for warming milk and special diets for invalids.
There will be a one-hundred bed hospital.
It will be up to each Center to plan its own design of community life.
There is no reason whatever for interfering with normal family arrangements.

Tony put the handbook down with horror for the fourth time. He had never heard the words "residents" or "dining room" or "safety councils" in all the weeks he had been here. And he had never seen any of the "facilities" described. The Caucasians did not mind lying. They taught it, practiced it, made a profession of it, built their society on it. But he would be reviled by the Japanese. The queues were beginning to move. He picked up his pen nervously.

Mrs. Noguchi, a tiny woman carrying a huge Whitman's Sampler chocolate box, approached timidly with her five children. The youngest, a girl of five, was hugging a Shirley Temple doll. Dr. Noguchi, a dentist, had been arrested a month after Pearl Harbor and sent to Fort Washington, a top security prison for "dangerous enemy aliens." Mrs. Noguchi was fashionably dressed in hat and gloves and high heels. She held herself erect and spoke English fluently. But her hat had worked its way to the back of her head, and she shifted uneasily in her Western shoes. She belonged in sandals and a cool cotton *yukata,* Tony thought, holding a teacup instead of that garish Whitman's Sampler. Most of her children, well-dressed, well-groomed, well-behaved, towered above her. But they were, no matter how big, only her children. She was clearly lost without her husband.

A family of eight, the Oshimas, arrived, six children ranging in age from five to twenty-five, and their parents who spoke very little English. Tony translated for them. The husband, a fierce-looking man in a red turtleneck sweater, frowned angrily, shook his head, and refused to say a word.

"You must," Tony said desperately in Japanese. "Otherwise they will send you to prison."

"They have already sent me to prison, stupid," Mr. Oshima roared. "I tell you nothing."

Tony turned to Mrs. Oshima, a scared-looking woman with swollen legs and swollen eyes. She bowed and smiled and bowed and smiled but clearly did not understand Tony's questions. She hurried away after her husband.

The mess hall was clearing at last. The woman on the stretcher was quiet now, as if her insides had finally been

whipped stiff. The teenagers had linked arms and were singing "Don't Fence Me In." The stout woman on the suitcase
had threatened to faint and was carried to one of the cots by
two oversized MPs while the young women followed, fanning
steadily. The two little nuns were talking to Mr. Ishii, peering
and smiling at little Ken-chan in his arms. "You must bring
him to St. Ursula's," one of the nuns said, "to play with our
children."

"Perhaps you would like to send him to our kindergarten,"
the other nun said.

"No!" Mr. Ishii hugged the boy closer. "No!" He turned
and hurried away.

A group of elderly Issei was shuffling toward Tony's table,
encouraged by the soldiers. Many of them had tattoos on
their arms: pine trees and flowers and dragons and whole
landscapes in black and red and blue. Fishermen and migrant
workers, Tony thought, and his heart sank; rough, tough,
angry men who would certainly resent his questions. They
moved sullenly toward him. Tony smiled and bowed. They
stared and frowned.

The first man was young and powerfully built, with the
posture of a man forever braced for attack. Tony bowed and
smiled again.

"Inu!" the man hissed. *"Inu."* He leaned over and slapped
the pen out of Tony's hand.

Tony sat gripping the table, watching as the others followed
him, muttering, *"Inu, Inu."* They were all, Tony noticed,
assigned to the grandstand, the Bachelors' Quarters. Tony
was living there too. He felt very small and very lonely and
very scared as he sat behind the official papers, waiting for
his smile to come back.

Outside it was dark except for the huge searchlights roaming through the camp, lighting up the luggage that lay strewn
across the fields like so many dead bodies.

TWO

THE Americanization ceremony was held outdoors six weeks after the camp opened. The director and his staff sat on an improvised platform protected by a canopy, an escort of armed soldiers, and a huge American flag with stripes like highways and stars like islands. An enthusiastic sun beamed down steadily, threatening to melt the stripes and sink the stars—and scorch the captive audience simmering in the heat.

The director, a tiny, far-off figure in a seersucker jacket, greeted them through a microphone. He was a familiar sight—from a distance—for he was often seen walking around the camp in the early morning and evening. But he always kept to the edges. As he spoke, a hot wind rose, lifting his hair, wrapping his tie around his neck, driving his words back into his throat, driving dust into the eyes of his audience.

After him, Colonel Collins, the chief security officer, was proud to announce the opening of the war bond drive. He was a thin man with a loud voice and a large face stuffed into a narrow collar. They must all buy war bonds, he told them. They must prove their loyalty. They must buy and buy and buy till it hurt. But it hurt already, trying to live on unpaid wages. For though most evacuees had camp jobs, none of them had been paid. They had been forced to leave almost everything behind. They had no money for clothes, or soap or toothbrushes or cigarettes. And they had no money for war bonds. The Issei, who did not know English, assumed the colonel was shouting accusations at them. As soon as the program was over, they would be rounded up and arrested. They might even be marched to the foot of that ugly mountain—like a crooked cannon with its nose in the air—and shot.

Schweiker, the chief executive officer, stood up to announce the Americanization program. A tall thin man in a dark, striped three-piece business suit, high-heeled boots, and a huge cowboy hat, he carried his old deputy marshal's pistol on his hip, agitating the stripes on his jacket.

"He keeps a walkie-talkie under that hat," Ray Noguchi said.

"That's why he never takes it off," Toyo Noguchi murmured.

"In case he's assaulted by an evacuee," Jack Oshima said.

"And can't shoot first," Josie Oshima said.

They were all young Nisei who worked as clerks with the Caucasians in the administration building. They had often seen Schweiker with that bulge on his hip striding past them in his seven-league boots, towering above them, sending down his stale air for them to breathe.

The Americanization program, he said, reading from a large document, would cover the following items: "What is a democracy?"

"And why isn't it practiced?" Jack Oshima said.

"What are the principles of the Constitution?" Schweiker said.

"And why aren't they practiced?" Sam Curry murmured.

"What is due process?" Schweiker said.

"And why isn't it practiced?" they all chanted.

Schweiker announced that he expected everyone to sign up for the course. Then he told them to stand and sing "America the Beautiful." They stood, opened their mouths, and the wind filled them with dust.

The young Nisei walked back to the administration building together. Tony Takahashi, the Kibei, fell into step beside Toyo Noguchi. Her father, a prisoner in Fort Washington, was regarded as a hero in the camp. "See you at the movies tonight?" Tony said softly. It was their code word.

She nodded and smiled.

They had met at the movies, which were shown once a week in one of the mess halls. People stood in line for hours in order to be sure of getting in and then sat jammed together on the floor on blankets and pillows, with the air thick as fur. Tony hated the movies, insultingly stupid, boring old films with dead actors and dead scripts, and shown with a film projector that broke down constantly. He hated being squashed on the floor among other people's bedding. But any place was better than the BQ.

One night he noticed Toyo sitting in front of him with her hair spilling into his lap. The next week he managed to sit beside her. When the projector broke down for the third time and the baby beside him squirmed and slobbered and alien bodies pressed against him till their sweat seemed to flow from his own pores, he took Toyo's hand. "Let's get out of here," he whispered.

They spent that evening, and every evening after that, walking round and round the racetrack, walking so lightly that their feet raised no dust. Sometimes they sat in the grandstand and stared at the stars spattered across the sky.

Sam Curry, with his hands in his pockets and his Caucasian wife close beside him, walked back to the stables with the Matsuis, mother and daughter. They had been close neighbors and close friends on Sullivan Street in the days before Mt. Hope.

Yet Nina with her pale hair and pale skin had always been slightly afraid of Emmy, who was sharp and shiny as an ice pick in smart black suits and hair cut short as a boy's and gleaming with lacquer. Her nails and her shoes and her tongue were all pointed. She had been a reporter for *Rafu Shimpo,* the Japanese-American newspaper, and was very clever at ferreting out news and reporting it and, Nina suspected, interpreting it.

"Don't expect me to congratulate you," Emmy told Nina the first time they met. "In marriage people ought at least to *start off* equal."

"Well," Nina said, "Sam is much smarter and quicker than I am. And so talented, of course. But we're equal in other ways: height and . . ."

"Equal? Dear God, look again. He's *Japanese,* in case you hadn't noticed."

"Oh, no. He's American. He was *born* here."

"He's *Japanese,* for God's sake."

"Well, I'm German. I was born there. *And* Jewish. A German Jew." She stared at Emmy defiantly.

"Don't be ridiculous," Emmy said. "You're Caucasian."

It was, Nina thought, the ugliest word in the language.

"I'll bet you could get quite a story out of that fascinating ceremony," Sam was saying to Emmy, who was a reporter again—for the *Mt. Hope Chronicle.*

Emmy grinned. "Nothing I'd be allowed to print," she said. At the stables she said good-bye and, with a hand on little Miko's head, steered her toward their stall.

At their own stall, the Currys found an elderly couple and a tiny baby surrounded by dozens of small bundles as if they had wrapped up bits of tables and chairs and parts of a sofa and brought them along. They were the Watanabes, the man explained with a smile and a bow.

Sam stared at the mounds of untidy packages. No more

than one hundred pounds, the evacuation orders had stated. "My God," he said. "This stall was designed for *one* horse, standing up. There must be some mistake."

"No mistake," Mrs. Watanabe said sharply. She was a short, heavy woman shaped like a kettle and prepared for any emergency in sneakers and slacks. But she clearly was not prepared for Nina. "Why *you* here?" she demanded.

"Because she's my wife," Sam said, putting his arm around her.

"She *hakujin*," Mrs. Watanabe said. "She should stay home."

"That's exactly what I told her," Sam said, leaning over to kiss Nina. "Many times."

Mrs. Watanabe's grandchild began to cry. Mrs. Watanabe picked it up from the top of a duffel bag. The baby stopped crying instantly. It was covered from head to toe, including the hands, in a long flannel kimono tied around the waist with a flannel belt. Mrs. Watanabe smiled at it and pushed its head down in the direction of the Currys in a deep bow. But she continued to glare at them.

"You must forgive my wife, please," Mr. Watanabe said. "She is not herself." He was a small, thin man with his head hung low, as though he had spent his life ducking flying fists. His son was in the Army, his daughter-in-law in some hospital far away. She had become very sick on the journey to Mt. Hope, and they had been forced to leave her behind in a strange town among strange people. He looked around the stall, unfurnished except for the cots and the dust and the bugs and the horsehair embalmed in the whitewash on the walls. And that strange-looking heater that stood like a sentinel beside the door. "I do not understand," he said softly. "First they send my son to the Army. Then they send the rest of us to a concentration camp." He sat down and put his face in his hands.

"I don't understand either," Nina said, staring at the Watanabes and the overcrowded stall. She sat down and buried her face in her hands too.

Sam sat down beside her. "You don't have to stay," he said softly. "You're Caucasian, don't forget."

"Don't say that," she hissed without raising her head. "Don't *ever* say that. Of course I have to stay. As long as you do. And don't call me a Caucasian."

He smiled and touched her hair. "Certainly not. I realized long ago that you were *sui generis*."

"Careful," she said, glaring through her hair. "I know Latin too, don't forget. I said my Hail Marys in Latin at St. Hedwig's, after all. Besides six years at the Waverley School for Girls."

But she had learned nothing useful in either place except to eat and sleep and breathe collectively. She had spent almost her whole life in institutions—on both sides of the Atlantic. And now she was in an institution again.

She longed to be a private person living a private life. She could hardly remember the time when she lived with her mother in their own apartment with a kitchen and a bathroom and a living room just for them and a whole bedroom just for her. But she had been too young to learn anything practical. And her life with Sam before Mt. Hope had been too short for her to grow into a housewife.

Besides, Sam had refused to allow her to settle into domesticity. "No!" he shouted when he found her in the kitchen bent over a Japanese cookbook. "Stop trying to please me." He was always accusing her of trying to please—everybody, from the newsboy to the neighbor's cat. "You should be spending your time painting pictures, not chopping and shredding and stirring. We'll do the cooking and the cleaning and the washing—everything—*together*. And we'll eat hamburgers and hot dogs and potato chips and ketchup. Like everyone else. And when we want Japanese food, we'll go to a Japanese restaurant. Like everyone else." He pulled her into his lap.

"But I want to learn."

"Learn painting, please," he said.

He had wanted her to paint ever since the day he found some of her sketches, sketches from the past: old Frau Felsheimer, so kind that she wore her watch pinned to her blouse, face front, so Nina could see what time it was; the trees in the garden at St. Hedwig's with blossoms deep as coffee cups; the rooftops from the dormitory windows at the Waverley School for Girls like broken steps across the sky. She had even sketched one of Sam's statues one evening when he was late getting home—of Anchises with the young Aeneas on his shoulders before they were displaced and their positions reversed. Her drawing was softer, more explicit than Sam's statue with the boy's arms around the man's neck and the boy's eyes gazing not out toward Rome and the empire to come but down on his father's head.

Sam grinned when he saw the sketches, and his eyebrows shot up. "They're good, damn good," he said. He hugged her and bought her an easel and canvases and brushes and tubes of oil. "Now you can paint," he said. "You must."

But she did not want to paint. She wanted to wear an apron and sweep their piece of the sidewalk and polish up their very own mailbox. She wanted to sing along with the vacuum cleaner and stir exotic sauces in a white and yellow kitchen.

"No!" Sam said. "Please! In the United States of America everyone is equal. Even women. Even wives. Even *you*. Paint pictures, *please!*"

"Is that what they mean by equality in the United States? I do what *you* want me to?"

"Of course. That way I can make sure we're equal."

She painted nothing but the kitchen. When that was finished she got a job in a drugstore behind the soda fountain, until the owner discovered that Curry was short for Kurihara. "My customers don't want no Jap-lover jerking their cherry smashes," he said. The pens in his white coat bristled. She found a job in the public library, shelving books.

She had never had a chance to become domesticated, she thought, peering through her hair at the horse's stall with the

Watanabes' dismembered possessions covering the floor and the narrow cots and the fine frenzy of dust everywhere. There was clearly no danger of settling into domesticity here. Here she went to work in the morning, like Sam. Here she was equal, at last, in a way poor Sam had never intended. She tossed back her hair and laughed.

He leaned over and kissed her. "If you're all right, I'll get back to work." He had a job on a cleanup crew.

"You're not going to that miserable job in this heat?" she said.

"Of course I am. I only came back here to make sure *you* don't go to *your* miserable job. In this heat." She was an aide at the camp hospital.

"Of course I'm going. Besides, we ought to give the Watanabes a chance to settle in."

"On the contrary. You ought to stay and protect our territory."

"No, thanks. I'd rather not watch."

On their way to work, they passed the site of the Americanization ceremony. It was almost deserted now. Only the director was still left, all alone on the platform, staring across the field as the last of the crowd dispersed. Even the flag was gone.

THREE

NINA awoke to the sounds of a siren and thought, for a moment, that she was back in St. Hedwig's, where the nuns had long skirts and hats like wings growing out of their heads and wrapped their faces in white bandages so stiff they could hardly smile or even talk except in a whisper. She had been taken there by Frau Felsheimer, an old lady with white hair and a wobbly chin. She lived across the hall in an apartment crowded with photographs of imposing Felsheimers in full sail, and enormous chairs and tiny tables covered with waxed fruit and dried flowers and lamps in wide, fringed skirts, and a large hatbox filled with macaroons which she shared with Nina every afternoon after school while they waited for Nina's mother to come home from the factory. Nina's father had stopped coming home long ago, the day he went to the hospital. So only Nina and her mother were there when the Nazis came.

One night Nina's mother did not come home at all. "I think it best, little one," Frau Felsheimer said, "that you go to the nuns. Come, we will go in a taxi. You will like that." Nina did not want to go to the nuns, even in a taxi. But Frau Felsheimer was firm. "It is possible that your mother may not come home for a long time," she said. She put on her hat and her little fox and took Nina's hand. "Come, little one," she said sadly. "The nuns will take good care of you." The little fox bit his own tail and looked sad too.

"Aha," Sam said when he heard. "I knew we had a lot in common. I spent twelve years in a Catholic orphanage and I'm not a Catholic either. I'm not even an orphan. Are you?"

"I am now. But then I wasn't sure. I kept expecting my mother every time I heard the visitors' bell." But it was always only Frau Felsheimer with a hat like a tea cozy and the little fox beginning to grow bald and the huge hatbox filled with macaroons. The nuns confiscated it as soon as she left.

What had happened to poor Frau Felsheimer? Was she still living in her crowded apartment, opening and closing her curtains and polishing her waxed fruit? Or had the Nazis removed her long ago for helping a Jewish child? And what about the others, all those children in the orphanage who had walked so quietly, two by two, and waited so patiently, and prayed so obediently? And what about the nuns with folded lips that asked no questions and folded hands that had unfolded to receive her?

But at St. Hedwig's she was always too cold, and here she was too hot and sticky and dusted like a doughnut. She had dust between her fingers and her toes and her teeth. St. Hedwig's had smelled of ammonia and damp flannel and homesickness. Mt. Hope smelled of sweat and manure and the musty odor of straw. She was sleeping on it. Like a horse, she thought. It even smelled of horse. She and Sam had spent hours, the night they arrived, stuffing it into sacks for mattresses.

She turned over but kept her eyes closed against the walls

where the horses had left their flies and their hair and their toothmarks embedded in the whitewash. But she could not keep out the faint smell of manure that still rose from the floorboards. Sometimes she awoke with the sense that the horse had moved back in. And she could not close her ears to the sounds around her: to the child four stalls down who cried most of the time—from hunger and diarrhea and colic and the horse-sized doses of typhoid vaccine—and the priest who chanted his New Testament in martyred English every morning.

Behind the sheet, Mr. Watanabe moaned. The Watanabes had settled into the other side of the stall, the side with the window and, originally, the only light, a forty-five-watt bulb that dangled on a cord from the ceiling. It gave a feeble but frenzied beam, for Mr. Watanabe banged his head on it every time he crossed the room.

The siren rang again. This time it reminded Nina of the fire alarm at the Waverley School for Girls. Her days had been bracketed by bells. Mr. Watanabe moaned again. He moaned often during the night but could not go to the hospital because Mrs. Watanabe did not trust *hakujin* doctors. Instead, she made him drink the strange messes she brewed for him on the hot plate she had smuggled in—herbal concoctions in strange colors and stranger smells. She blew fuses constantly, enraging the neighbors, plunging the stable into turbulence and total darkness. Nina could smell Mrs. Watanabe's brew now, a cloying, nauseating smell that suggested corruption far more than cure. Nina suspected that in her bizarre luggage Mrs. Watanabe had managed to smuggle in a great deal of contraband, which she hid in the soiled-diaper bag whenever the internal police arrived.

Perhaps she still had connections in the wholesale-food market, for the Watanabes had owned a small grocery shop before the war. One Sunday they were sitting in their tiny apartment above the snow peas and the bean sprouts and the water chestnuts, as they did most Sundays. But this Sunday was different. This Sunday was the memorial day of Mrs. Watanabe's mother, and Mrs. Watanabe had placed sweet cakes and candles in front of her mother's photograph on the *butsudan*.

Suddenly they heard shouts in the street and the sound of breaking glass. Soon the sounds came inside, just below them, sounds of smashing and wrecking. And they knew that their shop—their past, present, and future—was being destroyed. They did not try to investigate, to find out who was wrecking it and why. They simply blew out the candles, pulled down the shades, and sat in the darkness in front of the invisible photograph. They had never heard of that far-off place with the beautiful name, Pearl Harbor.

The smell of Mrs. Watanabe's brew became stronger. Nina's stomach stretched and heaved as if trying to slip its moorings. Suddenly the Oshimas on her left erupted into one of their bilingual arguments. There were eight of them jammed into the tiny stall, and they fought constantly, to the delight or despair of their neighbors.

"You speak Japanese!" Mr. Oshima shouted regularly in Japanese.

"No," his wife said quietly in English. "*You* speak *English*. We must learn English."

But Mr. Oshima went on shouting in Japanese, scolding his wife, raging at his children, especially the two oldest, who called themselves Jack and Josie. He shouted at them when they came in and when they went out. And they were always going out. "My children," he shouted, "going to work for the *hakujin*."

"Not children anymore," his wife said firmly, in English.

Mr. Oshima gave a roar of pain. "Yes, children," he shouted. "*My* children. He was strangling with rage, a fierce, proud man who had been deprived of everything—his home, his living, his language, his family, his self-respect. He was neither a Japanese nor an American. He was no longer a gardener or a husband or a father. He was merely a despised old man with an ulcer that was growing worse in a prison where members of his own family collaborated with their jailers. His wife wore trousers and worked beside strange men in the mess hall. His children worked beside Caucasians in the administration building. They no longer studied Japanese and were rapidly forgetting it. His wife was studying English and refused to speak Japanese. Soon he would not be able to speak to members of his own family.

He spent his days sitting in the doorway of the stall, blocking the entrance, choking inside his turtleneck sweater.

Lately the Oshimas' stall had grown quieter. The older children were never there. They were at work or roaming the camp during the day—after two months, there were still no schools—and at night they visited in other stalls or barracks or congregated for the weekly movies and dances, or simply gathered in the recreation hall, where there were a few old Ping-Pong tables and a phonograph. Or were they bedding down with their opposite sex in the Noguchi family, the gardener's daughters and the dentist's sons? For the gardener was powerless in this barren land and the dentist was locked up far away.

Yet there was no place at all that was private at the Mt. Hope Assembly Center. There were hardly even any bushes. Still, there had been several births—the girls were all named Hope—and a few "miscarriages." The "miscarriages" were increasing in spite of the saltpeter which, it was rumored, was sprinkled liberally into the food. The camp doctor was not allowed to give out contraceptives. The Authority had decided that "for moral reasons" only the ministers could sell them, and only to married couples. But the ministers were reluctant. "The Japanese are not an erotic people," a Baptist minister had said. "This will only encourage adulterous behavior." Instead, a pharmaceutical salesman from Roperville was said to be doing a lively business in contraceptives among the bachelors in the BQ. They had even sent an unsigned letter to the administration requesting a "licensed prostitute."

The letter was never answered, but at least one *un*licensed prostitute was believed to be practicing her trade in the barracks. But the young Noguchis and Oshimas of the camp would probably have no need of her services. Japanese girls were becoming Americanized.

To the right, the Noguchis' stall was quiet, as usual, as though they were waiting for Dr. Noguchi to arrive back from prison at any moment; for he would expect order and decorum even in a horse stall. Mrs. Noguchi never ventured outdoors without her white hat and white shoes and white gloves.

Smells from the broken sewer pipe rose with the shouts of Madame Sawada, who still wore her bright-flowered kimonos and her black wig and still shouted at her daughters-in-law, two very young women still dressed in *yukata* and *geta,* still fluttering around Madame Sawada like extra sleeves.

Now there was the noise of rustling newspaper. Someone was using a bedpan and trying to cover the sounds. But there was nothing to be done about the smell.

Nina turned toward Sam's cot and opened her eyes. He was sitting there in the dim light, fully dressed, watching her as usual. He got up very early but he always waited until she was awake before leaving.

"Morning." He smiled and kissed her. "I'm off. While there's some coffee left." He was still working on the cleanup crew.

"Terrible coffee," she murmured, rubbing her face on his sleeve. "Terrible job. Give it up. Sit behind a desk like all the other Nisei." But it was hopeless. Sam believed there ought to be *some* Nisei doing the hard physical work of the camp. Almost all of it was done by the elderly Issei. It was all they were allowed to do.

"What about *your* job?" Sam said. "Working in that hot, overcrowded pesthouse. Christ, you look like one of your patients already."

She sat up abruptly. "That's entirely different. I work with the *evacuees,* for the *evacuees*—for *us.* But you're breaking your back and risking heat prostration for *them.* Just because Chief Jailer Haydon asked you to."

"It's not for *them.* It's for us too. For the safety of the camp."

Haydon had made a special appeal at a mass meeting. The rubbish in the firebreaks and the construction sites constituted a serious threat, he said, his well-cut jacket rippling with sincerity and enthusiasm. At least two hundred men were needed. One hundred had volunteered. Fifty were still working. Sam's hands were raw from blisters that kept opening. The tools were inadequate and the pay—$8.00 a month for unskilled work—nonexistent. Nina, as a hospital worker, classified as semi-skilled, made $12.00 a month. Skilled workers earned $16.00. So far, no one in the camp had been paid at all.

"If it's such important work," Nina said, "why don't they pay you?"

"You know what Haydon said. It's because of the red tape in Washington, of course." It was what Sam always said.

"Then how come there's no red tape for the Caucasians?" Everyone knew that the Caucasian staff was always paid on time and paid far more than the Japanese for exactly the same work.

"We have to be patient," Sam said as he always did, at meals, at meetings, at work. "This is only a '*temporary* residence,' don't forget." The fact that the camp was so inadequate, so unfinished, so lacking in facilities and organization seemed proof to him that they would not be there long. Just till the war in the Pacific began to go well. "Then the hysteria will die down and we'll all be sent home," he had said at a meeting in his stall one evening.

"What home? Where?" Mr. Oshima shouted over the partition. But Sam refused to think about that.

He worked hard at being an American and had little sympathy for the Issei, like his father, who clung to their own language and their own traditions. The Authority was right, he thought, to allow only English in the camps, to insist on American food and American customs and Americanization in general. He threw himself into the work of the camp—but only the manual labor. "Not my medium," he said about clerical work and drafting and sign painting and even art. Was he trying to forget he was an artist, Nina wondered, trying to prove that he was simply a loyal citizen, a model evacuee? When he wasn't working, he kept his hands in his pockets as he had done ever since that terrible day, the day she found him in his studio, slumped in a corner with his back against the wall.

But most of the time his hands were busy. He was full of energy in spite of the heat, like a volunteer fireman putting out flames here, administering artificial respiration there, accepting responsibility for being both Japanese *and* American. He scrubbed their side of the stall and filled the knotholes and cracks as well as possible. He made rough chairs and tables and bookshelves out of wooden crates from the kitchen and scraps of lumber from the building sites. He had, as soon as he found their luggage, hung one of their precious sheets between them and the Watanabes and nailed Nina's drawings and her tiny British flag—acquired in transit from one country to another—on the wall opposite their beds. He hung wiring and bulbs and replaced the ramp outside the door with steps.

The smell from Mrs. Watanabe's brew was growing stronger. Nina's stomach kicked and stretched and seemed about to rise in protest.

"You all right?" Sam said. "You look feverish."

"Just hot."

"Then stay where you are."

He was about to kiss her good-bye when Mr. Tsuda, the block head-counter, arrived. "Good morning, good morning," he called, and peered myopically under the sheet. His glasses had been broken as he boarded the bus for Mt. Hope.

He had packed an extra pair, but his luggage, crammed with books, was three pounds overweight. It was left lying on the sidewalk as the bus drove away. He came every morning and evening at six to take the count and again at ten to shout, "Lights out."

He was a plump man shaped like a hot-water bottle and filled with woe. His wife had been killed by a bullet fired from a passing car full of large white men. Mr. Tsuda, reading *Leaves of Grass* on the front porch, had seen it all. One minute his wife was coming out of the house with hat and hymnal on her way to church, the next she was spread out like a mat at her own front door.

"Morning, Mr. Tsuda," Sam said. "We're all here. What about *your* family? Nick back yet?"

Mr. Tsuda shook his head sadly. "Maybe next week." Nick, his elder son, was in the camp jail, arrested in a fight in the BQ. He had been a college football star but was taken off the team after Pearl Harbor. He was always in trouble. Mr. Tsuda lived in terror that he would be sent to Fort Washington, that prison for the dangerous and disloyal, and eventually be deported to Japan. It had taken all the old man's persistence for them to be allowed to live together as a family instead of as bachelors in the BQ. But the boy spent most of his time there anyway. Mr. Tsuda would do anything to keep on the right side of the administration, even police the block for them, though he knew that his son's friends and perhaps even his son regarded him with contempt. *Inu,* dog, traitor, was the word they probably used.

"What about Yoshi?" Nina said. "Will he be coming home soon?" Yoshi, Mr. Tsuda's second son, had volunteered to pick sugar beets in Roperville, the nearest town, where he was boarded in barracks and marched to and from the fields under armed guard and the hostile glare of the townspeople. "We need the money," he had said, and sent Mr. Tsuda ugly green checks for very small amounts. So Mr. Tsuda lived alone in his share of the stall without his glasses or his books or his sons.

"No," he told Nina. "I do not know when Yoshi will come home. He does not write much. Only sends the green checks." He shrugged. *"Shikata ga nai."* It can't be helped. It was what they all said, Nina thought. Mr. Tsuda smiled and bowed his way out under the sheet.

Sam kissed Nina good-bye. "You feel feverish. Stay in bed. I'll ask Mrs. Watanabe to look in on you."

"I'm just hot," she insisted.

"Stay in bed!" He kissed her again. "I'll see you tonight." They had given up trying to eat together. In the beginning, people ate wherever was convenient. In some blocks the mess halls were not yet finished. In others the food was notoriously bad. In all of them it was insufficient. The young roamed from one to another trying to get enough. To prevent this, the administration had issued mess hall badges, assigning people to specific places. Those who worked in distant areas had to wait for an armed escort to march them back. At the mess hall, they were always the last in line. By the time they got inside, there was nothing left but bits of moldy bread and "alphabet soup," which was the color of prune juice and had a few unidentified objects floating on top. "Only four letters in that alphabet," someone said. It was known as shit soup. Because of that terrible job, Nina thought, Sam was getting almost nothing to eat. Because of that terrible job, she hardly saw him anymore.

She lay feeling the nausea like a live thing crawling around inside her. She closed her eyes. When she opened them again, Mrs. Watanabe was standing beside her with a large cup in her hand. "You sick? Your husband say you sick. You drink this. You feel better."

Nina raised her head. The drink was thick and yellowish and smelly. Terribly smelly. But Mrs. Watanabe looked stern and square as a karate artist in her baggy trousers. Nina thanked her and poured the drink between the floorboards as soon as she was gone. She felt much better. Just *not* drinking that mess had a therapeutic effect. She was about to get up when Mrs. Watanabe came back.

"You feel better?" she said, picking up the empty cup.

"Yes, thank you. What was in the medicine?"

"Oh. Was only a little broth with a little chopped up earthworms and a little snail juice and a little egg yolk. Was good, yes? You feel good now, yes?" She smiled and bowed.

Nina wondered if she was feeding that broth to her grandchild. The baby had not cried since that first night.

She got up and dressed and braided her hair into two tight pigtails that hung straight and stiff down her back. They made her look younger but more determined too.

She was starting for the door when the internal police arrived. Caucasians, they always came in pairs, different pairs. They came when they pleased, day or night, without warning and without knocking. They were, supposedly, looking for contraband goods and suspicious activities. But there were no firm definitions of either. They simply took what they liked: scissors, baseball bats, rubbing alcohol, tweezers, pipe knives, and anything Japanese they could find—clothes, scrolls, dolls, even Buddhas and books, including Bibles and diaries and letters.

Nina stood silently in the middle of the room, wondering what was left to take beside the spiders and the flies and the dust. She saw Sam's *Decline of the West*, a suspicious title, surely. But it was written by a German and they were interested only in *Japanese* subversives. But they didn't seem to be looking for contraband at all, she noticed. They were looking at her. Big, pale, flabby men with authority hanging over their belts and spilling over their collars, they filled the stall.

"Only contraband I see round here," the younger one said, "is this cute little white girl. An' cute little white girls don't belong in a place like this." He smiled like a man proud of his teeth and moved closer.

"Definitely not," the other man said. "Must be pretty awful living in a dump like this. With a *Jap*. Could be she's getting fed up. Could be she's ready to be confiscated." He took a step closer.

"Fraternizing between members of the staff and the eva-cuees is strictly forbidden," Nina said firmly. "It says so in the *Handbook*." But her voice sounded timid and girlish. They stood facing her, blocking the door. One more step and they would be upon her.

Around her, the stalls seemed empty. For once, even Mr. Oshima seemed to be out. The rest of the stable was com-pletely quiet too. Had the police confiscated everybody as well as everything before coming to her? She saw their enor-mous hands dangling loosely at their sides, twitching for something to grab. One flat palm, she thought, could cover her face and shut her mouth. She wanted to scream for Sam, but he was gone too. She took a step backward. They took a step forward.

Suddenly, next door, Mr. Oshima began to shout at his wife—in Japanese. "Foolish old woman," he screamed. "You are too old to learn a new language and you will forget the old one. They will all laugh at you, the Caucasians and the Japanese too."

"Holy Jesus," the younger policeman said. "Listen to that."

"Disturbin' the peace."

"Committin' a public nuisance."

"Incitin' to riot."

They dashed out.

Nina sent silent thanks to Mr. Oshima. How could she have forgotten that at the Mt. Hope Assembly Center she was never alone? But she was angry at Sam. She had come to this terrible place to be with him and he was never there.

FOUR

"WE'VE got problems," Chief Executive Officer Schweiker said at the meeting in the director's office, called at Schweiker's request. He was slumped in his chair with his long legs stretched out, taking up a good deal of the floor space in his three-piece suit and his cowboy hat and his cowboy boots, with his after-lunch Dentyne still wedged in his jaw. He wore his old deputy marshal's gun on one hip and a tiny pocket Bible on the other, but only the gun made a bulge. He was a stern, laconic man who kept to himself and his desk. He even ate his lunch there, brought from home every day in a ditty bag: one hamburger with no butter and no ketchup and no pickle. The rest was brought to him from the cafeteria by Toyo Noguchi at precisely 12:30—one Coca-Cola *in the bottle,* one straw, and three napkins—one for his fingers, one for his vest, and one to spread beneath the open Bible on his desk: ". . . the night cometh, when no man can work."

He was sitting close to the door, as usual, so close that Rigsbee, the comptroller, who always sat beside him, had one ear practically through the keyhole. He was a small, pale man who suffered agonies from the air-conditioning and seemed to be sinking inside an enormous woolen muffler. If he ever disappeared completely, Schweiker could pull him up again by the throat. He always arrived with Schweiker and left with him.

"Real problems," Schweiker repeated. Rigsbee nodded vigorously.

Behind his desk, Haydon, the director, nodded too. He was a tall man with the kind of restrained good looks that went with his narrow tie, his carefully subdued clothes and the mild tobacco he was stuffing into his pipe. But his shoes were scuffed. He had never expected to be the director, merely the assistant director to an older, more experienced man. But shortly after he arrived, the director was rushed to the hospital. He never came back. Haydon clung to the title of assistant, but no one else did. As time passed and no new director was appointed, he accepted the inevitable: that there was no one at all above him. The top of his head felt permanently cold.

He was staring out the window. In the distance, he could see Mt. Hope, crouched like the Sphinx against the darkening sky. He tipped his chair back slightly, his usual position, as if he preferred to see the world from a forty-five-degree angle. He lit his pipe and turned to gaze at Schweiker, his chief executive officer, a hardworking man with endless patience for details. "What kind of problems, Caspar?" he said.

"Discipline problems," Schweiker said. "Bad and getting worse. We don't do something real quick we're gonna have an explosion on our hands. Comes of being so soft. Which we are. We've got rules and regalations but no one's paying any attention to them." It was the longest speech anyone in the camp had ever heard him make. Schweiker put his hands in his pockets, one over the Bible and the other over the gun.

Rigsbee nodded and put his hands in his pockets too, one over his handkerchief and the other over his nasal spray.

"No attention at all," Schweiker went on.

"Damn right," Morrissey, the legal officer, said, polishing his glasses. He was short and plump, a lapsed Catholic from the slums of New York with soft, sandy hair that covered his head like a sponge and a round face forever red with emotion. He was furious at being forced to spend the war at home guarding civilians instead of in Europe fighting Nazis. "I can see perfectly well," he told Haydon the day he arrived. "Better than most."

Now he gave a last vigorous swipe to his glasses. "Case in point: the Wartime Civil Control Authority and the War Relocation Authority and the Army and the Bureau of Indian Affairs and all the other damn agencies responsible for running this place haven't obeyed their own regulations. The food here is *not* 'on a par with Army rations,' there is *no* 'one hundred-bed hospital.' Christ, they aren't even paying the miserable wages they promised." He rammed his glasses back on his nose. "Why the hell couldn't they have waited until the camps were ready before locking the poor bastards up? You'd think they were about to blow up the entire West Coast." Not a single case of espionage had been proved against the Japanese. "Christ, they barely moved the horses out before they shoveled these people in. The whole place still smells of shit. We're damn lucky we haven't had a riot by now."

There was an uncomfortable silence. Rigsbee blew his nose and stared at Schweiker, and Haydon leaned a bit farther back in his chair, increasing the distance between himself and Morrissey. Schweiker, who winced every time Morrissey swore, glared at him and adjusted his hat. He wore it all the time, even indoors, as though he were a visitor just passing through. "This place is a whale of a lot better than what our men are getting over there," he said. "From them."

"But that's hardly the point, is it?" Morrissey said. "Besides, these people aren't prisoners of war."

Schweiker's face tightened. A tight man, Morrissey thought, with a long thin body and a long pale face, suggesting that his arteries too were constricted. And he was much taller than necessary or even desirable for the job. He dwarfed the Japanese. The eternal distribution problem, Morrissey thought, embodied in Mt. Hope's chief executive officer, responsible for the goods and services and finances of the camp.

"The Japs not prisoners of war?" Schweiker said, shooting his eyebrows up under the brim of his hat. "That's news to me." He barely moved his lips when he spoke. Even his mouth seemed too tight.

"Most of them are American citizens," Morrissey said. "Born here." Schweiker's father was born in Germany and had fought for the kaiser in World War I.

Schweiker's eyebrows swooped down again into a sharp frown. Sharp enough to draw blood, Morrissey thought. "Maybe," Schweiker said. "But just let me remind you what the general himself said. 'It makes no difference whether a Jap is a citizen or not. He's still a Jap and can't change. A Jap is a Jap. You can't change him by giving him a piece of paper.' That's *eggzackly* what he said. And he oughta know." He leaned forward and pointed a long finger. "And we better pay attention. Remember it. Because we're too soft around here. Too blamed soft." He pulled his hat down lower over his eyes, leaned back, and stared out at the dusk settling like cinders all over the camp.

Rigsbee nodded encouragingly and applied a quick squirt of nasal spray. Morrissey's face looked blown up and ready to burst. Haydon reached for his knife and stirred the ashes in the bowl of his pipe. He remembered that as director he was responsible for the well-being of over six thousand uprooted, bewildered, possibly hostile people. He needed the cooperation of his staff. And he needed Schweiker, who had a large following among the Caucasian workers—something Morrissey, for all his sharp legal brains, did not understand.

Schweiker stood up. Invisible to the naked eye, Rigsbee stood up right behind him. "I said my piece, so I'll be getting on home," Schweiker announced. He was the only staff member who refused to live in one of the staff houses just outside the gate. Instead, he had taken a house fifty miles away and drove back and forth at a steady five miles above the speed limit. He towered over the other two still seated, and stared down at them from beneath his hat brim. "Don't misunderstand me," he said. "I know about prisoners and I know about colored. I've seen 'em all: black, red, yellow. I'm not saying we shouldn't treat 'em right. What I *am* saying is we should stick to regalations. Make sure they know *we* make the rules and *they* obey them. If they don't, we got ways of making sure they do. That's good administrative procedure, that is." He paused for a moment and resettled his hat. "I just want us to stick to the rules, is all. Just stick to the rules."

Yet Schweiker himself, Morrissey thought, broke one of the cardinal rules regularly by consistently carrying a gun.

Schweiker, with Rigsbee right behind him, strode off in his cowboy boots with his hat low over his eyes and his gun bulging from beneath his three-piece suit. He was a man who had covered all the angles. But from the back his neck looked naked.

He did not go home. Instead he went to his office, sat down at his desk, and opened his Bible. He read for a while and then began to write rapidly on camp stationery: "Grace be to you and peace from God the Father and our Lord Jesus Christ. . . . The powers that be are ordained of God. Whosoever, therefore, resisteth the power, resisteth the ordinance of God: and they that resist shall receive to themselves damnation."

The fields were dim now, with the racetrack slack as a noose waiting to be pulled. Alone in his office, Haydon stared at the sphinxlike mountain, a mere smudge on the darkened horizon suggesting that, like Oedipus, he had solved the riddle. And remembered what happened to Oedipus.

FIVE

In the days before Pearl Harbor, Sam Curry (born Kurihara), in tunic and cap and tightly wound puttees, drove Mrs. Willard Whitelaw all over town in her shiny, high-breasted Pierce-Arrow. In between he taught art in a neighboring town and worked on his statues of displaced persons from myth and literature and the Old Testament. Prometheus and Oedipus and Hagar and Lear, all the way back to Adam and Eve and beyond, to Satan himself, that first exile, who had dislodged the universe forever. They were huge, bold figures, designed to take their stand in public places: parks and hospitals and schools and libraries. Until then, they were lodged with Sam, crowding around him in his tiny studio. He could almost feel their breath on his neck, hemming him in, making him a prisoner of his own imagination.

It was raining hard the day he met Nina. He had delivered

Mrs. Whitelaw as close to her front door as possible—the Pierce-Arrow had settled one foot on the curb—and was taking the car back to the garage. He drove slowly, thinking about Persephone, his latest piece, who had been displaced from the earth itself. She would, he decided, be a *modern* Persephone, not a goddess abducted by a god but a mortal captured by soldiers.

He was thinking about her as the rain beat against the windshield, trying to imagine her form, her face, her expression, her stance. Suddenly he saw her, standing on the street corner waiting for the light to change, carrying an enormous suitcase as if she were all prepared for that trip to hell. He slowed down, staring at her drenched hair and her terrified eyes and her neck taut with silent screams. She looked thin and tired and soaking wet. She might have been standing in the rain for days. He pulled over to the curb, stopped the car, and opened the passenger door.

"May I give you a lift?" he said.

"Oh, no! Thank you."

"Please. You're very wet and I'm a very good driver."

"Thank you very much but I can't. I really can't."

"But you can, you know. All you have to do is get in. Wherever you're going, it's sure to be right on my way." Behind him, horns honked, drivers shouted. Across the street, a policeman began to swagger toward them.

"We're causing a traffic jam," he said. "Better get in or I'll be arrested. Please."

She got in and sat huddled in the corner with her soaked suitcase on her lap. She looked pathetically cold and wet and miserable and, increasingly, worried. He felt guilty.

He left the car at the garage and took her to dinner at a Japanese restaurant nearby. She was just his height, he realized, as they walked shoulder to shoulder under Mrs. Whitelaw's big umbrella.

At the door of the restaurant, she stopped. "I just remembered I have no money. I think I must have lost my wallet on the bus."

"Never mind. I have money."

"But I can't. . . ."

"Of course you can. And you must learn to stop saying you can't." He took her arm.

Inside, she looked around silently. It was the first time she had ever been to a Japanese restaurant. She had never seen chopsticks before or eaten Japanese food before or sat opposite a Japanese before or even been out with a man before. Her face was still wet and her hair was dripping. She licked the drops with her tongue.

"This," Sam said, pointing at her with his chopstick, "is the first time I've ever been out with a Caucasian."

"What's that?"

"You."

"But I'm not. I'm sorry to disappoint you but I'm a Jew. A *German* Jew."

He grinned. "That won't save you. You're still a Caucasian, a member of the white race, the *master* race."

"Don't be silly," she said. "I'm a Jew."

She looked like an American college girl, he thought, right out of Minnesota, with all that long pale hair and those strange blue eyes, the kind of girl who managed, always, to keep him just outside her line of vision. But Nina was looking straight at him with those blue eyes that reminded him of Father Luke's at St. Martin's when he was a boy. He had never seen blue eyes before. He thought it was a defect. He had felt sorry for poor Father Luke. Anyone who got close enough could see right through them, right down to Father Luke's soul. But Nina's eyes were darker. "And," he went on, "you sound much more like Boston than Berlin."

"Well, I started to learn English in London."

"But you don't sound English."

"That's because of Miss Motherwell," she said. "She's from Boston. She's head of the Waverley School for Girls."

"In Boston?"

"No. In California."

"Berlin, London, Boston, California?" he said. "Before

you've even come of age, by the look of you." He put down his chopsticks. "What happened?"

"Hitler."

"Go on."

She told him about her mother and Frau Felsheimer and the nuns and the little white-haired Fräuleins. Were they still traveling between Germany and England with their heads resting so calmly on contraband and their necks hanging by a thread?

They had fetched her from the convent one morning and smuggled her into England, where Uncle Willie and Tante Clara were waiting for her under an enormous umbrella. The train ride was frightening, with soldiers marching up and down the corridors. But the Fräuleins simply removed their hats, took two small pillows from their purses, settled them behind their heads, smiled at Nina, and closed their eyes.

"*Reisepasse,*" one of the soldiers demanded. He sounded very angry. His features surged. "You go back and forth to England very often, Fräulein?" he said with a sneer.

"*Natürlich, Herr Leutnant,*" Fräulein Ingeborn said.

"It is our duty," Fräulein Hildegard said.

"To make trade for the Reich."

"With contacts in Birmingham and Leeds." They handed him sheaves of papers.

The soldiers flipped through the papers quickly but examined their suitcases, their handbags, their pockets, and around and under their seats with great care. "*Und das Kind?*" the lieutenant said, staring down at Nina as if she were a pile of litter on the floor. Behind him, the second soldier stood looking ready to sweep her out.

The Fräuleins shrugged. "The child of friends," Fräulein Hildegard said.

"Her parents died in an auto crash," Fräulein Ingeborn said.

"We are taking her to relatives in London," Fräulein Hildegard said.

The soldiers left, the Fräuleins put their pillows back behind their heads, smiled at Nina, and closed their eyes.

Actually, their "business" was in smuggling—Jewish money and Jewish jewelry sewn up in those little white pillows on which they rested their aging heads so calmly for hours, to lift them, periodically, for the Nazis. But this time they had smuggled out a little Jewish girl as well.

At Dover they disappeared, their hats on, their pillows back in their purses. Instead, there were Tante Clara and Uncle Willie. They were small and thin. They both fitted easily under one umbrella. They kissed Nina and tucked her under the umbrella too.

Two months later they sent her to the United States, where she would be safe from the Nazis forever. For they were convinced that the Germans would overrun Europe without so much as pause at the Channel. They were sending her to a school in California, as far from Germany as possible, run by a friend of Uncle Willie's. They would stay in London and look after their bookshop until the Germans came.

They put her on a boat, kissed her good-bye, and gave her a tiny British flag to wave. She stood on the deck, waving her flag, watching them grow smaller and smaller under the big umbrella until it seemed to cover them completely. Then it too disappeared. Later she learned that they had both been killed in their shop during an air raid. "Buried beneath the debris," a neighbor wrote, "along with the great minds of the Western world."

Nina arrived on the doorstep of the Waverley School for Girls with a huge identification tag, a huge shabby suitcase, a few old clothes, and that tiny British flag. Uncle Willie's friend had died before Nina's boat had even docked. There was no money at all for her tuition. Besides, she was only ten years old, much younger than the others. Miss Motherwell took her in anyway. What else could she do with her?

Miss Motherwell had come to California from Boston in shirtwaist and oxfords to prepare girls for Radcliffe. But the girls wanted to be prepared for MGM. Miss Motherwell switched to V necks and high heels and offered classes in elocution and tap.

She regarded Nina with interest. The girl was always alone, set off by her strange speech—she knew very little English— and strange clothes: enormous cardigans and high woolen socks and high laced shoes that gripped her skinny legs. She curtseyed constantly and used her knife continuously and had never heard of Clark Gable or bobby socks or bubble gum. She still wore the stamp of the convent, forever waiting for instructions with her elbows and her toes turned in.

The other girls were suspicious.

"She's a spy, of course. A German spy."

"Don't be silly. She's a Jew. My father says all refugees are Jews. He should know. They've got millions of them at his studio. Besides, she's got those funny little eyes and a big nose."

"So? She could still be a spy, stupid. She's from Germany, isn't she?"

"My father says we shouldn't be allowing all these Jews in. He says soon they'll take over the whole country, just like the Japs are taking over the whole state. Soon there won't be any room left for us Americans at all."

Nina learned English very quickly. After a while she was never alone. She was constantly surrounded by girls who wanted her to mend their hems and brush their hair and correct their homework and help write their letters. Giving herself over and over again, Miss Motherwell thought; because she had nothing else to give? Paying for a debt that could never be settled? Paying for what, Miss Motherwell wondered. For being a Jew?

Miss Motherwell excused her from elocution and tap and taught her history and English and Latin instead. By the time she graduated, she was thoroughly Americanized. She ate like an American and talked like an American and even looked like an American: a tall girl with light hair and blue eyes. Her eyes had grown bigger and her nose smaller through the years, as though her genes had forgotten she was a Jew.

But Miss Motherwell could not give her a family. There was no "next of kin" for Nina on file in the school office, no one to notify in case of emergency. She did not even have a home address. She left school with her battered foreign suitcase, all straps and buckles, and a glowing recommendation from Miss Motherwell, along with fifty dollars. By the time Nina met Sam it was all gone.

For there were no jobs, not for her with no experience and no skills and no self-confidence. And there was no home for her, either. The rooms to let were all too expensive or too frightening, dark, damp little rooms with narrow beds crowded with nightmares even in the daytime. The buildings looked about to crumble with decay and despair. Unshaven men sat on the steps and reached for her ankles as she climbed the stairs. Many of the windows had signs that read: "No Japs wanted here"—she wondered why—or "Caucasians Only." What were they? She stayed away from both and slept in the homes of dead saints: Catherine and Anne and Mary of the Immaculate Conception. When Sam finally found her, she was standing on a street corner in the rain, holding her worn suitcase, feeling like a refugee again, a refugee who had just arrived.

She still looked like a refugee, Sam thought, still lugging that strange old suitcase. Suddenly he realized its significance. She had been carrying it around all day because, clearly, she had no place to leave it. He had noticed the initials, DLE, none of them hers, the initials, undoubtedly, of some remote ancestor; and the suitcase itself, with its frayed straps and dented buckles, suggested a long history of forced journeys and pitiful possessions and battered memories.

She was beginning to dry off, he noticed, which made her long hair look lighter and her whole appearance brighter, as if she were slowly rising from the deep.

"What about you?" she said.

"Oh, I'm lucky. I was *born* here. I'm a native American."

She thought of the Japanese she had seen; the gardeners at the Waverley School, forever bending over to tend other people's flowers and pull up other people's weeds; and always with their backs turned. She had never seen their faces. On school outings, from the windows of the bus she had seen the Japanese crowded into "Jap town," the oldest and poorest section of the city. "Sly, nasty things," Loretta, president of the senior class, called them. "With their eyes all squeezed together like that. It's not normal."

But Sam's eyes were large and wide open, with smooth eyebrows that went up and down so easily—in pleasure or sympathy or surprise—and his teeth were so white they might have been dipped in milk. He was handsome, she thought, remembering Loretta, who had a face like a piggy bank.

"What's so lucky about being born here?" she said.

"It means I'm an American citizen," he said, patting his chest—along with the buttons on his chauffeur's uniform.

"Which means you can be drafted."

"I don't mind. In fact, I was planning to enlist. Until today."

"What happened today?"

"I met you."

She looked startled and gazed around the restaurant in embarrassment. It was empty. "I must go," she said. "My landlady locks the door very early."

What landlady, he wondered. Which door? "Surely not *this* early?"

"Yes. I must go." She stood up.

He stood up too. "At least let me drive you home. It's still pouring."

"No. You mustn't. Please." She seemed about to cry.

They were standing close together, facing each other. Their features, he noted, were perfectly aligned. If he leaned forward, just slightly, they would meet. He leaned. For a long moment, they stood sealed together.

"Good-bye," she said abruptly, "I must go."

"Where?" He stared pointedly at the suitcase. "You have no money, remember? You lost it on the bus." He started for the door. "Wait here for a moment. I'll get the car. I wouldn't want that suitcase to get soaked again. You'd have nothing left but the buckles."

She stood staring after him. She could hear his footsteps and the rain beating steadily outside, waiting to beat on his bare head.

When he got back, Nina and the suitcase were gone.

He sat down at the empty table. How would he ever find her again? She had no address and no distinguishing marks except for that flick of a smile that pierced to the heart, and that ancient, worn-out suitcase.

He was driving Mrs. Whitelaw home, watching the pedestrians as he had been doing all week, slowing down for every lone woman he spotted while Mrs. Whitelaw recited snatches of Edward Lear through the speaking tube. But it was always someone else staring into a shop window or waiting for a bus or hurrying to cross the street against the lights.

The rain came suddenly, beating against the windows while the wipers chased each other frantically across the windshield. Mrs. Whitelaw switched from Edward Lear to King Lear and shouted above the storm.

Suddenly, Sam saw *her,* standing on a corner, holding her suitcase, waiting, once again, for the light to change. She seemed shorter and thinner. She's shrinking away, he thought.

He swerved over to the curb, slammed on the brakes, and opened the passenger door. "Get in," he said.

She merely stared.

"Don't argue, please! Just get in."

Mrs. Whitelaw left King Lear on the heath. "*Who* is that?" she said.

"Never mind her," Sam told Nina. "Just get in." Finally he grabbed her arm and pulled her into the car. "My fiancée, madam," he said.

"Good. She can do the silver and help with the laundry. But first she must have a bath and . . ."

"No, thank you, madam," Sam said. "It's very kind of you but no thank you."

"No?" Mrs. Whitelaw consulted a large hand-mirror that hung beside her seat and examined her face as if to make sure he was speaking to her.

"We have other plans, madam," Sam said.

"Oh?" She put the mirror back carefully. "In that case, I shall have to find another chauffeur."

"Yes, madam."

"Because you are fired."

"Yes, madam."

"As of now."

"Of course, madam." He stopped the car, got out, and removed Nina and her suitcase. Behind him Mrs. Whitelaw was still giving orders through the speaking tube. But he heard nothing except his own heart. He had found Nina at last. He would never lose her again.

Walking home, holding the soggy suitcase and Nina's wet hand, he realized that he had never seen her completely dry.

They would be married in Mexico, he told her that night, in a little town just over the border.

"Can we afford to?" she said.

"We can't afford *not* to. Marriage between Caucasians and Japanese is illegal in the sovereign state of California."

"That can't be true. There aren't any racial laws in the United States of America."

"It is and there are. In the South they're against Negroes. In California against Asians."

And in Germany against Jews, she thought. It seemed to be a matter of geography. "But you said you were *born* here. That you're a native, a *citizen*." But she had been born in Germany.

"Sure," he said. "But I'm still Japanese. As one of our newspapers put it: 'The Japanese can never be assimilated. They'll always have those short arms.'"

Like the hooked noses of the Jews, Nina thought. She began to cry.

"You can change your mind," he said.

"About what?"

"Getting married."

She stared at him. "Why would I want to do *that?*"

"You might not like short arms, for one thing. And you might not want to go all the way to Mexico."

"But I've *always* wanted to go to Mexico. I'd marry you just for that." He put his arms around her. They were, she thought, quite long enough. But suddenly she was aware of the huge dumb figures crowding around them, Sam's displaced persons. She imagined them chanting words and phrases she had read or heard but which had hardly registered before: "The Jap is and always will be a stabber in the back." "No Jap is fit to live with human beings." "Japs will do any kind of work for any kind of pay. They're dangerous." "Japs get out." "America for Americans." It was like Germany all over again, as if she had brought it with her. Poor Sam, who was so proud of being born in the United States. "I was lucky," he had said. And now he was going to marry a German Jew. But she was also, she had discovered to her amazement, a member of the master race! Perhaps that would be of some help to Sam. It was a strange thought for her, shy and scared as she was. It was an even stranger thought for a Jew.

SIX

HAYDON hurried to the sanctuary of his desk each morning and the protective arms of his easy chair each evening. He would have been happy to have the desk wider and the arms higher. He was ashamed of these feelings and kept them hidden behind a huge smile that switched on, like a light above the front door, as soon as anyone approached. He always made a point of getting up from behind his desk when anyone came to his office, and he preferred to hold staff meetings in a small conference room with a round table.

He took long walks all alone along the edge of the camp every morning and evening and spent the hours after dinner reading professional books—on the history and customs and psychology of the Japanese, for his job and for the work he planned to write on a psychological analysis of life in a Japanese internment camp—until eleven. At eleven, he lit a fresh pipe and allowed himself the indulgence of Condorcet or Constant or Montaigne or Mill, the enlightenment of earlier ages. Unless, of course, his wife required his attention.

She required it now, he realized, as he looked up and found her watching him. He wondered how long she had been waiting.

She smiled. "How much is three times two-thirds of a cup?"

"Exactly what it was last night."

"Last night it was sugar. Tonight it's flour."

"It's exactly the same."

"Oh, honey, you know I don't remember."

Her cheeks had gone pale in this harsh climate and her head drooped on her long neck. She's fading away, he thought. He lifted her face gently with both hands and kissed her. She smiled. She smiled easily. Then he got paper and pencil and worked through all the items in her recipe while she riffled through the pages of *On Liberty,* losing his place. Cordon Bleu, he thought, had left many gaps in her education.

She was a pretty girl who had left family and friends and the sunshine of Santa Monica to live with Haydon at Mt. Hope. Her sisters were all married by then and working on their careers. They were all going to make it big in Hollywood: Jackie sang and Gerry acted and Junie designed, which limited the choices left for Jenni, the youngest.

"Daddy says everyone should be good at *something,*" she told Haydon. "It doesn't matter what." Daddy was good at making money just by sitting at a desk. Jenni had been good at mixing his drinks and changing his cuff links and taking care of Mommy's migraines. But Daddy was not impressed. "Then I'll be a tap dancer," Jenni said. But Daddy said that was no career for a young girl. She should get married first, like her sisters, and let her husband worry about her career.

But now that Jenni was married there was no possibility of learning to tap dance—not at Mt. Hope. She considered photography, but it was too hot in summer and would certainly be too cold in winter and, besides, what was there to photograph? She tried the piano and went all the way to Roperville for lessons with Miss Sketchley, a tall bony woman in a hairnet and a long white smock like a lab coat with a clean cloth in the pocket for dusting the keys. "Aren't you afraid, living so close to all those Japs?" she said.

"Oh, no," Jenni said. "Why would I be?"

"I suppose your husband keeps them under strict surveillance."

Jenni, who had no idea what surveillance meant, looked surprised.

"Oh, no," she said vaguely. "They have to help run the camp, after all. Otherwise, Channi says, they'd have to close it down. I wish they would. Then we could *all* go home."

That was Jenni's last piano lesson. The next week, Miss Sketchley left for Albany to stay with her sister for the duration.

After that, Jenni turned to cooking, preparing elegant dinners for poor Channi, who was forced to eat lunch at the camp cafeteria. Jenni, who had never been inside a kitchen before her marriage except to get ice cubes, was sent by her mother to Cordon Bleu shortly before the wedding. The sight of her first cake, plump and firm in the pan, seemed to her like a miracle—a miracle *she* had performed. At Mt. Hope she took to cooking in earnest. It would be the thing she did well—like Jackie's singing and Gerry's acting and Junie's designing. Thanks to the PX, she could go on making dishes like *roulade de boeuf* and *médaillons de veau à la Suisse* and *suprème de volaille écossaise,* in spite of the war; though there were often a good many gaps and substitutions in her recipes. Sometimes all that remained was the name.

But Cordon Bleu had taught her nothing about cleaning up. The kitchen became a mess of greasy counters and charred pots and spattered stove. The maid could never get in to clean because Jenni was always cooking. When the pots and pans became too repulsive to sight and touch she bought new ones, but the old ones remained, crowding the cupboards, spreading their grease. Gadgets and appliances were often left unpacked or disassembled so that cupboards and drawers overflowed with bits and pieces of unidentified parts. Nothing fitted. Nothing was where it belonged. Opening a drawer one night, Haydon found wads of cotton, a bottle of aspirin, stray bobby pins, paper clips, an old powder puff, and a half-sucked lollipop mixed in with the knives and forks.

He stayed out of the kitchen as much as possible but was pursued by Jenni's cookbooks, which overflowed the kitchen cupboards and forced their way into the living room: *The Complete Gourmet's Peanut Butter Cook Book, The Cauliflower and Carrot Cook Book, The Soothing Soufflé Cook Book, The Just Desserts Cook Book.* They seemed to constitute her main reading except for the slogans that appeared on objects all over the house: on mugs and cups and glasses and ashtrays; on towels and napkins and aprons and sheets: NEVER SAY DIET on the refrigerator, WHO CARES? on the bathroom scale, KISS THE COOK on the dish towels, BOTTOMS UP! on the coasters, GET TO THE POINT on the pencil sharpener. Where words failed, there were pictures: of birds and flowers and Mickey Mouse.

He had married her without knowing anything about her except that she was beautiful. She was still beautiful, though her hair seemed to have faded since the wedding, as if all that cooking had steamed some of the color out of it. She had been a shining blonde for a short time before and after their marriage. Like a light turned on and off.

They had met in the dining car of a Pullman between Boston and Chicago, between fall and winter, when the country was still between war and peace. The draft was in full swing, but the fighting had not yet begun. Haydon, who had enlisted and expected to be called up very soon, was on his way to a conference—which might, very possibly, be his last. Jenni was on her way home from a visit to a school friend at the Boston Conservatory of Music. "I thought I might go there too," she announced to the three strange men at her table. "To study the harp. Like Lucy. No one in my family plays the harp. But Lucy said my hands are too small." She held them out and grinned. "Leastways, that's what I'm going to tell Daddy. Truth is, I'm much too stupid. All those notes. Like mouse droppings." She laughed.

Haydon, staring out the window, heard nothing, saw nothing but the lights of the engine curving around a bend, rushing into the darkness. He could see nothing of the countryside, only the lights up ahead—until the tracks straightened out. Then he could see nothing at all but his own reflection in the window, like a man traveling beside himself.

Jenni, sitting next to him, was tugging his sleeve and offering the gravy. The train lurched and the gravy landed in his lap. Jenni tried desperately to mop it up with her napkin and her handkerchief and wads of Kleenex, which only spread it around. Finally she begged him to come back to her compartment, where she had lots of the most wonderful cleaning fluid and a beautiful new traveling iron. She was close to tears. Haydon, who longed to change into dry clothes and go over his paper for the conference, thanked her and followed her out.

In her compartment, she turned and smiled at him. "Sit down while I find the cleaning fluid," she said. "My name's Jennifer Clarke but everyone calls me Jenni. Except Daddy, who calls me Flopsy. Because I'm so clumsy. Can't blame him, can you?" She laughed.

I can and I do, Haydon thought. She was very pretty, with soft, appealing looks so different from the women of Boston and Radcliffe, who were handsome and clean-cut, with no frayed edges, and so finished that they seemed to need nothing more. Certainly not a husband. He had never met anyone like Jenni. He wondered what he had been missing.

"Do, please sit," she said again.

He sat.

She stood smiling down at him, holding the cleaning fluid.

The train lurched, spilling Jenni and cleaning fluid all over him. But Haydon was aware only of Jenni who fitted his lap as if measured for it. The train continued to swerve and sway, hurling them through the darkness. But it was a darkness in which Haydon was no longer traveling beside himself. He was lying, securely coupled, in the cradle of a lower berth.

At breakfast, the first course was the news of Pearl Harbor. Jenni clutched his arm. "You'll probably have to go right away, won't you?"

"Probably."

In the taxi, she clung to him. "I'm coming with you," she said. "Wherever they send you. For as long as they let me."

"But Jenni, darling . . ." He began and stopped, for the cab had swerved and she was in his arms again and they were kissing like a couple being driven not to the other side of town but to the other side of Time. And he knew the meter was clicking away far more than the fare between the railroad station and the Palmer House Hotel. He never finished his sentence and Jenni never made that connecting train back home.

She had stuck to her promise to accompany him wherever he went, though she had undoubtedly expected an Army post with an officers' club complete with a beach and dances every Saturday night. But Haydon was transferred out of the Army even before they were married. "*We* need you," the attorney general had written. Jenni had accepted Mt. Hope gallantly and greeted him every evening with a smile and a kiss. "Get those trousers off fast," she would murmur in his arms. "I've got the cleaning fluid all ready."

But after a while she seemed too tired to greet him so effusively. After a while the cleaning fluid was forgotten and he no longer carried her up the stairs at six in the evening.

"We act just like an old married couple," she announced sadly, getting into bed one night.

He lay down beside her and put his arms around her.

"Well, I suppose that's what we are," he said. "Do you mind terribly?"

She snuggled up against him. "I suppose I do, in a way," she said.

So do I, he thought. They had been married for six months. But only pity and an accompanying guilt remained.

He handed her the revised recipe and returned to his book.

She smiled and thanked him and returned to her menu. She would wait patiently for him to look up again before putting another question. Often she had to wait a long time. Often he forgot she was there. When he remembered, he felt guilty. She was alone all day, he reminded himself, and, to all intents and purposes, all evening too. There was no one at the Mt. Hope Assembly Center who could possibly be company for Jenni—unless it was one of the young evacuees. And what, he wondered, would Schweiker and company make of that? "That's fratanizing, that is," Schweiker would say. "Against regalations, that is. Strickly against regalations."

Haydon thought of the wives of his immediate staff. But Mrs. Morrissey was in New York and Mrs. Schweiker was fifty miles away. Besides, she was probably a formidable woman with hands like oven mitts who forced Schweiker to live far removed from his colleagues and eat homemade sandwiches for lunch every day to save money. She probably taunted him mercilessly because he had always been *second* in command: *assistant* foreman, *assistant* bookkeeper, *deputy* sheriff. Perhaps that was why he had taken this job with "Chief" in the title, in spite of the Japanese, and insisted on his authority so rigorously. It pleased Haydon to think of Schweiker as the victim of a bullying wife. It justified his feelings of empathy with Schweiker which he could not otherwise explain and which, he knew, outraged Michael Morrissey, the liberal, humane, fair-minded Morrissey. Haydon resented Morrissey, a man who not only rode his conscience in public with the arrogance of a man proud of his mount but seemed to want to ride Haydon's too. Haydon felt more comfortable with Schweiker, whose prejudices seemed, at least, to be genuine, born of experience, not principles paraded for public display. Or did he, Haydon, envy Morrissey, who had left his wife in New York?

He made an effort to concentrate on his book and realized that he had been reading the same line over and over. "Liberty consists in doing what one desires." And what he desired now was to be alone with John Stuart Mill.

But Jenni was watching him with that pleading expression that brought pity, like a puppy, to his knee. "Recipe all right?" he said. "Measurements all clear?"

"Oh, yes. Thank you."

"Good." He was about to go back to his book.

"Oh, I forgot to tell you," she said quickly. "Mommy wants to know what you'd like for Christmas. She says she's absolutely, definitely coming. Isn't that wonderful? Only"—her head drooped slightly—"she says she can't stay very long." Haydon doubted that she would come at all. Wartime travel was not pleasant and Mt. Hope was not pleasant and Mommy liked things to be pleasant.

"She says how about some scotch," Jenni went on, "or a pair of those jade cuff links like Daddy's or a magnum of . . ."

He leaned forward suddenly. "Jenni," he said abruptly, "what I'd *really* like is a study."

"A *what?*"

"A room with a desk and a typewriter and . . ."

She began to laugh. "Oh, honey, I know what a study is. But you can't expect Mommy to bring you one of *those* from California. Besides, you've got one already. Only it's called an office. Down at that horrible camp."

"I know. But I need one here, a place where I can work at home in the evenings and on weekends and . . ."

"But Channi. You work all day, all week. I don't see why you should work nights and weekends too. Besides, why can't you have your study in here?"

He looked around. The living room was stuffed with tables and chairs and bookcases and a piano and a phonograph and records, and photographs of Jenni—with family, with friends, with classmates, with Amanda Sue, an enormous white angora cat—and Jenni's collection of huge toy koalas. Making sure, he thought, that almost all the life of the house went on in the living room. Together.

"But Jenni, there's hardly room for a paper clip in here."

"Well, there isn't any room anywhere else in this ugly old house." She looked about to cry. But suddenly she smiled instead. "I just remembered," she said happily. "Tomorrow's Wednesday. We *are* going to the PX, aren't we?"

"Of course." He took her to the PX every Wednesday evening. It was the high point of her week.

Morrissey stood in the middle of the PX holding a six-pack of beer. He longed to make it a barrel and invite all the Nisei clerks to help him drink it. Unlike Schweiker, who clung to his desk like a raft in rough waters, or Haydon, who walked discreetly around the edges of the camp as if afraid of getting his feet wet, Morrissey plunged into the very center, greeting people, defying Schweiker, and fraternizing as he went. He had learned to practice law but not discretion.

In the mornings, jogging around the racetrack in training for any future confrontations with Schweiker, he was joined by a string of small boys who cheered him on and followed along in his wake. On weekends he formed them into soccer and baseball and track teams and taught them to call him Uncle Mike.

In the administration building during the week, he met their older brothers and sisters and learned something of their histories. His secretary, Josie Oshima, was a lively girl with a wide smile, though she didn't have much to smile about. He gave her coffee from the Thermos on his desk every morning and she gave him details of her life in a horse stall. Not only was she miserable, she was scared. She lived in fear of her father, who had become quite savage since coming to

Mt. Hope. "I think he's just looking for an excuse to let go," she said. "And if he ever does . . . He can be real violent, you know." She was afraid of Schweiker too, who looked as if he'd like to shoot her dead if she so much as breathed out near any of the Caucasians. "Ever since he caught me talking to one of the MPs. Or rather one of the MPs talking to me."

"Do they often talk to you?" Morrissey said.

"Well, some of them are awfully nice. Private Miller, at the reception desk, always says good morning—when Schweiker's not around. Everyone knows he's just looking for a chance to use that handy little gun. But Papa would do it with his bare hands first." She wondered what would happen if they went on living in that stable much longer. And she wondered what would happen if they were ever let out again. "*Pushed* out," she said.

"You'd start living again," Morrissey said.

She looked at him angrily. "Where? How? On what?"

He had no answer. He should find an answer, he told himself. Discuss it with Haydon, though Haydon would say simply that there was nothing he could do. It was a phrase Haydon hid behind constantly. But Morrissey had spent his life fighting for underdogs: factory workers, domestic workers, endangered Jews. Besides, he was the legal officer, in charge of protecting the rights and liberties of the evacuees. *I* should do something, he thought. But what? There was, he realized like Haydon, nothing that he *could* do. He drove to the PX for a six-pack of beer.

He was standing in the middle of the aisle holding his beer when he saw Mrs. Haydon pulling cans off the shelves at a great rate. Haydon was trailing far behind her with his arms full. Morrissey had met her once before when she came to Haydon's office one afternoon with a bottle of kirsch for him to open. "Sorry, honey," she had said. "But I couldn't wait. I need this for the cherry torte and it's supposed to soak for four hours." Haydon had clearly been embarrassed and annoyed, but Morrissey had found her charming.

She was a pretty young woman with lots of blond hair and

blue eyes that darted from shelf to shelf, searching out goodies for Haydon, the lucky bastard. She seemed to be going a bit lumpy in places and in need of a good stirring. He glanced at Haydon. There was no distortion there, no bump or bulge anywhere. He was a thoroughly integrated man. But he was having trouble hanging on to all those cans. "Good God," Morrissey called to him, "having the troops to dinner?"

Haydon laughed. "Just the weekly grocery shopping," he said, looking at Morrissey's six-pack.

Jenni turned and smiled. "Hi there, Mr. Morrissey," she called. "Don't let Channi fool you. He *loves* coming here. That way he can be sure I buy the right beer. I never *can* remember. They all have those funny foreign names."

"Who cares?" Morrissey said, and smiled at her. He doubted that Haydon really did. She was very pretty and, obviously, a good cook. Morrissey's wife never cooked. She let the 86th Street Delicatessen do it for her. He had not thought of her for weeks. He did not want to think of her now.

She was a big woman who insisted on being called Mac, a piece of her maiden name that she clung to like the hockey stick hanging on the bedroom wall. She worked for a well-known fashion magazine and, though she cared nothing about style for herself, she enjoyed telling other women what to wear. It was no wonder, Morrissey thought, that the latest fashions always looked both ugly and uncomfortable.

She had never, for a moment, considered going with him to Mt. Hope. "You know I can't possibly leave New York," she had said.

"Well, *I* can," he said. "I hate it."

"Don't be ridiculous. It's the most beautiful, the most vital, the most exhilarating city in the world. It's the hub of the universe."

"Well, I'm tired of living in a hub. I'm tired of skyscrapers and subways and penthouses and slums. I'm sick of the law, and the Army won't have me. I might just be able to do a job out there."

"Running a jail?"

"I don't expect to be 'running a jail.' "

"No? What *do* you expect to be doing?"

"Protecting the civil liberties of several thousand innocent people who've been illegally incarcerated."

" 'Interned' is the word you want."

" 'Jailed' is the word I want."

"Well, don't expect me to play matron."

She had driven him to the station in her car with her monogram on the door. She had her own telephone and her own coffee cup and her own tube of toothpaste. Her hands were large and firm, more suitable for steering a horse than a car. At the station, she kissed him from behind the wheel. "Send me a picture postcard," she said.

Lifting his bag out of her car, he felt his spirits lift too. He had been anxious, depressed for weeks about this new job. But watching Mac disappear into the traffic, he felt like a man starting off on a long holiday.

Yet he had felt humiliated too. He refused to live alone in a staff house and had himself billeted in the Bachelor Officers' Quarters instead. He spent his evenings rereading Madison's *The Federalist* and Tocqueville's *Democracy in America*, and the Bill of Rights, and preparing briefs against the United States Government on behalf of the interned Japanese.

Mrs. Haydon was still browsing among the cans while Haydon, leaning against the wall, waited patiently. Finally she turned and waved. "Bye, Mr. Morrissey," she called. "Tell Channi to bring you home to dinner sometime soon." She hurried off down the aisle. In search of anchovies and truffles and marrons glacés for the Herr Director, Morrissey thought. Haydon followed slowly.

Smug bastard, Morrissey thought, a man so self-confident he could let his silence speak for him. At staff meetings, he was always quiet and relaxed at that round table, tilting his chair back on two legs. He said nothing until everyone else had spoken. Then he responded calmly, sensibly, from the special angle of that tilted chair, with his cupped hands raised as if offering, at last, his own carefully considered comments for their approval. Yet Morrissey was impressed by the compromises effected at that round table, where no sharp edges ever intruded.

At the far end of the aisle, Mrs. Haydon was still gathering food from the shelves to grace her husband's board. Though she herself was a dainty enough dish, Morrissey thought, hugging his six-pack. "You're a lucky bastard," he said as Haydon walked by with his arms full. Haydon merely smiled.

SEVEN

THE siren screamed and Madame Sawada shouted and Nina rolled over but kept her eyes closed so that when she opened them the first thing she would see would be Sam waiting, as always, for her to wake up. But this morning he was gone, leaving not so much as a dent in that hard, flat bed. She had not seen him last night either. He was block manager now and a member of the council and on several committees for this and that. He was out at meetings almost every night. It was natural, she thought, that he should be chosen, but it left no time for her. She hated being without him at night in the stall, where she was never alone, merely lonely. Without him she felt caged in that tiny space, assaulted by other people's sounds and smells and emotions, tossed in at her over the low partitions. Without him she remembered that she was living in a stable in a concentration camp with nothing to go back to and nothing ahead. Like a horse, she thought. She gave his cot a hard angry pat and got up.

Even in the early morning the air seemed thick as custard. The sun spread out over the camp, looking for a resting place: a tree, a bit of grass, a stretch of water. But there was nothing; only the dry, scrubby land and the converted stables and the blocks of barracks, ugly as warehouses and stuffed with used goods. In the center the racetrack seemed to be shriveling in the sun. She passed crude street signs made by the evacuees. The Authority had forbidden them to use the names of American military and naval leaders, but the Japanese preferred racehorses anyway, in alphabetical order: Azúcar, Bay View, Challedon, Discovery, Equipoise. There was a Bridle Path and a Rotten Row and a Burlap Row. Stables and barracks had signs that read: "Seabiscuit Slept Here," "Bridle Suite," "Faint Hope Hotel."

It was a landscape done in charcoal, Nina thought, and for a moment she wanted to draw it: the long horizontal lines of the barracks, the vertical thrusts of the guard towers, and, in the distance, Mt. Hope like an old wrinkled snout sniffing the clouds. The only color lay in the sky, which seemed far away, as though it too had been confiscated.

Still, in only a few months the Japanese had managed to provide some color of their own. Their laundry hung like banners from the clotheslines, and rows of flowers—chrysanthemums, violets, hyacinths, zinnias, even vegetables, grown by lugging water laboriously from the wash houses—made fringes of color around the barracks and stables. There were rock gardens and even a "victory garden" with VICTORY spelled out in pebbles. American flags and gold stars hung in some of the windows, while others showed striped or flowered curtains. The wash house, built by the Issei with traditional tubs instead of the barbaric communal showers, squatted comfortably near the grandstand, and in the distance their orange Shinto shrine rose like some exotic blossom.

Up ahead she saw another splash of color. It was Mrs. Noguchi, the dentist's wife, her neighbor on the right, carrying a black and gold parasol. She always carried it back and forth to the latrine and put it up when she sat on the toilet, for there were no walls around the seats. From the front all one could see was the top of her head and the points of her shoes, but from the sides she was completely exposed. She always offered to lend it to Nina. Other women used sheets or cardboard cartons. They all suffered agonies of embarrassment at the lack of privacy. Small children had to be watched constantly. One morning, Keiko, the youngest Oshima child, was found hanging by her elbows down the hole, screaming her head off.

Mrs. Noguchi was a tiny, delicate woman, incongruously dressed in trousers and *geta* to lift her above the dust of the camp. She had finally given up wearing dresses and her white hats and white gloves and white shoes. Now she wore pants like the other women, ordered from the Sears Roebuck catalogue, like the other women. The pants were all too wide and too long and made the women look, from the back, like inverted frying pans. *"Shikata ga nai"*—"it can't be helped"— they said.

Mrs. Noguchi was expecting her husband to arrive from prison any day now, though she did not know exactly when, for his letters came with most of the words blacked out. She kept them anyway as she always had, though no longer in the lacquered box inlaid with tortoiseshell and a gold crest. Here she kept them in a gaudy Whitman's Sampler box instead. *Shikata ga nai.* She was eager to see her husband but worried too. Dr. Noguchi, she knew, would not like his wife's new Western ways. She had even allowed Toyo, her elder daughter, to cut her hair. Whatever would Dr. Noguchi think of *that?*

"He will think how beautiful you look, Mama-san," Toyo said. "And how young. The camp has made you young again. No more cooking and scrubbing and polishing all day, alone with the tables and chairs all day. Here when you scrub it's for *people,* not furniture. Here you go out when you please. Not wait for Papa-san to take you in his big car in your hat and gloves where you sit in the back with your hands folded. Here you go out when you please. You're free here, Mama-san."

Mrs. Noguchi was shocked. Her children were becoming bold, crude in this coarse place. But perceptive too. Toyo was right. She was freer here than she ever was at home: freer to come and go as she pleased, to wear comfortable clothes, to speak the English she had learned so well at the Women's University in Tokyo but which she had almost forgotten in America. At Dr. Noguchi's home only Japanese was spoken, and Mrs. Noguchi was always at home. She was glad to be out of that house where she spent her days and nights bent over the chopping board preparing traditional Japanese meals for her husband's friends—the endlessly tedious *chirashi-zushi* which he loved—and the thick cream puffs for the thick wives of his Caucasian colleagues; where she sewed and embroidered tableclothes and guest towels and handkerchiefs and tea sets for family and friends who had too many of them already. In desperation, she had recited reams of poetry to herself as she worked: tanka and haiku: Lady Kasa and Fujiwara no Teika and Bashō; and English poems of the nineteenth century: Byron and Keats and Matthew Arnold. She had even begun to compose her own tanka as she shredded and sewed.

But at Mt. Hope she was never at home. Here she worked in the hospital, scrubbing strange floors and making strange beds and bathing strange people—women *and* men—and found, to her surprise, that in many ways she liked it. She enjoyed meeting new people and was pleased at the idea of being useful to someone besides Dr. Noguchi and her children; of engaging in work more important than embroidering tea towels and baking cream puffs. She would be sorry to give it up when Dr. Noguchi came home.

In the evenings, when the youngest child was in bed and the older ones were out, she sat down beneath the single bulb and read the Japanese poems she kept hidden in the

lining of her Whitman's Sampler box, verses as carefully arranged as the flowers in the *tokonoma* or the movements of
the tea ceremony:

> *Orange blossoms that came*
> *with the fifth month—*
>
> *breathing their scent,*
> *I catch the fragrance of the sleeve*
> *of someone from long ago.*

Sometimes she went back to composing poems herself,
poems about the scenes of her childhood in Japan, where she
had lived not in the steady unblinking glare of the West but
in a gentler landscape, where the houses wore their broad-
brimmed roofs tilted against the sun; where they dressed their
rooms not in the glitter of glass and steel and chrome but in
the subdued and pensive tones of lacquer and wood. But Dr.
Noguchi would expect her to play the koto to him in the
evening, not sit silently writing poetry. And she realized that
the stall without him was far less cramped than their huge
house with him. Perhaps she would keep her job after all—
even after he came home.

Seeing Nina, she smiled and bowed. "It is filthy in there,"
she said. "Broken again. All over the floor." She smiled
again. "*Shikata ga nai.* Shall we go to the grandstand?"

People went to the grandstand latrines whenever possible
because they were built for gamblers, not evacuees. They had
enclosed cubicles and smooth seats. There was one for "Ladies" and one for "Gentlemen" and one for "Colored," which
mystified Mrs. Noguchi. "For the stable boys, probably," Nina
explained. It was an old American custom. The other latrines
were open to the wind. Sometimes an old man or an old
woman wandered into the wrong building and left—ashamed
or amused—with a full bladder. Sometimes old people lost
their way at night. Some women were afraid to venture out
alone at night. The old and the sick were often reduced to

chamberpots. "We live like animals," Mrs. Noguchi had said, and packed away her white hat and her white shoes and her white gloves.

In the wash house, she crouched behind her umbrella while Nina turned on the faucets, which were out of reach for most of the Japanese. The other women made a point of not seeing her. Some were bathing in pails or dishpans, some in underwear. Some cowered behind sheets or the protective bodies of relatives or friends. Some bathed in the middle of the night. They envied the Issei their cozy, comfortable tubs. Everyone stepped carefully over the mysterious pool at the entrance as if it were holy water, and foot infections continued to plague the camp. Everyone refused to use the long, ugly tin sink that ran like a cattle trough down one side of the room except that it was much too high—for cattle and for the Japanese women. One old woman was struggling to empy a bedpan into it. Mrs. Noguchi, squatting down behind her umbrella, shivered with shame and cold. There was no hot water.

Madame Sawada arrived with a leopard-skin coat over her kimono and a shower cap over her wig. Her daughters-in-law followed, several paces behind, lugging a huge barrel. They lurched and slipped on the wet floor while Madame Sawada shouted steady insults to them in Japanese. "Lazy, ignorant, sly," she screamed. They had tricked her stupid sons into marriage while she and her husband were in Japan. He was an important industrialist who had been sent to the States to represent his firm. He had gone back to Japan on business just before Pearl Harbor, taking his sons with him. They had been trapped there and Madame Sawada was interned in the United States like all the other Japanese. Locked up like a common criminal, she claimed, because her jealous daughters-in-law had told lies about her. She made them carry that heavy barrel down to the wash house every day so she could have privacy while she bathed. No one else, not even her daughters-in-law, was ever allowed to use it.

She stood staring contemptuously around her at the other

women while her tiny daughters-in-law struggled to fill the barrel at the high tin sink. Mrs. Noguchi, hurrying out of the shower, covered with embarrassment and her umbrella, walked straight into Madame Sawada and sent her sprawling on the wet floor. Her daughters-in-law rushed to help. Behind them the old woman gave up trying to empty her bedpan into the sink and spilled it into Madame Sawada's barrel instead.

People were waiting in long lines outside the mess hall with the sun spread out on their shoulders. Men, women, and children stood silently, melting into each other. Mrs. Noguchi skipped breakfast, as usual, to hurry back to her stall. Dr. Noguchi might be coming today. She must tidy the stall. But she would arrive at the hospital hot and breathless and on time, as always.

Nina skipped breakfast too. She had no appetite without Sam and certainly none for Block B mess hall food. It was purported to be the worst in the camp.

"What can you expect on thirty-seven cents a day?" Sam said.

"Tastes more like seven," Nina had said.

Hackett, the chief chef in Block B, was a short, powerfully built Caucasian with a narrow fringe of red hair. The rest, people said, had been lost in the mess hall soup. He had been a butcher before the war and was believed to keep a supply of knives and cleavers hidden in the storeroom. His apron was always bloody, which was strange since the meat served in the mess hall came almost entirely from cans.

Mr. Ishii stood at the end of the queue, sweating in his American army uniform, like an oversized hairshirt, with his grandson in his arms. The Ishiis and the Currys had been neighbors on Sullivan Street, but Nina rarely saw Mr. Ishii now, though he lived with the Tsudas only a few stalls away. He seemed to spend most of his time alone, hugging his grandson and his privacy to his chest. Like Sam's statue of Anchises and Aeneas, Nina thought. But that statue was vertical, one generation growing out of the other. The Ishiis were circular, the one contained by the other. Someday, she thought, she might want to draw them.

The hospital was just another long rickety barracks and, like the others, had no plumbing. Water was hauled from the nearest wash house in fire buckets. Dr. Landau, the only fully qualified doctor, was a German refugee, a tall, thin man with thin gray hair, a long nose, and dark eyes drowning with fatigue. He worked round the clock and through the week and seemed to slide rather than walk, as if to save energy. He said little and that hardly above a whisper, as if to save energy there too. He had been saved from the Nazis by a grateful patient and smuggled out by the Underground. He had sent his wife and children to Holland months before and had not heard from them since. Rejected by the United States Army, he had volunteered for Mt. Hope, which was as close to a concentration camp as he could get. He worked steadily, often without food and without sleep, trying to get closer still.

The other "doctors" were evacuees who had been expelled from medical school. Ray Noguchi, who had had one year of internship in surgery and whose services Dr. Landau desperately needed, was not allowed anywhere near the hospital because his father was a prisoner in Fort Washington.

"What has that to do with it?" Dr. Landau demanded.

"Because of the drugs."

"What drugs?"

Most of the medical equipment came out of the doctors' own kits.

A tall, solid concrete building was crowded up against one end of the hospital, breathing down its neck. This was the crematorium built by the Friendly Funeral Home of Roperville with camp labor at camp wages and so close to the hospital that Mr. Friendly could save the expense of a hearse. Anyone going in or out of the hospital or just looking out a window was confronted by it. Sometimes patients not only saw it but breathed it. Funeral urns were available only from the Friendly Funeral Home at inflated prices. The evacuees were convinced of collusion between the administration and Mr. Friendly. After two months the crematorium broke down. People were delighted to see it go cold, but it meant that any cremating had to be done in Roperville, and no one liked the idea of being sent to Roperville, not even dead. In Roperville, they suspected, dead Japanese were burned with the garbage in the city dump.

Nina nodded to the old men sitting in front of the building on wooden crates. They were watching the road for old Mr. Sato, who came every morning and afternoon to read to them from the contraband Japanese books he smuggled in under his jacket. The patients gathered around to listen and the staff merely smiled and hurried by, refusing to notice that Mr. Sato was engaged in subversive activities. They were glad to have him there to act as interpreter, for his English was perfect. He was a mild, gentle man who had once, in a note to the administration, suggested that the Japanese be called "cooperators" instead of evacuees. He had no family and lived in the BQ, where he was immensely popular, as he translated everything from the camp newspaper to the fine print on the cigarette wrappers. The old men on the crates nodded to Nina and went on watching.

Inside, some people still lay on mattresses on the floor or in the corridors. Some were patients, others simply had nowhere else to sleep. They used up all the space and all the air. Sometimes relatives tried to spend the night beside the sick. There were rumors that cremation might, occasionally, be premature.

Nina glanced at the bed in the corner where the dead were laid out surrounded by screens, objects of mystery and fear to the other patients. They watched it continuously, noting whether the screens were up or down, wondering who lay there and who would be next. Last month it was a woman in childbirth who had hemorrhaged to death because of lack of plasma. Last week it was a boy with a ruptured appendix who had come to the hospital too late. Many came too late—

defying Dr. Landau to bring them back from the dead. This morning it was another difficult birth, but this time Dr. Landau had been able to send for the husband immediately, to give a blood transfusion. The doctor was still in his cap and gown. He looked gaunt and exhausted, but the screens around that bed in the corner were gone. The bed was empty. Thank God, Nina thought. "The maternity case?" she said.

He smiled with the corners of his lips. "Another girl."

"Another Hope?" Another brand-new prisoner given, as a constant reminder, the name of her jail.

He nodded. "What else can they give her?"

It struck her that if anything happened to him, there would be, for many, no hope at all. "Mother all right?"

This time he merely nodded.

"Go to bed," she said.

He shuffled toward the door. "Let me know," he began, and stopped.

"Of course," she said quickly. She hurried toward the "nursery," where the new baby was asleep in a wooden box. Like a coffin, she thought. She picked up the youngest, newest Hope, sleeping peacefully with her fists up. Perhaps it was a good name after all.

Toward evening, Mr. Ishii arrived with his grandson in his arms. He had grown pale and thin since coming to Mt. Hope, and his World War I uniform hung loosely on him. "Good evening," Nina said, peering into the little boy's face. It was pale and thin too, and tinged with pain. "He doesn't look well, Mr. Ishii," she said. "I'm glad you brought him. We'll find a bed for him right away."

Mr. Ishii looked around at the mess in the ward, at the bedding on the floor, at the bedpans waiting to be emptied, at the patients sweating silently, motionlessly, pinned to their pain.

"No," he said quickly, "I've changed my mind."

"We'll take good care of him, Mr. Ishii. I promise you. We'll take very good care of him."

"No. I cannot leave him here. I could never leave him in such a place. He should be in a *real* hospital."

"If we find we can't help him here," Nina said, "we'll send him to the hospital in Roperville."

Mr. Ishii's face and arms tightened, and she knew she had said the wrong thing. No one, alive or dead, the evacuees believed, should be sent to Roperville. There were rumors that the Japanese beet workers there had been cheated and robbed and even attacked. Besides, evacuees were never allowed out of the camp except on work permits, not even to visit sick relatives in the hospital. If Ken-chan went to Roperville, Mr. Ishii might never see him again—except in his coffin. He thanked Nina, bowed formally, and hurried away. He was bent over now. Was the burden in his arms becoming too great?

He had once been a proud, handsome man who walked at the head of his family with his back straight and his head high, with little Ken-chan and his enormous dog at his side. Mr. Ishii had named the dog after Woodrow Wilson, a good president and a good man, a man of peace. Mr. Ishii had served under him in World War I and stood at attention for two minutes every year on the anniversary of his death. Behind him, silently, invisibly, walked the spirits of Ken-chan's parents, Mr. Ishii's children.

They had been killed in a mysterious fire that broke out shortly after Pearl Harbor. Mr. Ishii had grabbed little Ken-chan from his bed but could do nothing for the parents. He stood staring at the blaze with the boy in his arms and his eyes full of smoke and shame and tears. He had failed his children. Ken-chan would grow up without parents and his children without grandparents. Mr. Ishii was ashamed to be alive. His life hung heavily, awkwardly on him, an ill-fitting coat he longed to shed. But it was no longer his to shed. It belonged to Ken-chan now.

After that he and the boy were always together, walking hand in hand with Ken-chan's left arm resting on Woodrow Wilson's shoulder. They went to the stores and the library and the park together; and to the tailor shop, where Mr. Ishii worked with the boy and the dog at his feet. And wherever they went, Ken-chan's parents went too, walking right behind them. Ken-chan's mother was short of breath so Mr. Ishii always walked slowly.

Now he walked stooped over and alone, except for the child in his arms. Woodrow Wilson had been left behind. "No pets of any kind," the evacuation orders had warned. For days a neat, hand-printed sign was seen in Ken-chan's bedroom window: "My dog needs a home. He is very gentle. Will someone please take him?" But no one did. The day before they left, Mr. Ishii and Ken-chan walked Woodrow Wilson for the last time, the boy's hand on the dog's shoulder. They never saw the dog again. He had stayed on Sullivan Street, in the garden beneath the pepper tree. Ken-chan's parents had stayed behind too. They would never have allowed themselves to be "evacuated." They were no longer following Mr. Ishii. They were with Woodrow Wilson on Sullivan Street.

Only the boy remained, always in Mr. Ishii's arms. He might have been soldered there. Mr. Ishii refused to go to work because of the boy in his arms. He refused to send Ken-chan to the kindergarten run by the nuns. And he refused to leave him at the hospital. They had taken everything from him. He would not let them take his grandson too. He left, hunched over the child, hugging his treasure, his face angry with suspicion.

As he walked, he stared ahead at the mountain in the distance, not tall and graceful but squat, deformed, as if the Caucasians had cut it down to size. In Japan, mountains were sacred, mysterious, beautiful, like gods with one foot on the earth. The ancient Japanese had been content to leave them alone, to worship them from below. Later they built shrines and buried their dead there. Only in the West did men climb mountains in order to conquer them. Mr. Ishii felt a certain sympathy for Mt. Hope, so lonely, so battered, so despised.

EIGHT

Mrs. Oshima sat in the mess hall drinking tea the color of urine in tiny sips to avoid the taste, with her youngest daughter, Keiko, beside her. Only mothers and very young children still ate together. Even her husband would not eat with her, claiming that just sitting in the mess hall irritated his ulcer. Recently he had developed a toothache as well but refused to see a doctor. He didn't want any damn *keto* sticking hairy fingers into his mouth.

He stayed in the stall all day waiting for her to bring back something he could eat from the mess hall or the canteen. But the mess hall food only sent him into a rage and the canteen sold nothing but cookies and candy and Cokes and potato chips, food fit only for children—Caucasian children who would grow up fat and pasty-faced with weak teeth and floppy tongues. Besides, the canteen required money, and Mrs. Oshima had no money to buy anything, not even soap or toothpaste or shoes for little Keiko, whose old ones had grown too small. Mrs. Oshima cut off the ends and suffered agonies of shame at her daughter's exposed toes.

Mrs. Oshima suffered over her husband too, who had been a strong, cheerful, energetic man in the days before Pearl Harbor and had done many things to support his family. He had worked hard as a farm laborer until he earned enough money to buy some land. When he discovered he was not allowed to own land, he rented it and spent twelve hours a day with his back bent, growing chrysanthemums big as melons. Other Japanese sent their sons to work for him, to develop muscles and self-reliance. The owner, watching all this from behind the fence of his dilapidated farm, decided he wanted the land back. Mr. Oshima produced his lease. The owner raised the rent. Mr. Oshima paid.

One morning, he found that all his flowers, acres and acres of them, had been beheaded. He planted more and sat in shifts with his assistants, a cutlass across his lap, until the last flower was picked.

After Pearl Harbor, when the bus refused to stop for him, he walked the seven miles to his land and back each day. But he was defeated by the curfew ordering all Japanese to remain at home between 8:00 P.M. and 6:00 A.M. and forbidding them to travel more than five miles in any direction at any time. The owner got his land back, fertile and profitable, with the huge crop Mr. Oshima had cultivated. But Mr. Oshima refused to move away—off the West Coast—as the government urged all the Japanese to do. Instead, he bought an old barber chair and taught himself to give haircuts by practicing on himself and his sons, though it was considered shameful to be a barber, like butchering and caring for corpses and graves, occupations fit only for the despised *eta*.

But he had changed, Mrs. Oshima thought, sipping her tea. In the camp he did nothing but complain, sitting on the steps his sons had built, with his hands dangling between his knees, spoiling the view, getting angrier and angrier. Someday he would lose his temper at the Caucasian police and they would shoot him dead. Meantime, he raged at his own family. Mrs. Oshima got up at last and walked back to the stall slowly, fearfully, holding little Keiko with one hand and her husband's dinner with the other.

"You know I can't eat that," he told her, scowling at the two naked-looking little sausages. "Not with my ulcer. Is that all?"

"That is all that was left."

"The rest was even worse," Josie said.

He got up and walked angrily to the door, staring at the sunset churning up the clouds, turning them into huge red waves, ready to drown the sky in blood.

"You will die of hunger," Mrs. Oshima said.

"He'll die of apoplexy first," Josie murmured.

Mrs. Oshima handed Jack, her oldest son, the *Handbook*. "Read, please," she said. "About special food, please."

"Special food," Jack read, translating as he went, "will be provided for babies and invalids. . . ."

"Go find it, please," Mrs. Oshima said. "The special foods. For your father. He is an invalid, yes?"

"Yes. But there isn't any special food, Mama."

"Of course there is. It says so. In the handbook. *Their* book."

"Never mind what it says, Mama. There isn't any."

"They lie? Is that what they do in that big angry building up there? Make up lies?"

"Maybe they'll have special food later, when the camp is better organized."

"Maybe later is too late for your father," Mrs. Oshima said.

"It is already too late," Mr. Oshima shouted from the doorway. "I am weak from not eating, from sitting in a horse stall all day, smelling horse shit, staring at horseflies, sleeping on hay. Soon I will die of glanders, like a horse." He said it all in Japanese, as always, but his family, he knew, understood. Just as he understood their English when he chose. They were staring at him in dismay.

"Oh, Papa," Josie said. "Why don't you go to work? It

would be good for you, Papa. Really it would. Give you something to do, to think about instead of . . ."

"Work? What work? I am a gardener. I grow flowers. I do not dig ditches for the *hakujin*."

"It wouldn't be for *them*, Papa," Jack said in Japanese. "It would be for *us*. For the *evacuees*."

"No!" he shouted. "Positively no!"

"Then be a gardener, Papa," Josie said. "They need gardeners. To plant grass and . . ."

"For what? For their horses to eat?"

"Why not be a barber?" the second son said. "You're a good barber, Papa. And they need them here."

"Besides," Josie said, "it would make a good impression on the administration. They think all Issei are either traitors or bums or both."

Mr. Oshima stared at her in horror, his own daughter calling him a traitor and a bum. She was wearing trousers like a man and paint on her face like a prostitute. He looked at his wife, but she was nodding in agreement. She was wearing trousers too. Freaks of nature, he thought, women in men's clothes, Americans with Japanese faces. They were neither women nor Japanese anymore. "You!" he screamed at Josie. "*You* telling *me* what to do?" He had taken a step toward her with his fists clenched when Jack moved quickly between them. Mr. Oshima gave a howl of rage and ran out of the stall.

Poor man, Mrs. Oshima thought, staring after him. He was no longer Mr. Oshima, her husband. He belonged to the *hakujin*, who had locked him up body and soul. He was no longer himself. He was theirs, their creation, and the more he struggled, the tighter they squeezed. His heart had become small and hard as a nut, so that he had almost attacked poor Josie. His brain too, probably, sending him out of the stall like a madman. But he would come back. Where else could he and his anger go? He would come back again and sit in the doorway again and spew his rage all over them again. They were knee-deep in it already.

Mr. Oshima, rushing out into the night, longed to run far away into the silence and privacy of total darkness. But the long black buildings lay all around him like enormous crates packed with people, ready to be shipped out. Beyond lay the barbed-wire fence. As he ran, the huge searchlight caught him and smothered him in a blanket of light. He spent the night facedown on the racetrack, waiting for the horses to trample him into the dust.

In the morning he sat in the bleachers, shivering with shame in the hot sun, remembering how his fists had clenched against his own daughter, remembering Jack's face as he stepped between them, remembering, too, his shouts of rage that could be heard all up and down the stable.

Around him, old men lay sleeping on the benches. Others played *goh* or *shogi* or dice. One old man was playing Japanese music on a bamboo flute, delicate, elusive, plaintive as a wisp of smoke—until it was drowned out by a group of teenagers playing guitars and singing "We're Here, Because We're Here." Teenaged girls walked round and round the racetrack for exercise inside a pocket of dust, carrying black umbrellas against the sun. Teenaged boys played softball and young men practiced sumo and karate, and judo under the stern eyes of the judo master and his assistants from the BQ. On the benches around him, little girls giggled steadily over a game of jacks and two little boys played *jankempo*—(stone, paper, scissor)—in the dust below. A noisy group of young toughs sat on the bottom bench and shouted crude comments: *"dai-kon-ashi"*—"legs like white radishes"—to the women going by; and *"bootchi"* or "Buddhahead" to the shambling old Issei. In the center of the track, an old man in a long white robe preached an incoherent sermon on the theme of Jesus the outcast, Jesus the despised, who lived in a stable and slept on straw. "Jesus, the evacuee!" he shouted.

Mr. Oshima stared around him in disgust. The old here were finished, the middle-aged stalled, the young stunted. Living in two cultures, they were degraded by both. They were neither Japanese nor American. They were, simply, evacuees.

He longed for the sight of green grass spreading out soft and cool around him. But here even the sky looked hard, glazed. The soldiers could shoot holes in it, but his prayers would only bounce off it. In the distance, he could see the crooked mountain with its head cut off. Like his chrysanthemums, he thought. The white man destroyed everything he saw, including Mr. Oshima. He had been, as his children said, "Pearl Harbored" as much as any battleship in the fleet. Only he refused to sink. Not like his neighbor, Mr. Fakuda, who committed suicide after hearing of the attack. "I am ashamed of being Japanese," he had said. Then he went into the bathroom and shut the door. Mr. Oshima had felt shock, grief, regret at the news, but he refused to feel shame. When the *hakujin* took their revenge by punishing the innocent, he became permanently outraged.

He refused to cooperate from the very beginning. He refused to move off the West Coast. Not like the Yamamotos next door, who shut up their shop and set off in their rickety old pickup truck, bound for relatives in Arizona. "We must leave California," they explained. "The government said so." One week later they were back.

They had met hostile signs all along the way. "No Japs Wanted Here." "No Jap Rats Fed Here." Gas stations and hotels and restaurants refused to serve them. At one motel, the owner greeted them with a shotgun and began to fire as soon as they stepped out of the truck. A crowd gathered, laughing and laying bets on which Jap he would hit first. Farther along, they saw a huge notice signed by the governor: "Japs keep out," it read. "If you're not good enough for California, you're not good enough for us." At the Arizona border they were turned back by the police.

In the burning sun, Mr. Oshima began to feel weak and dizzy. He thought of the cellar Sam Curry and the Noguchis and even his own sons had built beneath the stables. It was

always much cooler down there. But he refused to have anything to do with such "improvements," refused even to enjoy
them. Suddenly he saw his second daughter, "Mary," with
one of the Noguchi boys. They were sitting close together,
their heads almost touching. As he watched, they got up and
walked slowly away, their hands locked, their faces turned
toward each other. He watched until they disappeared behind
the grandstand. He wanted to get up and shout at them to
stop, to race after them and drag them back. But his throat
felt dry and the top of his head was burning as if the sun had
landed there. He could not shout. He could not move. He
could only go on sitting in the grandstand, a captive spectator
at some terrible game.

That night the soldiers came to the hospital carrying old
Mr. Sato. Nina, working late, took one look at him, pointed
to the bed in the corner, and put the screens up around him.
Mr. Sato would not be reading to the patients anymore.

"Heart attack," one of the soldiers said. "Poor old bastard."

Nina saw the blood seeping through Mr. Sato's coat.

Later, in his office, Dr. Landau lit a cigarette and told Nina,
in his precise and cultivated English, that Mr. Sato had been
shot during the night on his way to the latrine. He had evidently become confused and wandered too close to the fence.
He had not heard the soldier's command to halt, or had not
understood it. He had not halted.

"So they *killed* him?"

The doctor nodded. "We have been ordered to keep
this . . . this . . . to keep it quiet," he said, pulling on his cigarette, pulling smoke deep into that perpetual hole inside him.

"Keep it quiet? We can't *possibly* keep it quiet. For one
thing, he'll be missed. The men in the BQ, the patients here.
Everybody knew him. He came every day. They waited for
him."

"They will be told he died of a heart attack—on his way
to the latrine."

"But the administration mustn't be allowed to cover it up. It was murder."

"Of course it was murder. But if we say so, there will be more murders."

"And if the soldiers get away with it this time they'll do it again. Why not? Out of sheer boredom." She was close to tears.

He leaned forward. "If we do not cover it up," he said gently, "the following may very possibly occur: there will be a riot, the Army will come in, and your bored soldiers will have something active and exciting to do. Yes? You remember Pine Gap?" Everyone in the camp knew about Pine Gap, another internment camp. There had been a riot there last month during a contraband raid. The Army was called in, two evacuees were killed and ten wounded.

"So," Dr. Landau went on, "we will keep it quiet, please. Yes?" He stared at the limp ash growing between his fingers. "Yes, he will be missed," he said softly. "Of course he will be missed." He stubbed his cigarette out carefully. "*I* shall miss him."

The next day the old men were sitting in front of the hospital as usual, waiting for Mr. Sato's hearse as they had once waited for Mr. Sato. They had been awake when the soldiers came, had seen them put Mr. Sato in that special bed in the corner with the screens around it. It was Mr. Sato, they were told in the morning, Mr. Sato who had had a fatal heart attack during the night on his way to the latrine. They had known Mr. Sato very well. He was a kind, gentle man. They knew there was nothing wrong with his heart. They were thankful, at least, that the crematorium had broken down, thankful that they would not have to sit quietly while poor Mr. Sato drifted past their noses.

They were there, watching, when the hearse bumped its way across the field beyond the barbed-wire fence, through the nettles and the stones and the scrub, jolting poor Mr. Sato, rattling his bones, rocking his brains. There were no mourners at the grave. Only immediate relatives were allowed to attend funerals and Mr. Sato had no relatives, only friends—many, many friends. But friends were not permitted, only soldiers with guns, as if they expected Mr. Sato to wander too close to the fence again. There were no mourners and no crepe-paper flowers made by sorrowing relatives to decorate his grave. There were only the soldiers and a strange clergyman administering an alien comfort—and the old men watching behind the fence.

And Nina. She was watching too, sitting on a mound of stones behind the hospital as she sometimes did when she was free for a few moments, to escape from the sights and sounds and smells of the wards. She sat with her back to the hospital, oblivious of the guards in the tower above her and the long straight rows of barracks on her right, drawn up in battle formation. She was staring at the soldiers burying Mr. Sato in the wilderness. As she watched, she saw an old man picking his way slowly across the field toward the funeral and the barbed-wire fence—and a "heart attack"? She dug her hands into her pockets and found the pen and pad she always carried as part of her nurse's equipment. She pulled them out and, with her eyes on the old man, began to sketch.

She told no one but Sam the truth about Mr. Sato's death. "Dr. Landau was perfectly right," Sam said.

NINE

THE cold came suddenly, freezing the ground and the evacuees in their thin summer clothes, which were all they had and all they had ever needed at home, where it was always summer. But the Mt. Hope Racetrack, off season, turned bitterly cold. The Authority was forced to issue bits of secondhand army uniforms to those who could not afford to buy winter clothes. Men, women, and children stood on line for hours in the icy wind with the sand like broken glass in their faces. They developed colds, flu, strep throats, chilblains. After that they moved slowly, weighed down by secondhand long johns and khaki trousers and ear muffs and caps and twenty-pound jackets, patched and darned and rent with agony.

Tony Takahashi, the small, scared Kibei with a desk beside the director's office and a bed beside the judo instructor's, shivered. He was lying on a hard cot with two army blankets that smelled of blood and a straw mattress that smelled of manure. He hated waking in the Bachelors' Quarters instead of in his own room at the Lawsons', an apartment, really, with its own bathroom and a hot plate and bookcases and sprigs of cherry blossoms climbing the wall. His desk overlooked the garden with a lilac tree that, it seemed to him now, was always in bloom, its scent perpetually in the air.

In the crowded BQ, he awoke to a different smell, so strong he bumped his nose on it: of sake and old men and old money that changed hands every night—and burnt flesh. He imagined he could even smell the ashes of Mr. Wada's father, who had been found dead on arrival. Mr. Wada could not afford to buy the undertaker's urn. He kept the remains in a cardboard box beneath his bed.

Tony heard groans from the next bed as he did every morning, though the judo instructor, known simply as "Judo," was among the youngest in the barracks and certainly the toughest, a short fierce man adored by Issei and Kibei alike—except Tony. Tony had hated him ever since that first night when Judo had knocked the pen out of his hand and the smile off his face and called him *inu,* traitor; hated the squat powerful body with the heavy legs curved like a giant turtle's, moving slowly, silently, menacingly. He hated the contempt that bubbled in the corners of Judo's mouth and dripped from his voice when he called Tony *hakujin*-lover, so eager to help his jailers keep his fellow prisoners locked up so he could have a nice, comfortable job behind a desk and be paid $16.00 a month for filing papers and hanging up the *keto* boss's coat; instead of $8.00 for digging in the frozen earth with the wind freezing his ass.

"How come you're not sleeping up there too, with the *keto* bosses?" he shouted. "In one of their nice, comfortable houses with lots of air-conditioning in summer and heat in winter and plenty of hot water and your own flush toilet with a real seat and a door to close so you can be all nice and private and cozy while you shit? So how come you're still down here with us? Huh? So you can inform on us? Like the fucking little *inu* you are?" Tony was terrified of him.

He was the real leader of the BQ who did as he pleased. He had been elected block manager unanimously (Tony had been careful to be out that night), but the administration vetoed it because he had been arrested several times for gambling. So much for *hakujin* democracy, he announced, and hung an enormous Japanese flag above his bed which extended over Tony's as well. He kept an ancient samurai sword in its silken bag beneath his mattress and took it out once a month to polish it. Kneeling on the floor, he would hold the long, elegantly curved blade to the light until it looked as if his whole arm had burst into flame. He no longer had the finely powdered stone used for polishing, but he wiped the blade lovingly, twice, with a carefully preserved piece of Japanese paper kept in its own little red pouch. Tony watched these proceedings with terror and hid his Berkeley banner in the bottom of his suitcase.

Judo continued to be the real leader of the BQ and held meetings in the barracks almost every night to which Tony was never invited. "We're trying to decide what to do about rotten little *inu*s," Judo told him. Once, when the camp radio piped in news of an American victory in the Pacific, Judo hacked the speaker to pieces with his bare fists. It was Judo who organized the building of the Japanese bathhouse for the BQ with decent individual tubs instead of primitive communal showers. It was Judo who designed the dainty Shinto temple and recruited the Issei to build it. He led the gambling and the drinking in the barracks every night and often the brawling as well. He refused to work because, as an Issei, he would be allowed to do only the most menial jobs at the lowest wages. He earned more by giving judo lessons, though it was strictly illegal to take money for anything but regularly authorized work. Yet he was attracting young men from all over the camp.

But now he lay flat on his back. He had been sick on and

off for weeks but refused to go to the hospital with its Caucasian doctor. Instead, he stayed in the barracks, where Mr. Wada, a slender man with sad eyes and arms like pylons, nursed him tenderly with traditional Japanese methods. Judo's body was covered with scars from the burning *mogusa* cones Mr. Wada applied all over him; and Tony's bed was covered with smoke and the odor of burning incense and burning flesh and the sounds of Judo gasping with pain.

Tony buried his nose in his pillow and thought of the Lawsons, wondering what they were doing at this exact moment, though he had no idea what time it was in Emerson, California, except that it was certainly earlier. He imagined them walking behind him, stepping over his discarded hours. He should be clearing their path, not littering it.

His own parents had disappeared. His father was a plump, shiny little man: shiny shoes, shiny gold-rimmed glasses, even the pinstripes on his suits seemed to shine. He had spent his life in his office, attending to imports and exports, making money to pay for his wife's seventeenth-century Sotatsu fans and French perfumes. In the end, Tony thought, his wife and sons did not interest him nearly as much as the buttons on his desk and the golf clubs in his bag. A thoroughly Westernized man, he had, nevertheless, strong Japanese business connections and would certainly be among the first to be arrested after Pearl Harbor. Poor Papa, Tony thought. But he felt no pain. He hardly knew his father.

The thought of his mother in an internment camp gave Tony real pleasure. He had hated her ever since he could remember. She was a tall, terrifying woman with an enormous edifice of gleaming black hair set on a dead white face. Everything else was covered with silk and brocade. She had arranged the marriage of Tony's elder brother and insisted that the couple live with her in traditional Japanese manner. As the young husband grew to love his wife, Mrs. Takahashi treated her with increasing contempt. She never allowed the girl to eat with the family or sit with them or go out with them. She ate alone, spent her evenings alone in her room and her days washing and ironing Mrs. Takahashi's underclothes and scrubbing her drawers. She brushed Mrs. Takahashi's hair and gave her daily massages but was forbidden to speak to her—except to answer her questions. When the baby came, she was not permitted to care for it—except to nurse it. When she stopped nursing, Mrs. Takahashi sent her away. Her family, filled with shame, refused to take her back. Tony's brother, a good son, accepted his mother's authority. The young wife, less cooperative, committed suicide—brazenly, openly—by throwing herself into the river. Her husband grieved in silence and finally stabbed himself in secret. His mother sent the baby to an orphanage.

Tony stayed out of her sight as much as possible, but when he was twelve his mother sent him to a monastery in Japan anyway, to become a Buddhist monk. "So you won't grow up crooked like the *hakujin*," she said, "who cannot tell the straight path from the twisted." So I won't grow up to get in your way, Tony thought.

By now she must surely be living in an internment camp, he thought, sleeping on straw, eating slop from a tin dish, breaking her long, lacquered nails on the washboard. She would sit on hard, backless benches at meals, surrounded by *eta:* a butcher on one side, a gravedigger on the other. He imagined her in the wash house, looking for somewhere to lay her rings; standing in the public shower while Mrs. Watanabe, who told fortunes, examined her naked body like a palm, or stood over her as she squatted on the toilet. "You want to eat a little less starch, dear," Mrs. Watanabe might say, bowing formally with her handkerchief over her nose while Mrs. Takahashi looked around for a bit of newspaper. She might even die of outrage and constipation. But she had probably gone back to Japan long ago.

Tony hated the Buddhist monastery, where he was hemmed in on all sides by a ritual that limited his world to the excruciating pains in his back and legs and the incense stick burning away his life. Working outdoors—weeding, chopping, sweeping—he was aware of the mountain rising tall and stern above him. Sometimes he stared at it until he imagined he could see a face staring back. He longed to climb it, to see its features more clearly, to see the trees that fanned its brow and the shreds of clouds that circled its throat. For he could not fit himself into the narrow, rigidly anonymous life of the monastery below. He had grown up in the West and his legs were the wrong shape for the lotus position. He was accustomed to heavy shoes and heavy knickers that fell below the knee so that his walk, in the loose sandals and long robes that teased his ankles, was sloppy and undisciplined, not the gait of a man certain of his own path. Without his usual covering of hair, he could hardly keep his head. Besides, he did not want to empty his mind; he wanted to fill it. He did not want to live in the present; he wanted to escape from it. After five years, with the blessing of the mountain and the monk in the next cell, he fled.

He found the Lawsons on the deck of the SS *San Francisco,* bound for California. He adored them from the start, from the moment he emerged from his hiding place in the lifeboat and saw them lying side by side in their deck chairs, their long thin bodies clothed in blue with touches of white—white hair, white hands, white shirts—like strips of sky dropped softly on the upper deck. They were the Reverend and Mrs. Theodore Lawson, from Emerson, California, returning from a visit to church schools in Japan. They spent the day in their deck chairs, reading, dozing, gazing at the sea, remembering aspects of their long, dedicated but quiet lives. Good deeds, they felt, had been all too easily available to them, landing like tame pigeons at their feet, requiring only the tiniest crumbs from the Lawsons' enormous store. Nothing very difficult, they believed, had ever been demanded of them. Tony had been simply another tame pigeon.

They took him home to their tiny house with the extra room over the garage. It was a quiet, modest house, done in soft tones: white and blue and gray. Even the garden seemed especially gentle, with no thorns, no pointed leaves, no strident colors. They sent Tony to high school and then to the university. When the draft came, he enlisted.

"I must," he said. If there should be war between Japan and the United States, he must be clearly identified—in khaki. After Pearl Harbor he was discharged. He came home with no protective coloration.

At first he thought the Lawsons could help him. At first they thought so too. In the end, they shook their heads. "My dear boy," Mr. Lawson said.

"The only way," Tony's anthropology professor said, "is to get a new face. But it will cost a lot of money." Tony did not have a lot of money.

He could not believe that, for once, his charm and his wits had failed him. Always before, everyone but his mother had succumbed to them. Even old Mokichi, in the cell next to his in the monastery, an intensely pious, even holy monk in spite of his two silver teeth, had helped him to escape with directions, instructions, food, coins, prayers, and tears.

Lying in bed, Tony felt the tears in his own eyes—from memory or the fumes from Judo's *mogusa* treatment.

The head counter for the block, known as "Block Head," knocked on the door but dared not come in. The only time he had shown his face, he was met by jeers and threats and flying sandals. Mr. Wada gave the count for Judo, who was still groaning in his sleep.

Tony got up quickly. Cold as it was, he preferred the outdoors to the noises and smells of the BQ with the Japanese hemming him in. He was not used to them anymore. For years he had been surrounded by Caucasians, at home and at school. He had been happy among them, had been accepted by them, had thought of himself as American, like them, the son of the Reverend and Mrs. Theodore Lawson.

He dressed, grabbed a towel, and hurried out into the frozen world with the wind whipping his face and the mountain like a thick stalagtite ready to topple over and crush them all. Racing back, his wet towel froze and his wet hair turned to ice; he imagined it breaking off, piece by piece. At the BQ, his palm stuck to the doorknob. Inside, the hostility rose like steam. He hung up his towel and fled.

He hurried past the latrine, past the long queue and the short, rounded figures with their heads sucked in between their shoulders. He would use the men's room in the administration building, though it was restricted to "Staff Only"—which meant Caucasians only. At the mess hall the line was even longer. He would get breakfast at the staff cafeteria, thanks to Toyo Noguchi who worked there.

The thought of her cheered him. He could warm his hands in her long black hair. If he married her, he could move out of the BQ, away from Judo and his thugs. She was the first Japanese girl who had ever been kind to him. Nisei girls would have nothing to do with Kibei, whom they regarded as "foreigners" with their stiff, formal manners and slight accents. But Tony had been sent to Japan so late—his mother had probably forgotten all about him—that his English and his manners were completely American. Even so, as soon as a Nisei girl discovered he was a Kibei, she backed away. Did Toyo know he was a Kibei? In Japan, people took great pains to check on family background before a marriage, often tracing it for several generations. Certain clans were taboo. Even in America, people like the Noguchis would be sure to continue the custom. Tony did not have a single relative in the camp. He did not know where his parents were or even if they were still alive. A good son always knows where his parents are. The Noguchis might even suspect him of being *eta.*

Yet Tony did not really want to marry Toyo, despite her kindness and her beautiful hair. He did not want to marry anyone yet, even to escape from the BQ. If he ever got out of Mt. Hope, he wanted to go back to the Lawsons and to Berkeley to learn to be an anthropologist. Among Indians and Eskimos and Africans, no one would know or care whether he was Issei or Nisei or Kibei. He had applied for a fellowship at dozens of Eastern universities. The replies had all been the same: they were not accepting any more fellowship applications for the present. Any more *Japanese* applications, he thought.

In the administration building he hurried into the men's room. Coming out, he saw Schweiker, the chief executive officer, known as the chief executing officer, walking toward him down the hall; a man who covered miles in minutes in those high, pointed boots and saw into distant secret places from under that huge black hat. He had undoubtedly seen the bacon-lettuce-and-tomato sandwich from the cafeteria yesterday, hidden under Tony's jacket.

"Morning, sir," Tony said. Schweiker merely nodded and walked on, and into Haydon's office. To report that Tony Takahashi had been caught using the staff men's room and carrying food from the cafeteria into his office? Tony would never get that fellowship. He would never go to graduate school with a library big as a church, a church stuffed with books. He was hungry for books. The camp library had only a few provided by the Authority—textbooks on citizenship and American history—and a box of secondhand publications of the twenties donated by the Roperville Baptist Church: *Spiritual Principles in Advertising; Moses: The First Entrepreneur; Jesus, Founder of Modern Business;* and ten Gideon Bibles.

Toyo Noguchi came hurrying toward him, with coffee and two doughnuts under a napkin. "To Tony from Toyo," she whispered, shoving the food into his hands. "Toyo and Tony. They go together, don't you think?"

"Definitely." He grinned and thanked her.

"Movies tonight?" she said shyly.

"Of course. Same time. New place."

They had found the new place one night when a cold wind rose, lifting the sand, tumbling the clouds, blowing out the stars, forcing them closer together as they sat side by side in the grandstand. Instinctively, they put their arms around each other and walked slowly down the steps to a quiet, secluded spot far back beneath the grandstand where the wind never came. Even the searchlight, they thought, could not reach them there. When Tony got home, the BQ seemed more sinister, more frightening than ever.

Last night it had reeked of homemade brandy and hatred and burnt flesh. As soon as he came in, all talking stopped. There had been another raid that evening, Mr. Wada told him in his carefully lowered voice. Forty men were arrested and much money confiscated. Strange, he said, letting his voice drop even lower, how the raids always occurred when Tony was out.

"But I'm *always* out," Tony said.

Mr. Wada nodded silently—they all nodded silently—and bent over to apply another *mogusa* cone to Judo's back. The smell of burning flesh filled the barracks, and the sound of Judo sucking in his breath.

Sitting at his desk in the administration building, Tony could still hear that sound and buried his nose in his handkerchief to avoid that smell. He hid the doughnuts and coffee in the bottom drawer of his desk under a pile of papers and heard Haydon's door open and close and Schweiker's heels clicking down the hall. He wondered what the penalty would be for urinating in the Caucasian latrine and eating food from the Caucasian cafeteria. He thought of the prison camps for Japanese traitors, where he would certainly be killed by the guards or the inmates. Unless he was shot by the soldiers at Mt. Hope first—by order of Chief Executive Officer Schweiker for "attempting to escape."

He sat staring out the window, at the barracks beaten by the wind, at the poor mangled mountain clinging to the horizon, as though afraid of being blown away.

TEN

"WE got troubles," Schweiker said. "Like I warned you we would." He was sitting in his usual place near the door in Haydon's office with his legs stretched out and his pre-lunch Dentyne revolving between his jaws. He kept his face toward the window, watching the gate to make sure that the flag and the soldiers were still there. His hands lay low in his pockets, the left curled around the Bible, the right fingering his gun. Beside him Rigsbee stared out the window, too, with his hands in his pockets, too, clutching his handkerchief and his nasal spray.

"What kind of troubles?" Haydon said. He was leaning back in his chair with his head tilted, studying Schweiker like a painting, examining his boots and his three-piece suit and the exaggerated angle of his hat. Haydon, who had swum and sailed on the shores of Martha's Vineyard, was fascinated by that hat. He found it daring, colorful, "a touch of the authentic." "Just what do you have in mind, Caspar?" he said.

"The Isseis, for one thing. They're bad news. Won't work, won't obey regalations. Just sit around playing those Jap games and brewing sake and gambling and fighting. In and out of jail all the time and thinking up new ways to make trouble. Like organizing a Black Society right there in the BQ and building that there temple and their own private bathhouse. With stolen wood."

The Japanese were certainly loosening Schweiker's tongue, Morrissey thought. Silent Schweiker was becoming a preacher with a singularly unattractive text.

"Anyone ever give them permission?" Schweiker went on. "That's bad 'ministration, that is. You don't stick to the rules, you don't have control. First thing we know, everyone'll be doing what he blasted well pleases. Like that judo instructor giving judo lessons and taking money for it. Which is strictly against regalations." Beside him, Rigsbee nodded vigorously.

Nodded, Haydon knew, for almost the entire staff of clerks and petty bureaucrats, not to mention Security and the internal police.

An attack on his whole administration, Morrissey thought. But Haydon was taking it calmly, gazing at Schweiker as he might have gazed at a student who had raised an interesting point. Nothing, Morrissey thought, seemed to shake him. In all the months they had worked together Morrissey had never seen Haydon angry or irritated or depressed or even impatient. He was always pleasant, cheerful, even buoyant, with his smile floating like a banner above any turbulence below. He was taller than most, perhaps he saw farther. Morrissey felt his glasses sliding down his nose and shoved them back up again. He was filled with irritation at Haydon's bland style, but he felt admiration, too, for his ability to keep the balance between Schweiker's prejudices and Morrissey's passions. Haydon was, Morrissey decided, that rare and precious creature, a rational man. Ideal in an administrator but terrible in a husband, he thought, remembering poor Mrs. Haydon rushing around the PX in search of delicacies for him. Yet she had been willing to come with him to Mt. Hope. His own wife, he reminded himself, was spending the war in New York.

Haydon was contemplating Schweiker, a hardworking man with endless patience for detail. He arrived at his office early and left late. A dedicated man, Haydon thought. "You're right, of course, Caspar," he said. "The Issei *are* a problem." It was a problem they had discussed at every staff meeting since the camp opened. "But we can't *force* them to work."

"Of course not," Morrissey said impatiently. "And murdering one of their mates didn't help. We're damned lucky they didn't start a riot when it happened. And there aren't any regulations that say we can shoot down a harmless old man in the middle of the night. . . ."

"For trying to escape," Schweiker said.

"For trying to find the latrine. Besides, do you know what the legal penalty is for a *prisoner of war attempting to escape? Prisoner of war,* mind you, not a civilian internee. *For trying to escape,* mind you, not for getting lost. Know what the punishment for *that* is?" He leaned over, glaring at Schweiker. "A maximum of thirty days in jail," he said slowly. "Not death."

There was a long pause. Schweiker shifted his hat. Morrissey, who had played cowboys and Indians on the streets of Hell's Kitchen, hated that hat. Pathological bully, he thought, in a three-piece suit.

"That soldier was court-martialed, wasn't he?" Schweiker said.

"And sentenced to a one-dollar fine. For 'unauthorized use of government property.' "

The room was silent except for the sound of Haydon tilting his chair and Rigsbee blowing his nose and Schweiker stretching his legs out still farther. A little more, Morrissey thought, and his feet would be right under Haydon's desk. "Trouble is," he said, "there's nothing we *can* do to integrate the Issei into camp life. Not as long as we insist on treating them like enemies."

"Which is *egg-zackly* what they are," Schweiker said. "Only solution is to get them transferred out. Before they contaminate the whole blasted camp. Never should have been dumped here in the first place. Should have been sent to Fort Washington. Direct."

"A prison," Morrissey said, "for *'dangerous enemy aliens.'*"

"Well?" Schweiker said.

"You have to prove it," Morrissey said. But he knew that was not true. He had come to Mt. Hope to protect the rights of the Japanese. But the Japanese, he realized, had no rights. He was spending his time trying to protect them from Schweiker.

"The best we can do for them now," Haydon said, bringing his chair to an upright position, "is to let the Issei remain segregated. Let them carry on their traditional practices, even encourage them. Let them have their temple and their judo and their baths and their clubs." It was what they had decided to do at every meeting since the camp opened. He looked at Schweiker. "At least for the time being," he said.

"It's not enough," Morrissey said. "But it's something."

"It's appeasement," Schweiker said while Rigsbee sneezed and nodded. "And it's dangerous."

Could he be right? Haydon wondered. Schweiker, after all, had been many things in his life and all of them practical, useful, tough-minded: an assistant foreman in a factory, an assistant comptroller in a mining company, even a deputy sheriff in Texas. He would certainly understand that mysterious being, "the man in the street," whom Haydon had spent his life studying but never met—until Schweiker. Schweiker, after all, had spent his days consorting with men, not ideas, and working with numbers, hard, precise numbers, not soft, slippery words. He did not teeter back and forth between one position and another. Even Morrissey, with his wide trousers and loose loafers and his glasses forever wandering around his nose, looked flabby and sloppy beside Schweiker, in spite of his sharp legal mind. Morrissey would do better, Haydon thought, to stop fighting Schweiker and start studying him; to try to understand him, even learn from him.

"What we *should* have done," Schweiker was saying, "was send them *all* to Roperville to pick sugar beets like the farmers wanted. We should do it now. They still need help there—in the canning factories. And these here Isseis still need work. What's more, it's the kinda work they're used to. Ship 'em out. Fast."

Haydon frowned. He had been enthusiastic about the project at first, had urged the evacuees to sign up. He welcomed anything that would allow them to get out of the camp for a while and to earn regular wages. It would also, he thought, be good for town-camp relations. But the project had not been popular.

"Damn few signed up," Rigsbee said. "And most of them quit." He buried his face in his handkerchief.

"Not surprising," Morrissey said. "Considering that they had to sign up 'for the duration' and pledge themselves to do any job they were given and accept the 'going wage.' They know damn well that no Japanese ever gets the 'going wage,' least of all when he's an interned 'enemy alien.' "

"That," Schweiker said, "is hogwash. They didn't sign up because they didn't have to. Just like they don't sign up for any work right here in the camp. Because they can get along just fine by sitting around and playing Japanese checkers and drinking sake. We should ship them *all* out, every Jap in this camp without a job. That way we help the farmers get their beets in and we get the Isseis out—out of camp and out of trouble."

"We can't force them to work," Morrissey said again.

"But we sure as blazes could use a little more persuasion," Schweiker said. He leaned forward toward Morrissey and quoted softly, almost inaudibly: " 'This we commanded you, that if any would not work neither should they eat.' "

Oh my God, Morrissey thought. Saint Paul in cowboy boots.

"We've got no system, no regalations around here," Schweiker went on in his normal tone. "Take this building, for instance. Overrun with Japs. Which is against the rules. Besides being unfair."

"What rules?" Morrissey said.

"Unfair to whom?" Haydon said.

"Look around you. Dozens of Japs up here with nice cushy jobs, punching a few keys and pushing a few papers. Just like the whites. Nice and cool in summer and all toasty warm in winter. While the rest of them down there are sweating in the kitchens or freezing in the fields. Course it's unfair. And what's more it's illegal. Working 'longside of the whites like they are. Even senior officers." He glared at Morrissey. "That's *fratanizing,* that is, and that's against regalations. Article Five, Section Two. Besides which, it's dangerous."

"Dangerous?" Haydon and Morrissey said together.

Schweiker adjusted his hat to ease his forehead. "You're darned right." He glared at Morrissey again. "Getting cozy with the enemy is always dangerous. We shouldn't allow Japs up here at all, handling confidential information and . . ."

"Confidential information?" Morrissey's voice rose. "What confidential information? Plans for the school? Requests for more medicine and more . . ."

"You're not careful," Schweiker went on, "you're gonna have a case of sabotage on your hands. Right here."

"Sabotage?" Morrissey howled. "In the middle of a desert?"

"Snooping around all the time like they are." Schweiker turned to Haydon. "Like that assistant of yours."

"Tony?" Haydon said with surprise. "Tony Takahashi?" Mild, inoffensive, eager-to-please Tony?

"I see him using the men's room up here all the time. Like he's a member of the administration. And smuggling food out of the staff cafeteria."

"Well, he won't be here much longer," Haydon said. "He's

applied for a fellowship in the East and he's certain to get it. He's very bright. He'll probably be leaving very soon now."

"You better watch him till he does. Lives down in the BQ with all those Isseis. They've got Japanese flags all over the place down there, including one right over his bed."

"Tony lives in the BQ?" Haydon said with surprise; that small defenseless boy with his American accent and American sympathies?

"If he does," Morrissey said, "you'd better get him out of there fast. He doesn't belong there."

"Course he does," Schweiker said. "He's a Kibei, isn't he? Spent all those years in Japan, didn't he? Just like an Issei. Course he belongs there. He's one of them."

"Get him out of there," Morrissey told Haydon. "We have a legal responsibility to protect these people, and it's dangerous for him down there."

"Well, it's dangerous for the rest of us having him up here, using staff facilities, messing around with our files. No Jap should be allowed up here at all."

"We can't possibly run the camp without them," Haydon said.

"Precisely," Morrissey said. "We're supposed to be self-sustaining. That's regulations too. Article Ten, Section Two."

Schweiker stood up. "Look," he said slowly. "You're forgetting one thing. These people are *Japs*. They hate us. Why wouldn't they? We're at war with their country. We pulled them out of their homes, locked them up here. Course they hate us. I don't say I blame them. I don't say I wouldn't feel the same way. But it's them or us. And there are *ten thousand* of them."

"Six thousand four hundred forty-two," Morrissey said.

"You mark my words," Schweiker went on. "We're gonna have trouble, and we're not ready for it. The least we can do is see that the staff is armed."

"And that's against regulations too," Morrissey said. But Schweiker was already out the door, with Rigsbee right behind him.

"What was all that about, I wonder," Haydon said.

"Guadalcanal, probably. Every time things get rough in the Pacific, he starts talking as if he'd like to lynch them all. What's the matter with him? Got a son fighting the Japanese? But he couldn't possibly sire a son. Hell, the man secretes nothing but pickle juice. I wonder if he even has a wife."

"I've always assumed so," Haydon said. "Though I've never seen her."

"He probably keeps her locked up with his gun collection." Poor Mrs. Schweiker, Morrissey thought. He imagined her as a tiny woman in an enormous apron, standing behind Schweiker at dinner, ready to pour his Coke and butter his bread. "He's probably scared to death to bring her anywhere near the camp," Morrissey went on. "Terrified of murder or rape or yellow fever."

"I wonder," Haydon said slowly, "if he knows something we don't."

"And I wonder," Morrissey said, "if he's just *predicting* trouble or *creating* it."

"Meaning what?"

"Wanting to clamp down on the Issei like that. He'd probably love a little riot. Then he could call in the troops and the FBI and . . ."

"Oh, no," Haydon said. "He has no authority to do that. Still, it's just possible that he understands the evacuees better than we do. In some ways, he's a lot closer to them."

"Closer to them? Good God, man, he loathes them. And what's worse, he's terrified of them. Why, he's so paranoid he won't live anywhere near them and won't eat anything on the premises except what he brings from home, and drinks his Coke straight from the bottle—*through a straw!*"

"Oh, I don't believe it's as bad as all that," Haydon said.

You wouldn't, Morrissey thought, looking at Haydon's handsome features, carefully controlled through centuries of good breeding and good living; features designed to fit well under a polo cap or a yachting cap. Morrissey had been to Harvard too, but it had been the Harvard of the impecunious law student, the Harvard of boarding houses where the heat was always off and the bathroom always occupied; the Harvard of baked beans at Bickford's and a fellowship supplemented by delivering milk every morning at dawn, dawns that were filled with freezing winds and friendly maids. He had spent his free time organizing Harvard's waiters and biddies, joining pickets, distributing leaflets, aiding Loyalist Spain and Nazi refugees. He had loved every minute of it, but it left him with little sympathy or patience with Channing Haydon.

"Maybe Schweiker just prefers his own cooking," Haydon said. He smiled. "And the taste of a straw."

Morrissey stood up. He wanted to get away from Haydon, a man so bland, so bloodless that he could sit through the stormiest staff meetings at a discreet forty-five-degree angle. For the first time he wondered if the compromises effected at that round conference table, where no sharp edges ever intruded, weren't more concerned with peace than principle. Or was he, Morrissey, the sawed-off mick from Hell's Kitchen, simply jealous of Channing Haydon, so elegantly constructed from all the best materials: good looks and good family, a beautiful wife and a chair at Harvard when most of his contemporaries were still wobbling precariously on stools? He collected his papers and turned to say good night.

"What do you propose we do?" Haydon said abruptly. "Assuming you're right."

"About Schweiker? Get rid of him."

"How?"

"Send him to Roperville to supervise the sugar beet workers. Or make him take a nice long vacation—in the Philippines. But get him out. Fast."

And what would Collins of Security and Rigsbee the comptroller and the rows and rows of staff workers at all levels think of *that?* Haydon wondered. "We've no reason to fire him," he said. "Except that he hates the Japanese. Which would hardly be considered a crime by the WCCA or the Army or any of the other myopic agencies running this camp. So there's really nothing we *can* do."

Nothing you *want* to do, Morrissey thought. "And *that*," he said from the doorway, "is the most dangerous thing of all."

Alone in his office, Haydon felt vaguely upset. Images kept coming back: Schweiker with his long snakelike body insinuating himself farther and farther into Haydon's office, into Haydon's affairs; Morrissey's round red face about to burst with frustration at Schweiker—and at *him?* Haydon had failed them both. But it was impossible to please them both. Someday, he was afraid, he might have to choose. It was a choice he would, if possible, avoid.

It was six o'clock, but he was reluctant to go home to Jenni and a succession of enormous portions of rich dishes which she served up daily—a trial to body and soul in the middle of a war, in the midst of food shortages, on the edge of a camp whose inhabitants were fed on thirty-seven cents a day. To compensate, he left before Jenni was up so he could skip breakfast, and had a bowl of Jell-O for lunch. Going without food during the day made him irritable. Eating huge dinners at night ruined his sleep. Poor Jenni, married to a man whose favorite motto was plain living and high thinking.

He stared out the window, though there was nothing to see but the searchlight rolling around in a frenzy, lighting up that crazy mountain crouched on the horizon, ready to pounce. He heard the click of Tony's door. A good boy, he thought, eager, hardworking, and very bright. He must remember to have him removed from the BQ right away. Just then he heard the tap of heels at the other end of the hall and had a vision of Schweiker in his black suit, smooth and tight—except for the bump on his hip—and his huge black cloud of a hat and his face dented with anger. Actually, Haydon decided, there was no need to move Tony. He was certain to win a fellowship any day now.

Haydon turned back to his desk and felt a terrible sense of oppression, as if Mt. Hope, tired of crouching, had leaped at last and landed on his back.

ELEVEN

IN her dream, Nina saw the mountain guarded by two soldiers, one on each side. Beneath them, two lines of tiny people were laboriously climbing the slopes. As they reached the peak, the soldiers picked them up, one by one, and dropped them into that hole at the top. Each time Nina heard a faint moan.

She awoke shivering and pressed closer to Sam, pulling the two thin army blankets up under her chin. There was no top sheet—it was used as a room divider—and the blankets felt scratchy and smelled . . . of sweat, semen, blood? Beneath her, the straw had matted into hard lumps, leaving bare spots so that in some places she lay directly on the springs. No fresh straw had been delivered for weeks. She lived, constantly, with the memory of displaced horses and dead soldiers, and crowded by displaced people.

She and Sam were never alone, not even at night. Bodies

lay stretched out right and left behind halfhearted walls that stopped too soon. In the silence of the darkness, she could hear Mrs. Watanabe swallow, and Mr. Tsuda, who never slept, turn a page, and Madame Sawada dream of baths at the Waldorf. Every cough, every sigh, every moan—of ecstasy or anguish—was a public announcement. People stifled them as far as possible and lived, so to speak, under their breath. And all night long, at regular intervals—Sam claimed he knew to the exact minute—the searchlights attacked them, shattering privacy and intimacy and blessed oblivion. *There is no reason whatsoever for interfering with normal family arrangements,* the Handbook said.

She heard the moans again, coming from the Oshimas' stall, not the harsh groans of the old man who had been suffering from toothache on and off but long low moans that might have been left over from her dream. They were growing longer and louder. No one else seemed to hear them. People dived headfirst into sleep here, not only from exhaustion but for escape, until the shriek of the siren catapulted them into another day.

Nina lay listening, wondering if she should get up to help. But Sam suddenly flung an arm over her, pinning her down, still protecting her—when he was there. Besides, he had warned her from the very beginning not to interfere. "These people are very proud and very private," he had said.

Suddenly, there was a sharp cry, then silence. Someone had probably stuffed a sock into that suffering mouth. Soon she heard footsteps and the door opening and closing. She fell asleep.

In the morning when she awoke, Sam had gone as usual, rushing to work on still another camp project, rushing to lay pipes in the bitter cold so that he could freeze in winter as he had burned in summer—for the good of the camp. He no longer waited for her to open her eyes to wish her good morning, to kiss her good-bye. He simply hurried out, leaving no dent in that hard bed beside her. At night and on weekends he was at meetings of this and that, to discuss this and that—for the good of the camp. Lately she had hardly seen him at all, only felt him beside her in the darkness like a dropped stone. It might have been anybody, any evacuee, lying there, for the camp had worn away all distinctions except Issei and Nisei, cooperative and disruptive. There was no category at all for her, the Caucasian, or for Sam, husband and artist; only Sam the evacuee. Sam, the old Sam, had disappeared except for his blankets, piled neatly over her every morning against the cold dawn. Otherwise, he might have been dropped, like the people in her dream, into that mountain's huge gullet.

Last night he had come home very late. She had been in bed for hours, reading by the beam of a flashlight. "It's a wonder you weren't arrested for breaking the curfew," she said.

It was a tone he had never heard her use before. "Hello, darling." He leaned over, way over, to kiss her. "You shouldn't wait up."

"Of course I should. I *must*. If I ever want to see you again."

He stared at her. Not only did she sound different, she looked different. He turned on the light. "When did you cut your hair?" he said.

"Weeks ago."

"Oh, darling, your beautiful hair."

"What does it matter? You never noticed it. Because you're never here."

He sat down beside her on the bed. "I thought you understood about this new project."

"What new project? Something else for the 'good of the camp'? To help the administration keep us in line?"

"Didn't I explain it? We've *both* been so busy lately we've hardly even seen each other."

It was true that she was working harder than ever now, for there had been an outbreak of measles recently and the Authority had refused to provide funds and materials for isolation beds and inoculations. "They have to get measles sometime," Dr. Landau was told. "They might as well get it now." He had worked feverishly—they all had—but one boy in Block C died anyway.

"*I* come home at night," she said.

He stared at her for a moment. "But, darling, so do I." He moved closer and put his arms around her.

"How in the world would I know? You're not here when I go to bed and you're not here when I get up. You're *never* here." She was sobbing into his shoulder. "You never think about anything but this horrible camp. I'm not married to Sam Curry anymore. I'm married to the Mt. Hope Assembly Center."

"Oh, darling. What nonsense. Stop crying and let me explain." He kissed her and stroked her hair and wiped her eyes and told her, in a low but excited voice, about the new project. There were six of them, Nisei and Issei, three of each, working on a constitution for the camp. "A *democratic* constitution with equal rights for Issei and Nisei. Self-government in a concentration camp!"

She could feel his excitement, almost smell it and taste it: a slightly salty taste. "We meet every night," he went on, "and weekends and any other chance we get. In the Americanization Room. Appropriate, isn't it? But we've got to keep it quiet, Haydon says. Not to raise hopes prematurely."

"Not to raise objections, you mean," Nina said. "From people like Schweiker right here and from people like Schweiker in Washington. They'll never let you do it."

"But it's Haydon's idea. Of course they'll let us do it."

"You know perfectly well he hasn't any power against Washington. You've been saying that yourself for months. He won't be able to save you. He probably won't even try."

"Save me? From what? I'm only trying to help write a constitution. By appointment of the director. Not start a revolution."

"They murdered Mr. Sato just for losing his way to the latrine."

Was Sam about to lose his way too? she wondered now,

wiggling out from beneath the extra weight of his blankets. But the sense of oppression remained.

She dressed quickly and picked up the sketch pad and charcoal that she had been carrying around ever since the death of Mr. Sato; like an alcoholic with a hip flask, interposing a piece of paper between herself and reality; reducing the world to a series of black lines and white spaces, which she could arrange as she pleased. Drawing while she waited on endless queues gave her patience. Holding charcoal, like holding Sam's hand, gave her confidence. It seemed a long time since she had held Sam's hand.

But there was another piece of paper in her pocket, shoved way down so she would not have to think about it. It was from the director. He wanted to see her and her drawings in his office "as soon as it is convenient." It would never be convenient. What right did he have to summon her and her drawings to his office? She stuffed the paper back into her pocket. But she felt a sudden chill, felt the camp's long, frozen arms close around her. Had they already closed around Sam?

Outside, it was gray, as always, as if the mountain spent the night spewing ash all over the camp. This morning the mountain looked taller, sharper, with its neck stretched up to pierce the sky. She thought of the sounds she had heard in the Oshimas' stall and the "miscarriages" at the hospital. And she thought of Sam out so late every night.

Near the latrine, she saw Mrs. Oshima in her wide khaki pants that flapped around her like empty sails. She was carrying an old suitcase which she stood on end, like a screen, for privacy. She bowed and smiled, though she looked very tired and the empty suitcase seemed to weigh her down. She must have been awake all night, Nina thought. But she greeted Nina with her usual cheerfulness. "Broke again," she said, "all over the floor." She shrugged and smiled again. *"Shikata ga nai."*

Nina thought of the moans during the night and that silent exit from the stables. Was that why the toilets broke down so often? Had Mrs. Oshima said, *"Shikata ga nai"* to *that* too? Nina looked at her with new interest. Mr. Oshima, it seemed, knew nothing. Camp clothes were big and sloppy and Mr. Oshima was, evidently, a sound sleeper. But what would happen if Mr. Oshima ever woke up?

"I thought I heard someone in pain last night," Nina said. "Was it Josie?"

"Oh, no. Only Mary. But she fine now. Was nothing. Too much hot dog maybe. But she fine now. Fine." She smiled and nodded.

"Tell her to come to the hospital, just to make sure," Nina said. "So Dr. Landau can have a look at her. Just to make sure."

"Oh, no," Mrs. Oshima said. "No hospital. Hospital not necessary. Thank you very much." She smiled apologetically.

There was the usual long queue outside the mess hall. People stood pressed against each other with their heads down and their mouths closed against the wind, trying to keep whatever spark of warmth they had inside them from escaping. Mr. Ishii stood near the end of the line, as usual, wearing bits of a World War II uniform now, with his grandson wrapped up inside his coat. They had finally become one.

"Morning, Mr. Ishii," Nina said. She smiled at the old man and peered at the boy. His face was very thin and blotchy and covered with perspiration. His eyes seemed not so much closed as stuck. "Ken-chan doesn't look at all well, Mr. Ishii," she said gently. "I think you'd better bring him to the hospital."

"No!" he said, hugging the boy closer. "No hospital."

"Please," Nina said. "I'll see that he's very well taken care of. You can even stay with him. I'll fix it with Dr. Landau. He's a very good doctor." She wondered if Mr. Ishii had heard about the little boy in Block C.

"No. Thank you. No." Mr. Ishii put his hand protectively over Ken-chan's head. "*I* take care of him. No one else." He turned and hurried away toward the stables.

Everyone, Nina thought staring after him, tried to avoid the hospital. Because Dr. Landau was Caucasian? But so am I, she thought suddenly. Was she making Dr. Landau's position even more difficult?

Family groups hurried past her, dressed in their best: high heels and hats and even ties. It was Sunday, she realized, and they were on their way to services—Catholic and Baptist and Buddhist and Seventh Day Adventist—held in the old barns. If only there were as much space for medicine as for praying, she thought, and as many doctors as there were ministers. But there was no Sunday for her. Sam was gone all day, so she went to work all day too. There was never any Sunday at the hospital either.

There had been many Sundays before Mt. Hope, one every week in fact, when Sam went to visit his parents. The Sunday after his marriage, he took Nina with him.

The Kuriharas lived in Fish Harbor on Terminal Island, a tiny dot of land set in the bay and surrounded by a naval station, an Army fort, the federal customs office, a yacht club, and the Terminal Island Prison. Fish Harbor was inhabited almost entirely by poor Japanese who fished industriously. The sea took its revenge by swallowing a good many of them, leaving their poor families even poorer. Their houses were mere shacks with jagged shingled roofs and no yards.

Sam's parents, the Kuriharas, were a thin little couple who greeted Nina politely and offered her the only chair that had four legs and two arms. The tiny living room was almost bare except for the pictures that covered the walls: a photograph of Sam in his First Communion suit, looking as if he wanted to pee; and Japanese landscapes done on brown paper with inkstone and brush in blacks and grays, delicate and graceful as butterflies. "My mother's," Sam said proudly. "An exceptional woman."

Nina studied her. She did not look exceptional, only tired. Every now and then, she pressed her hand to her heart as if she had a secret joy or a private pain. She talked quietly to her son, in English, about his work and his teaching. Across the room, Mr. Kurihara sat alone on a three-legged stool and watched. He refused to talk English and his son hated to talk Japanese. Only Mrs. Kurihara spoke both easily and willingly.

Mr. Kurihara had chosen her from the photographs sent from his native village. Yuki was the oldest and the plainest, but she looked both strong and gentle with her hair like a cushion on top of her head. When he first saw her limping toward him across the dock, he had been furious, had longed to push her back into the sea, had refused even to look at her. "How do you do, Mr. Kurihara?" she said in perfect English learned at a mission school. "I am very pleased to meet you." He raised his head and saw her eyes, large, calm eyes, anchored in the placid harbor of her face. He felt his anger drain away, felt that he, too, had finally reached port.

She went to work in one of the canneries, as most of the women on the island did. She worked at all hours, whenever the boats came in: at the end of the day, in the middle of the night, in the early morning. She learned to recognize the whistles of the various factories. When she wasn't working in the cannery, she worked at home: cleaning, scrubbing and— sometimes—painting on grocery bags and brown wrapping paper. But she was always on the dock waiting for Mr. Kurihara when he returned from fishing. She named her only child Sami after an ancient poet, Sami Mansei, whose tanka she had read long ago: "To what shall I compare this world? A boat that rows off with morning, leaving no trace behind." It seemed appropriate for a fisherman's son. After Sami came she waited on the dock for Mr. Kurihara with the baby like a gift in her arms.

When Sami was six, she insisted on sending him to a Catholic school on the mainland. The schools on the island were very poor, with very little equipment and very few teachers. The children ran wild. They spoke the rough dialects of their parents' native village, full of oaths and insults and obscenities. Even Yuki could hardly understand them. "My son must learn to speak proper English," she said. During the week he would live in the orphanage run by the fathers to avoid the long trip back and forth.

"But he is not an orphan," her husband shouted. "He is not even a Catholic."

"He is *Japanese*," she said. "He must learn to be a Japanese-*American*. The Fathers will teach him."

Mr. Kurihara was furious, as he had been that day he first saw her limping across the dock. She had steadily refused to talk about it, that mysterious limp. She had done it to herself, he thought angrily, to give her the courage to be different, to send her only son away to live with strangers. But the boy was *his* son too, the son who would fish with him in the morning and smoke with him in the evening, who would help him pay off his debt to the Crown Can Company so that he could own his boat before he died. If Sami went away, he would lose him forever.

"It's hard for us," Yuki was saying. "But it will be better for Sami." She limped toward him. For the first time since he'd known her she was crying. His anger evaporated. He felt ashamed. She was losing her son too.

The Fathers at St. Martin's began by changing "Sami" to "Sam" and chopping "Kurihara" to "Kuri," which they spelled "Curry." They taught Sam to speak good English and to worship a white god who had been poor and suffered and wanted everyone else to be poor and suffer too. They taught him to kneel for hours in front of the priest and the cross and the saints in the chapel.

He learned to doze on his knees, to shut out the sounds of prayers and sermons, to study the saints in their anguish and the stained-glass windows that changed with the changing light. At first the painted saints fascinated him: the folds of their robes, the veins in their hands, the blood on their bodies. As he grew older, he found them too gaudy. He was not moved to pray to figures whose souls seemed drowned in a wash of red and blue and gold. Compared to the soft, subtle blacks and whites and grays of his mother's landscapes the stained-glass windows seemed garish. The religion of the Fathers seemed overwrought too. The act of eating and drinking the body and blood of their dead god made him feel sick. The thought of hell terrified him but made him hate the fathers who preached it and the god who created it. When he left St. Martin's, he found that he had left his faith behind too. It had simply dropped from him. He stepped out of it easily, like stepping out of his trousers at the end of the day.

He might have been saved by St. John, an unpainted stone figure of the Baptist as a boy, half naked, half starved, and half mad, banished to a dark corner of the church. Sam stole back there often when no one was around, to study him. Assaulted constantly by the California sun and the California decor, Sam was moved by the force and subtlety of stark, unadorned stone. "In Japan, unlike the West," his mother told him, "we have a taste for shadows." St. Martin's had failed to turn him into a Catholic. But St. John the Baptist had turned him into a sculptor.

When Sam announced that he was coming home with a Caucasian wife, Mr. Kurihara was shocked. He considered all Caucasian women extravagant, lazy, domineering, and shameless. He had seen them from his fishing boat, stretched out on their shining white yachts wearing almost nothing but sunglasses and earrings, holding drinks and cigarettes, waving and laughing at him in his dirty little fishing boat. He had watched angrily while his wife kissed his new daughter-in-law. Like an American, he thought with disgust. The girl looked at him shyly and held out her hand like a man.

He was aware of her looking at him now from across the room. She was not at all like the women on the yachts, he thought. She was quiet and spoke softly and her hair was the color of dried bamboo. She caught his eye and smiled. A Caucasian smile, he thought warily. He was not sure what it meant: contempt, pity, ridicule? Until he remembered that she was not an American either. She was an alien too, an *enemy* alien. He bowed slightly and smiled back.

That was the last time Sam and Nina ever saw the Kuriharas. The next Sunday was December 7.

On December 7 Mr. Kurihara, like all the other fishermen, turned his boat back to Terminal Island as soon as he heard the news of Pearl Harbor on his radio. Like the others, he was met at the dock by a mob of shouting Caucasians who beat him up the moment his foot touched land. They confiscated his catch and his log—written in Japanese—insisting that it was a spy diary, and hauled him off to jail with the others like a netload of fish. For the first time, Yuki was not waiting for him. She had been forced off the street by soldiers from Fort Arthur who arrived in jeeps with machine guns and drove all the inhabitants indoors. Later the FBI came and ransacked the houses, confiscating radios, cameras, tools, and everything Japanese. The men were lined up, interrogated, and carried off to prison.

The Currys never saw Terminal Island again either. No one was allowed in or out—but the military. Telephone wires were cut and newspapers closed. The island was sealed off from the rest of the world, and its remaining inhabitants, women and children, isolated. All Japanese employees were fired, all Japanese shops closed. People starved while food rotted. Military patrols roamed the village. People were locked in their houses, others attacked on the street. In the end they were all ordered off the island within twenty-four hours—with no money, no known destination, and no public transport.

Weeks later, the Currys received a letter from Mr. Kurihara in tottering English. He was all right. They were not to worry. He expected to be shot soon. They must take care of Yuki. She must lie down more often and rest her bad leg.

But Yuki, with her hand over her heart, had gone to lie down forever, the day her husband was arrested.

"Could he be right?" Nina asked.

"About what?"

"Being executed."

"Of course not," Sam said. "This is the United States of America, remember? Not Nazi Germany. He'll be released as soon as the hysteria is over."

TWELVE

DANNY Matsui arrived from prison with a cropped head, a cane, and a pronounced limp from having been locked in an unheated cell all night. Nina and Sam gave a party for him in their stall. As many people as possible crowded in, eager to give Danny a hero's welcome. Sam provided peanuts and potato chips and Oreos and Cokes from the canteen, and Mrs. Oshima brought large quantities of rice cakes and *surume* from no one knew where. Mrs. Noguchi, in well-bred Japanese style, came very late, lugging buckets of tea.

Danny sat on a cot with one arm around his wife and the other around little Miko and sang songs and told jokes and gave impersonations: of FDR and Bing Crosby and Adolf Hitler, and of Congressman Rankin shouting, "The Japs should be removed even to the third and fourth generation. . . . Damn them! Let's get rid of them *now!*" The whole stable listened and laughed and applauded and shouted for more.

He had been a movie actor before Pearl Harbor, descended from generations of Kabuki players, with a face he could change in an instant, like the little "basic black" featured in the fashion ads that was completely transformed merely by the addition of a necklace or a scarf or a pin. He could look funny or sad, young or old, healthy or sick, saintly or sinister. He could look Chinese, Korean, Hawaiian, even American Indian. The white man couldn't tell the difference. Two days after Pearl Harbor he was fired. He could not look Caucasian.

"They're all doing it," Emmy had said the night she and Danny came to break the news, with Miko asleep in Danny's arms. "All the big studios. Firing every Japanese on the payroll."

And they're all run by Jews, Nina had thought. Not just Caucasians but *Jews*. No one looked at her. She slumped lower and lower, wishing her hair, her eyes, her skin would change color. On the opposite wall she saw her tiny British flag and her sketch of the boy, Aeneas, settled securely on his father's shoulders. But he had grown up to be displaced. The world seemed to be full of displaced people. What would happen to Sam, she wondered, if he were displaced from his art? What would happen to her if she were displaced from her marriage?

"What will you do?" Sam had said.

"Work for my brother-in-law. He owns a radio shop."

"But you don't know anything about radios," Sam said.

"Don't have to. All I have to do is sell them."

"Why not *act* on the radio?" Nina said.

"Yes!" Sam said. "On the radio no one will know which way your eyes slant."

"The sponsors will know," Emmy said.

A week later, Danny was arrested—for consorting with radios?

"But he doesn't know a damn thing about radios, for God's sake," Sam shouted. "All he did was *sell* them. So why Danny?"

"Because he's Japanese," Emmy said. She was standing on the doorstep holding little Miko by the hand. She refused to come in. She was used to standing on doorsteps.

"But Danny doesn't know or care anything about Japan. He's *American!* He can't even speak Japanese."

"It's his *face,* not his tongue," Emmy had said. She was going to stay with a friend. In a strange house she would stop listening for Danny's key in the lock.

Nina watched her go. She imagined herself walking away someday, a displaced person again; only instead of a child she would be holding a soggy suitcase.

Now Sam, squeezed into a horse stall, stared at Danny. He was laughing and singing, enjoying the first audience he had had for a long time; perhaps the only one he would ever have. But he hardly looked like Danny anymore, with that cane propped up beside him and his hair cut off. They had clipped him at both ends. Sam thought of his father, that fiery old man who could pull a net apart with his bare hands or yank a man's arm out of its socket. He thought of that letter, the only letter he had ever received from his father, written, with great difficulty, in English; an enormous concession, he realized with a pang, to his Americanized son and his Caucasian daughter-in-law. But where was he? Sam had never heard from him again, though he had tried for months to find him: through the police, the Red Cross, the Quakers, even congressmen and senators. Some responses had been rude, some sympathetic. By evacuation time he had learned nothing.

He felt guilty, remembering his father sitting so silently while he and his mother talked about his school, his art, his teaching—in English. He had tried so hard to become a good artist and a good American. But he had become a bad son.

As the evening wore on, Danny grew more subdued. Someone brought him a samisen. He took it gently and began to sing, to chant, to recite bits of the ancient *Naniwabushi*. The audience, surprised, turned sad.

Mrs. Noguchi began to cry. She had never even said good-bye to her husband, a stubborn man who refused to see what was going on around him. But Mrs. Noguchi saw: her neighbors kneeling beside their incinerators, burning Japanese scrolls and books and dolls. Sitting quietly in the car behind her husband with her hands folded, she noted the signs in the streets—on shop windows and billboards and car bumpers: JAPS SHAVED HERE—NOT RESPONSIBLE FOR ACCIDENTS. JAP HUNTING LICENSES—FREE! NO JAP RATS HERE. FOR SALE. CLOSED. UNDER NEW MANAGEMENT. Reading the newspapers was worse. A Chinese man had been found scalped in an alley; he had been taken for a Japanese. Asians wore buttons proclaiming: I am Korean, or Hawaiian, or Vietnamese, or Chinese. Japanese shops were attacked, Japanese families evicted, and more and more Japanese men arrested, men Mrs. Noguchi had known for years: the Reverend Tayama of the local Methodist church, Mr. Yamazaki from the bank, old Mr. Nagashima who owned the laundry and had lost an arm in World War I. The other wives kept suitcases for their husbands, packed and ready, beside the front door.

But Dr. Noguchi had been scornful. "Please to remember that I am president of the Japanese Professional and Businessmen's Society in this town and founder of the local chapter of the Japanese-American Dental Association and a charter member of the local chapter of the Japanese-American Citizens' League. And, also, please to remember, I am a most generous contributor to the hospital, the Red Cross, the Boy Scouts, St. Christopher's Home, and *both* political parties." He flipped back the sleeves of his kimono. "I don't think *we* need worry," he said.

His oldest daughter, Toyo, was fired from her job as a nursery school teacher; "to protect the children." His oldest son, Ray, an intern at the local hospital, was fired; "to protect the patients."

"Terribly efficient, aren't they?" Toyo said.

"Too bad they weren't as efficient at Pearl Harbor," Ray said.

But Dr. Noguchi was not worried. "I am not in a sensitive occupation," he said.

"I doubt if your patients would agree," Ray murmured.

Mrs. Noguchi packed a suitcase for her husband and kept it beside the front door, like her neighbors.

They came toward evening, four men with shoulders like sideboards, and waited for Dr. Noguchi to come home: one at the front door, one at the back door, and two in the living room. Only Mrs. Noguchi and her youngest daughter were at home. She had just come in and was still wearing her Western clothes. She smoothed her skirt, straightened her hat, stared at her gloves, and tried to make conversation. The men said "Yes, ma'am" and occasionally "No, ma'am." They sat with their hats on and their hands in their coat pockets, like men on a bus, ready to get off at the next stop. When she offered them tea, they thanked her but said they didn't use tea. They sat. The phone rang. They let it ring. They waited.

When Dr. Noguchi finally arrived, they took him away without allowing him to set foot inside his own house. His suitcase was left standing beside the front door.

Mrs. Noguchi stared at Danny's cane and wondered if her husband, too, would come home with a part of him frozen forever and a piece of dead wood in its place. Would he come home at all?

Nina was sketching Miko, asleep on Danny's lap. The little girl stirred and whimpered. She had been sick almost steadily at Mt. Hope, from the shots and the food and the water and the heat. She was no longer the adventurous little girl Nina remembered who loved to walk across the lawn on her hands on Sullivan Street, examining the world upside down. At camp she stayed close to Emmy. "She's afraid I'll disappear like her father," Emmy had said.

It was not the same Emmy either, Nina thought. Smooth, sharp Emmy looked blurred and sloppy in her army clothes, and her hair was long and uneven, as if it had crept unnoticed down her neck.

Once the party was over and the other guests had left, Nina realized that the old Danny had gone too. The new Danny began to talk. He talked of how he was arrested and carted away just as he was, in shirt and trousers. They emptied his pockets of everything, including tobacco crumbs. When he tried to invoke his rights, insisting that he was not an enemy and not an alien and not dangerous, he was told that as a dangerous enemy alien he had no rights. He was herded with the others—farmers, businessmen, bankers, Buddhist priests, Protestant ministers, teachers, journalists, fishermen—from one place to another until, finally, they were all packed into a train and shipped out. They had no idea where they were going except—from the fall in temperature—that it was north. They prayed that it would not be to a regular prison where they would certainly be killed by the inmates if not by the guards. They were dumped, at last, in a desolate landscape where even the buffalo, they were certain, could not survive. For a month they shivered in their light clothes until the Army handed out secondhand military gear. They lived in a huge, half-built camp in underheated dormitories and worked at finishing the buildings. They cooked and cleaned and did the prison laundry and stared at the icicles hanging down like a second set of bars at the windows. All mail was censored—in and out. All paper was stripped from packages and cans; cigarettes were removed from their packets, chocolates from their wrappers. The men were photographed and interrogated.

"Who do you think will win the war?"

"If you had a gun, would you shoot an American or a Japanese?"

The old Issei stood staring at the young American for whom trickery and lies were no problem, for whom success was the only goal. How could he say he would kill a Japanese? It would be a lie and an act of shame. But if he said an American, he would be shot. The old man lifted his head and stared at the young lieutenant. "I shoot myself," he said with dignity.

Occasionally, one of the men was taken away. The others waited nervously. They believed they would all be killed sooner or later as reprisals against the Japanese.

There was no hospital at the prison. Sick men stayed in the dormitories. One old man in the bed next to Danny's died there in great pain. Danny sat beside him through the night and listened to his screams. "Christ, can't you see he's in agony?" Danny had shouted at the officer on duty. "And probably dying? Get him to a hospital, for God's sake."

"What hospital?" the lieutenant asked.

"*Any* hospital, you damn sadist."

Danny spent that night in an unheated jail. The lieutenant had merely intended to cool Danny's blood, not freeze his foot.

"Can't get that old man out of my mind," Danny said, stroking Miko, asleep on his lap. "Seemed familiar, somehow. Amazing man! Sick as he was, he'd have flashes of temper— from the pain, I suppose—when he became strong as a bear, upsetting trays, throwing dishes. Once he even picked up the bedside table. But most of the time he was gentle, apologizing to everyone, obeying instructions meekly. Toward the end he talked about his family, his wife and his son, as if he knew they were special though he didn't understand them. Sometimes I thought that perhaps *they* didn't understand *him*. Anyway, he was enormously proud of them. Seemed surprisingly enlightened for a fisherman from Terminal Island."

"He was," Sam said.

"His name," Danny said slowly, staring at Sam, "was Kurihara."

After that night, Sam found himself calling Danny simply Dan. The others followed suit. "Danny," like Mr. Ishii's children and Ken-chan's Woodrow Wilson, had been left behind on Sullivan Street.

"Dan never talks about the future anymore," Emmy said in the mess hall one morning. "Only about the here and now. Like a reporter. I wish to God he were a reporter—instead of slaving away in that ghastly kitchen."

Opposite her, Nina was working on a sketch of Miko with her head on her mother's arm looking too weak to hold it up herself. "How's the *Mt. Hope Chronicle?*" Nina said.

"You mean the *Lost Hope Chronicle,* don't you? Publishing nothing but cheery lies. I should change my byline to Pollyanna. Today, for instance, I'm supposed to cover the opening of the elementary school. Only, of course, it's not opening because it's not finished. Just like the high school. Which would, at least, make a good story. Only it's been censored." A makeshift school had begun at last, squeezed into drab, drafty barracks, displacing dozens of families who were jammed into already overcrowded quarters. Even so, there was not nearly enough room for the school. Classes were run on double sessions so that the children went for only a few hours a day. There were not nearly enough teachers—no Japanese were allowed on the faculty—and hardly any books. So far, the best-housed, best-staffed, and best-equipped courses were those in English and Americanization, teaching the evacuees the constitutional rights they had been denied.

Emmy, with her chin in her hands, stared at the oatmeal, like a glob of glue, on Miko's plate and at the coffee in her own cup, thick as motor oil. "Disgusting food," she said. "Dan insists that they ought to do better than this even on thirty-seven cents a day. He's convinced there's dirty work in the kitchen. He wants an investigation. But I wish he wouldn't get involved. That chef, Hackett, looks as if he's just itching to carve someone up. He used to be a butcher, after all. I wish Dan would get out of there. Now."

He did get out, in the evenings, when he turned the mess

hall into a theater and himself into a one-man production staff: director, set designer, costume designer, makeup man, even playwright and actor. He organized bands of teenagers to help—on stage and off. He ran talent shows, musicals, Western and Japanese plays, and concerts with whatever instruments he could find: guitars, trumpets, violins, and drums, as well as bamboo flutes, bells, samisen, and even a koto. New and unusual sounds were heard in the camp, suggesting solitude and contemplation and a gentle melancholy. He even gave a shortened version of a traditional Bunraku play, *The Love Suicide,* translated by Mr. Tsuda, whose eyes, without his glasses, were dim but whose mind and memory were remarkably sharp. The Issei played the accompaniment and teenagers helped to build and work the puppets. Between productions, Sam performed alone: with readings, songs, mime, and monologues. He did everything but dance, with his cane as an important part of his act. It became a scepter, a sword, a wand. The evacuees adored him. They cheered him on stage and shook his hand when he ladled out their beans in the mess hall. He joked with them and laughed with them and was grateful to them for providing him with an audience again.

He came home as late as possible, postponing as long as possible the sight of his family living in a stable. He had his cane for company. It seemed as much a part of him as his moods: swung jauntily like a swagger stick, waved like a baton, propped like a crutch, or stretched across his lap and stroked like a cat. There were times when Emmy was jealous of that cane.

She stared across the table at Nina, absorbed in her sketch. "How's Sam?" she said.

Nina kept her eyes on her drawing. "Fine," she said brightly, and rubbed out a line. "I guess."

Emmy looked at her sharply. "Another camp widow? Funny how this place manages to squeeze us together and drive us apart at the same time."

"It's *their* fault," Nina burst out. "Our husbands'. Why do they have to be such good citizens, such cooperative evacuees?"

"Dan's not a good citizen or a cooperative one. He's just an actor turned manager. And he thinks this whole production is very badly directed. I think he's just itching to direct it himself, to show what a good professional could do."

It's different with Sam, Nina thought. He seemed to identify completely with the administration. He was more of a Caucasian than she. The camp infuriated, embarrassed, shamed her while he defended it constantly. In their eagerness, they had each overshot the mark. Were they in danger of losing touch with each other completely?

Emmy, with her head twisted, was squinting at Nina's drawing. "You're lucky to have *that,*" she said.

"I know. Thanks to Sam." The old Sam, she thought, who had known months before she did what she really wanted, even needed; to stand behind an easel with a canvas between her and the world. He had been right to urge her to substitute a sketch pad. But it was no substitute for Sam.

It might also be making trouble for her, she thought, remembering the director's note. Why should he want to see her—and her drawings? Which drawings did he want to see? What right did he have to see any of them? Could she simply refuse?

Her fingers were sketching rapidly, but Miko, she thought, looked paler and thinner than ever, as if just copying her made her fade; like the old Japanese belief that looking at a picture wears it out.

Was that—or even worse—what had happened to Sam? Had his own wife worn away not his picture but *him?* She remembered the passages she had read on Japanese perceptions of Caucasians when she was working in the public library. Caucasians were loud and boastful and rude, the Japanese thought, with coarse manners and repugnant physical features: protruding noses and fishy eyes and hairy bodies and a distinctly fatty smell—*bata-kusai*—from eating so much meat and wearing animal skins. Was that how Sam felt? She had gone reeling down the library steps, afraid to go home. But Sam always greeted her with open arms.

Yet in the close intimacy of the camp, surrounded by his own kind, her traits had probably become more obvious and more offensive. Was she, as a Caucasian, not a *help* to Sam as she had thought, but an *embarrassment;* as she undoubtedly was to Dr. Landau?

She thought of her coming interview with the director, for she knew she would have to go. She had seen him at mass meetings and, occasionally, walking around the camp. She hated him from a distance, on principle, the walking embodiment of the WCCA and the WRA and the BIA and all the other possible combinations of letters in the Western alphabet guilty of crimes against the Japanese. "It's not his fault," Sam kept saying. But it was. Of course it was. And it was his fault that Sam was out all the time, working on projects for the camp, working so hard that he had no time to eat or sleep or see his wife. That was Haydon's fault too. Of course it was.

Suddenly she decided that she was looking forward to her meeting with Haydon. Sam was right. She had spent her life trying to please everyone who had so much as glanced over those institution walls: all those girls and nuns and Frau Felsheimer and Miss Motherwell. Yet they had all, except Sam, disappeared. It was shameful to be so timid. As a Caucasian at Mt. Hope, she had a responsibility. She could do what even Sam and Dan and the others dared not do. She would tell the director exactly what she thought of him and his camp. Would he have her removed immediately? Even deported back to Germany?

THIRTEEN

THE director came out from behind his desk, shook hands with Nina, waved her into a large upholstered armchair, and poured coffee for her from the Thermos on the small table between them; *real* coffee—she could tell from the smell—and hot. There was even a fat little pitcher of cream. She wrapped her hands around the cup and warmed her nose in the steam. Though the heat in the office was solid as a wall, she was still cold from the wind outside and her own nervousness inside.

"Sorry," Haydon was saying. "They seemed to have forgotten the sugar."

"*Sugar?*"

"Don't they serve sugar in the mess halls?"

"Of course not. We'd be happy for just coffee, *real* coffee, *hot* coffee. Like this."

"Don't they serve coffee in the mess halls either?"

"Well . . . it's *supposed* to be coffee."

"What is it?"

"No one knows. But it's called Hackett's Tobacco Juice."

"Good God." He laughed, then frowned. "I'm sorry about that too," he said.

Then *do* something, she thought. But he had obviously forgotten all about it already and was concentrating on her dossier. He looked more like a scout leader than a jailer, she thought. He should be running a boys' camp, not a concentration camp. A jailer in a tweed jacket, walking around the edges of the camp, smiling vaguely at the "residents," careful not to come too close.

She had hated him the very first time she saw him at the Americanization ceremony, though she had seen only a tiny, distant figure shouting into the wind. She glanced at him now, a mild-mannered man reading her dossier with great care.

He looked up. "Nina Dorfman Curry," he said. "A good international mix."

"The Wandering Jew," she said. "Nina, Russian; Dorfman, German; Kurihara-Curry, Japanese-American."

"Displaced three times?" He remembered her that very first day, a pale, frightened girl, leaning against the wall waiting to be processed—for the *third* time?

"But this is the first time I've ever been in a camp—or, rather, an 'Assembly Center.'"

"I'm sorry about that too," he said.

She wondered if he knew that she had *chosen* to come, had in fact, *begged* to be allowed to come. If so, he did not remind her of it. Decent of him, she acknowledged reluctantly. "I've spent most of my life in institutions, of one kind or another," she said. "Which is why I've never learned to cook." She was talking too much, she thought. Eager to please, as always. Even the head jailer of a concentration camp.

"You can't cook?" Wonderful woman, he thought. After Jenni, it seemed a major virtue. He examined her again. She did not seem to suffer from any other inadequacies. "But you can draw," he said. "May I see your drawings?"

Why should he want to see them? she wondered again.

How did he even *know* about them? They had spies, inform-ers, *everywhere*. Everybody said so. *Inu,* they called them, but she had never really believed it. Was it against regulations to make sketches of the queues, the stalls, the latrines? Would they lock her up, the first woman and only Caucasian to be sent to Fort Washington? "How did you know about my drawings?" she said.

"Why shouldn't I?" He smiled.

He had a nice smile, she thought. In fact, he had a nice face, the kind she considered "typically American"; the kind that showed up in movies starring young men who flirted with old ladies and snubbed young ones and were deadly serious with children; techniques that seemed to charm them all. She could feel her hatred slipping through her fingers. She closed her fists.

Haydon, still smiling, was holding out his hand for her drawings. "Been sketching secret weapons?" he said.

She stiffened. He was, after all, the enemy. He would arrest her for spying and Sam would go crazy with guilt.

"I know about your drawings," he said, "because I've seen you at it. That's all. Quite often, in fact. You're almost a part of the landscape." The best part, he thought.

He remembered the first time he had seen her sketching on one of his evening walks around the camp. It was his favorite time, when the sun, grown fat and red on the nour-ishing day, took its last stand on Mt. Hope and sent long reluctant glances across the fields. For a moment it stood there, balanced like a penny. Then it dropped—he could almost hear the click—leaving wisps of peach and pink and blue and gold, like scattered thoughts, behind.

On such an evening, he had seen Nina with the sky turning wistful behind her. A rather tall, thin, pale figure, she had seemed almost emaciated beside the sturdy dark shapes around her. She was leaning against a post in the grandstand, drawing not the sky, streaked as a palette above, but the children playing in the dust below. She had, he realized, no colors with which to paint a sunset.

He had seen her often since then, but never close up. Looking at her now, he could see that, though slim, she was solid and her skin, darkened by the sun, no longer seemed so pale. She even looked younger. She had cut her hair. An admirably adaptable young woman, he thought, and began to examine her sketches.

She had caught it all, he realized, as he turned the pages, showing him parts of the camp he had never seen before: the stalls crowded with people—old and young, eating, reading, scrubbing, sweeping, crying, staring—and filled with home-made furniture, including a baby's potty and a homemade wheelchair. He saw women lugging heavy buckets of water and bent over endless washing—floors and clothes and a baby in a pail. He saw them crouched under showers and sitting with bowed heads on the exposed toilets. He saw men bent over shovels, lugging wood, standing in doorways with their hands hanging down and their eyes staring out. He saw an old man on an orange crate carving a piece of linoleum with a pocket knife and a young man nailing a horseshoe over the door of his stall. He saw a large woman with a tiny child on her back, watering a row of petunias in front of her barracks. And over and over, he saw a small boy caught in a huge empty landscape like a pin on a map.

He was studying her drawings like incriminating evidence, Nina thought. She folded her cold hands and looked around the office. It was just an office, with a desk, a phone, a filing cabinet, four chairs, and a map of the camp on the wall. There was no American flag, no pictures, no photographs, no ci-tations; nothing of *him* at all. She wondered why he was there, spending his days keeping thousands of people locked up. Mt. Hope was the second largest city in the state, with a warden instead of a mayor. She wondered if he liked his job.

"They're very good," he said, finally, putting down the last sheet almost reluctantly. "Just what we're looking for."

"What *are* you looking for?"

"An official camp artist."

She felt surprised, flattered, and finally, suspicious. Why

had he chosen *her?* Because she was Caucasian? Was it some sort of plot or just simple racial favoritism? Her sketching, like her cooking, was primitive, for home consumption only. She couldn't possibly be an "official artist" any more than she could be an "official cook." "Why me?" she said. "I'm not nearly good enough. I'm not really an artist at all. And I couldn't be an *official* anything."

"But you'd be doing exactly what you've been doing all along," he said. "Only you'd be doing it full-time, for pay."

"I couldn't possibly. I already have a job."

"I know. I've spoken to Dr. Landau. He agrees . . ."

"No. They need me at the hospital. Besides, I couldn't just stand around all day playing with charcoal when everyone else is doing hard physical work. *Necessary* work."

"This is necessary too."

"Then you should give it to an artist, a *real* artist, a *Japanese* artist."

"Race has nothing to do with it."

"Of course it does. And there are lots of Japanese artists in the camp. Real, *professional* artists."

"There are?" He sounded genuinely surprised. "We haven't been able to find any. Who are they?"

"My husband, Sam Curry, for one. He's really a sculptor, of course, but he does marvelous sketches. Much, much better than mine."

"But he refuses to do anything except manual labor. He said so on his questionnaire, he said so to the personnel officer, and he said so to me."

She nodded. "He's been saying that ever since that day."

"What day?"

She hesitated. She and Sam had never mentioned that day to anyone, not even to each other. It was sealed up and buried. The very thought of it made her sick, as if she'd swallowed it. And now Haydon was forcing her to bring it up again. She would do just that, she thought, spew it out all over him. Let him have it, all over that beautiful tweed jacket. He was waiting with patience, with sympathy. She began slowly.

It had happened a week after Sam was forced to give up his job at the art school because of the curfew. He had spent all his time in the studio working on his Persephone, like a man who knew his hours were limited. But that evening, when she came home from work, the house was quiet. There were no sounds from the studio, no chipping or sanding or whistling. Worried, she opened the door.

At first, the room seemed completely empty. Even the statues were gone, their stands bare. And then she saw them, bits of them, strewn around the room: severed heads and arms and legs and torsos; blind Oedipus's fingers still grasping his staff; Hagar's disembodied hand still holding Ishmael's; a tip of Satan's wing. She half expected to see blood all over the floor.

Sam was sitting in a corner with his back against the wall and the head of Persephone in his lap. She knelt beside him and put her arms around him. His whole body was shaking. At last he put the head down carefully on the floor and stood up. Then, leaning heavily on her, he walked slowly to the door. Like a cripple, she thought.

For the next few days, he stopped eating and sleeping and speaking. He sat at the kitchen table with his head bent and his fingers working rapidly, folding paper: newspaper and napkins and towels and old shopping lists; folding them into boats and birds and flowers and figures. When he finally got up, his movements were slow and his speech muffled, like a man moving around in the dark. After a while, he managed to find a series of jobs: in restaurant kitchens, on garbage trucks, even down a manhole—places where he would not have to show his face. He never went into the studio again, but his fingers twitched and his hands moved constantly. He would put them down—on a table, the back of a chair, Nina's shoulders—as if he longed to walk away and leave them there. Now, whenever his hands were empty, he kept them in his pockets.

Nina stopped talking and put her hands into her pockets too. Haydon got up and stood looking out of the window in silence, at the rows and rows of barracks, lined up like military graves. "I'm shocked," he said at last with his back turned. "And ashamed."

"You *should* be," she said, hanging on to her hostility with her fingernails. "So am I."

"What in the world are *you* ashamed of?"

"Being Caucasian."

"But you're a victim too." He came back, sat down, and looked at her silently for a moment. "As a Caucasian," he began hesitantly, "are you . . . have you . . . what I mean is, have you had any special problems here?"

Suddenly, she felt very hot. She stood up. "If you mean with the *Japanese,* the answer is *no!* Absolutely *not.* The only 'problems' I've had have been with your *Caucasians.*" She thought of the internal police who had offered to "remove" her as contraband; of Schweiker glaring at her in the hall this morning, ready to squash her beneath his enormous boots. And the soldier outside the administration building who greeted her with a wink and a leer.

"Applyin' for a discharge, at last?" he said. "How come you stuck it so long? Wait'll I tell my buddies. They been layin' odds. . . ."

She had grown rigid with anger as he went on. How could she have forgotten that she was never alone, that the Army was always watching, staring down from those tall towers? She thought of the small mound of rocks behind the hospital where she sat, occasionally, to be alone for a little while; to grieve in private and to spew out her rage at the sun and punch holes in that hard blue sky. And all the while the soldiers had been looking down, dropping ridicule and insults on her head. She could almost feel the lacerations on her skull.

"I have an appointment with the director," she said coldly, "about my work here."

"You mean you're *stayin'?* You sure got crazy tastes." He grinned and shook his head. "But anytime you get tired a the dirt and the slop and those bowed legs, lemme know. I could find you some nice lil spot. . . ."

"Thanks," she said, trying to move past him. "I prefer to stay where I am."

"In a stable? With a *Jap?* You a traitor? Or just a pro, not too fussy about your customers? I'll bet business is pretty good in there, huh?"

As she hurried by him, she noticed a faint, unpleasant odor. *Bata-kusai,* she thought. The smell of the Caucasian. She had detected it at last.

Would she smell it in Haydon's office, she wondered. She took a deep breath. But all she could smell was tobacco.

Haydon was frowning. "They're hardly *my* Caucasians," he said. "Which Caucasians were they?"

"How can I possibly tell? You know all Caucasians look alike."

"I mean it."

"I don't know and it doesn't matter. We're all fair game for all of them, aren't we? Just being here. The guards watching us all day and squirting that huge searchlight on us all night." She was almost shouting now, glaring down on him with clenched fists. "And those horrible internal police, your so-called safety councils, though they're the most dangerous animals around, bursting in when they please, taking what they please, threatening . . ."

"Threatening? Threatening what?"

She merely shook her head. "Not to mention poor old Mr. Sato."

He nodded. "That's not my jurisdiction, you know," he said quietly. "That's Security. But I'll speak to Collins." Yet if Collins refused to discipline his men, Haydon knew that he could not interfere. "There must be lots of other complaints," he said. "I'd like to hear them. All of them. But won't you sit down first, please?"

She went on standing, glaring down at him, suspecting that only from that position could she continue the attack.

"There *are* other things," she said. "*Lots* of other things."

"Let's have them." He pulled out his pipe.

She made a grasping motion, taking her courage in both hands. "The crematorium, for instance," she said.

He raised his eyebrows. "Ghoulish but necessary."

"Not stuck right down beside the hospital, it isn't, blowing smoke all over the wards. The only thing to be said for it is that it broke down so soon. Besides, everyone is convinced that . . ."

"The administration has been too friendly to Mr. Friendly? Go on."

She went on with her face flushed and her voice high: about the food and the plumbing and the crowding and the unpaid wages. She paused for breath.

"Anything else?"

"Lots. That pathetic excuse for a school and the censorship and the hospital. Want to hear about the hospital? Much too many patients and not enough of anything else. Beds or equipment or drugs or doctors. Dr. Landau is a genius and a saint combined, but even *he* can't operate with a can opener. All we can do for the patients is to let them suffer. They're not even allowed to read Japanese and many of them can't read English. So all they can do is stare at us—and the bugs on the wall." She was almost in tears.

"I know," he said, staring into the bowl of his pipe.

"Then why don't you *do* something? *You're* the director."

"I'm *only* the director. And that's *all* I am. The director. I don't make policy and I don't supply equipment, which is what's needed to take care of almost all the problems in this place. I can order it, beg for it, shout for it, pray for it. But I can't make it come. I can't make them send material for building, or money for wages, or qualified doctors. The Caucasians won't come and only a very few Japanese have been trained, thanks to the prejudices of the medical schools in this country. I don't even make the rules here. All I do is enforce them." He paused, then said emphatically, "But you could help. Through your drawings. They're very effective, you know." He leaned forward, looking up at her, and began to speak earnestly, even passionately. "What I'd like is a record of what goes on here. Not the Army version taken by military photographers but a factual, day-to-day description of life at Mt. Hope—as the evacuees experience it. 'Official' just means you have the administration's blessing. But if you don't like that word, we'll use another. 'Authorized,' perhaps. If you don't do it, we'll have only the Army version of what happened here. Wouldn't you like to leave a record too?"

He was wickedly persuasive, she thought. She was aware of him holding her drawings, aware of his eyes watching her, eyes that had been watching her on and off for weeks without her knowing it. The eyes of a spy, she told herself firmly.

She thought of Sam, who had declined the director's flattering offer. His eyebrows would lift in surprise and pride at the thought of Nina as an Authorized Artist. "You see," he would say. "I was right. As usual. You're damned good."

"Well," she said, looking down at Haydon, "not full-time and not for pay. I go on with my job at the hospital, as always, and sketch whenever I want, *whatever* I want, as always."

"Good! Now will you please sit down? Please?"

He was smiling at her. He had a nice smile. But she did not smile back. "Will they be censored, my drawings?" she said sternly.

His smile disappeared. "Not in *this* office, certainly. But I can't say what the Army or the WCCA or the FBI or the WRA or any of the rest of them will do."

Sam was right, she thought. Poor Mr. Haydon. He was just as much a prisoner as the rest of them. She remembered him that day at the end of the Americanization ceremony when he stood all alone on the bare platform, staring out at the disappearing crowd. Like a captain going down with his ship, she thought, as she sat down beside him at last.

FOURTEEN

I*T will be up to each Center,* the section on self-government in the *Handbook* read, *to plan its own design of community life.* Sam and the other members of the Committee to Draft a Constitution had worked hard for six weeks, meeting far into the night. Even Judo, who had required a good deal of persuasion to join, had come faithfully. When it was finished, they were pleased. It was practical, fair, democratic, with no distinctions among Issei and Kibei and Nisei.

"My wife's going to be terribly disappointed," O'Donnell said, "when I bring home a constitution instead of a pocket full of cash. She thinks I've been gambling in the BQ every night for the past six weeks." He was a cheerful man who had been a distinguished law professor until they discovered he was one-quarter Japanese. "I couldn't convince them that that was the legal-theory part. The rest was all baseball and

Ginger Rogers movies." He grinned at the brand-new constitution in his hands. "It's a damn good document," he said.

"Agreed!" Sam said. "It might even bring the Issei out of the BQ. Right, Judo?"

"It ought to please poor old Haydon," O'Donnell said. "He hates feeling like the head warden." Like Sam, he was always defending Haydon. And now Haydon had given him the chance to help write a constitution. "Let's go back to my place and celebrate," he said. "I just happen to have . . ."

"Just a minute." Colonel Collins, the chief security officer, with a head like a soup bowl, was standing in the doorway. He walked to the front of the room and began to read in a stern voice from the latest Washington directive: all forms of self-government in the centers were herewith abolished; councils of evacuees would be permitted but their members were to be chosen by the directors, and only American citizens, Nisei, could serve; the only powers of said council were to make recommendations and to cooperate with the administration. When he was finished, Collins folded the document carefully and lifted his head slowly as if to avoid any possible spill.

"Does Haydon know about this?" Sam asked.

"Irrelevant. This comes direct from the top brass in Washington."

"When was it issued?"

"Also irrelevant. November first."

"That was over two weeks ago!"

"Why weren't we told sooner?"

"We've been breaking our backs every night for the last . . ."

"And breaking curfew every night," Collins said.

They sat listening to his steps retreating down the hall. Then there was silence, except for the sound of ripping. Judo was tearing his copy of the constitution into strips. "For the latrine," he said.

The other Issei picked up their copies and tore them into strips too. Then they all followed Judo out of the room.

"How about having that drink anyway?" O'Donnell asked the others. But there was no longer anything to celebrate.

Sam sat alone in the Americanization Room staring at the huge flag drooping on its pole in the corner. He longed to turn its face to the wall. Walking home at last, with the darkness beginning to fray around the edges, he felt worn and heavy and carved in stone. Like one of his own statues, he thought.

In the icy stall, he sat down on his cot and stared at Nina, asleep with her flashlight still on and her book still open beside her. She was lying in the fetal position with her head down and her legs curled up. Dreaming she's still waiting to be born, he thought, into a life without Sam Curry and the Mt. Hope Assembly Center. Though God knows he had tried to spare her that, had reminded her often enough, even before the evacuation orders, that she was not Japanese. "A fact you seem to have forgotten," he said.

"Well, I'm not American and I'm certainly not German anymore. I have to be *something*."

"You might try being sensible," he had said.

The evacuation orders appeared, nailed like circus posters to telephone poles all over town. The soldiers appeared with them, lined up along the streets with their guns ready. Groups of people gathered in silence around the poles and stared up at the notices. Some could not read them because they were in English; some because they were too high up. Sam read the orders aloud.

"May ninth! But that's less than a week away!"

"What's 'PWT time'?"

"What are 'essential personal effects'?"

"And 'temporary residence elsewhere'?"

"Yeah. Where in hell is 'elsewhere'?"

"And how long is 'temporary'?"

"What's the difference? They'll never let us back."

"And what would we come back *to?*"

"My landlord says it's for our own protection."

"Sure. Punish the victim."

"There's a war on, don't forget."

"Then how come the Italians and the Germans aren't moving?"

"They are. Right along with the Caucasians. Into our farms and our shops and our jobs and our homes."

"It's only temporary. Just till they get us sorted out."

"Don't be stupid. They're not planning to 'sort us out.' They're rounding us up and moving us out so they can get rid of all of us at once. Nice and easy and quick and quiet."

Sam and Nina walked home in silence. But the voice of the Lieutenant General in Command of Western Defense went with them: "All evacuees must . . . All personal effects will be . . . No pets of any kind may be . . ."

Outside their front door, the eucalyptus tree still stood in its saucer of grass, but the tiny house looked different, as if it had stirred slightly and resettled itself, all ready for the new tenants. Inside, Nina looked around. "I shall miss my easel," she said in a small, tight voice. "Even though I never used it. But now I'd like to paint it all, all the people and houses and trees on Sullivan Street. Right down to the cracks in the sidewalk." She turned to Sam with a sad little smile. "You were right," she said. "Absolutely right."

"Of course, darling. I always am. And you *will* paint. Why shouldn't you? You're not going anywhere."

"Of course I'm going. I'm an enemy alien too, don't forget."

Sam's eyebrows shot up. "Sorry, but they don't give a damn about Germans. This little operation is strictly for Japanese only."

"Well, I'm a Japanese-in-law. By marriage."

"Don't be ridiculous. You're Caucasian. They won't let you go."

"Oh yes they will. Says so in writing. Right here. From the colonel himself." She reached into her pocket and pulled out a large, official-looking paper, carefully folded. She opened

it and read it proudly, like a citation, in her clear, high voice:
" 'There is absolutely no objection to your leaving with your
husband,' " the Colonel, Infantry, Provost Marshal, Western
Defense Command, had written. "You and your husband will
be allowed to evacuate together. . . .' "

"My God," Sam roared, "it sounds positively indecent."

" '. . . according to the rules and regulations governing all
other evacuees,' " she went on, " 'which will, of course, be
your status too.' " A new status, she thought; and, in fact, a
brand-new word.

"No!" Sam said. "Absolutely not. I refuse to be evacuated
with you." She was refolding her letter carefully. He put his
arms around her. "Please, darling," he said, and gave her a
long, deep kiss, to be framed and hung when he was gone.

"But I can't disappoint that poor man," she said at last.
"The Colonel Infantry Provost Marshal Western Defense
Command. Not after he's gone to all that trouble to turn me
into an evacuee."

"You damn well can," Sam said angrily, "and you damn
well will. Has it ever occurred to you that you may be resented? That the others won't want you around?"

He was frowning at her as if she were a piece of stone he
was getting ready to carve, to turn into something completely
different. He was, she reminded herself, very skillful at handling intractable material. He had never been angry with her
before. But she had never really crossed him before.

"Or do you think it will make things easier for me to have
a blonde, blue-eyed Caucasian wife around? Is that what you
think?"

"I think I should decide for myself," she said, still clutching
her letter.

"You don't seem capable of doing that. If you want to
know what will make things easier for me, it will be . . ."

"But I'm not thinking of making things easier for you. I'm
thinking of *me*. Isn't that what you've been telling me to do
all along? Well, now I'm doing it, being selfish, just as you
ordered. Now I'm not trying to please anyone but me. Not

even you. Now I'm going to do what *I* want. And I want to become an evacuee."

They were facing each other, looking straight into each other's eyes. Hers were filling with tears. He could not see in.

"Please, Sam," she begged. "Everyone I've ever known has disappeared. I can't let you disappear too."

He had a sudden vision of her as he had first seen her, looking half drowned with her suitcase disintegrating in her hand, standing on a street corner staring at the red light as if she expected to go on standing there forever, as if she knew that, for her, the light would never change. It was only a temporary residence, after all, he told himself as he put his arms around her, turning her into a displaced person again.

In the camp, in the beginning, he had waited every morning until she opened her eyes to assure himself that she had survived another night at Mt. Hope. But watching her sleep now he felt that, thanks to him, she was still waiting for the light to change.

He thought of the days before Mt. Hope when they had shopped and cooked and cleaned together; when they had gone to bed together—in private—and gotten up together; when they had spent their evenings together: Sam sketching Nina as she sewed or ironed or read or posed for Persephone with her ancient suitcase and chattered on about the people she met in the neighborhood and in the library and in the books she read.

"I've reserved the new Faulkner for you," she told him. "But you're only allowed to keep it for seven days."

"I shouldn't be expected to gulp down Faulkner," he said, squinting around his charcoal. "Those Snopeses have to be well chewed."

"Oh, no. The trick is to swallow them whole. Without tasting them." She turned to laugh at him.

"Hold that pose, woman," he shouted.

He opened his eyes and realized that he had been dreaming.

Nina opened her eyes too. She smiled. "I dreamed we

were back on Sullivan Street," she said, "and you were shouting at me to hold that pose."

He grinned. "At least we're still dreaming together," he said as he crawled in beside her.

For the next week, Sam was always there when she got home at night and still there when she awoke in the morning. But he seemed quiet, subdued, even depressed. He did not seem to be dreaming anymore.

"What about that constitution?" she asked him one evening.

"There won't be any constitution."

"I thought Haydon . . ."

"Nothing to do with Haydon," he said angrily. "It was vetoed by the Authority."

The next morning she heard him laughing softly beside her. "Christ, I was a fool to think they'd ever let us have a constitution in this place," he said.

"Yes," she said. "You were."

He rolled over and kissed her left eyebrow. "Because this is only a *temporary* residence, after all." He kissed her left cheek. "But there *is* something we can do." He kissed her squarely on the mouth and began to get up.

"Hold that pose," she shouted.

"Sorry, darling. No time now."

"But I haven't a single sketch of you."

"Okay. But not now. I'm late already."

"Tonight then?"

He hesitated. "I'll try. But there's a council meeting tonight. I think it's time we tried to do something about the mess hall food."

Suddenly she remembered what Emmy had said about Dan and his campaign against the chief chef. No wonder Sam was feeling so bouncy again. He had thought of another project "for the good of the camp." "You're not going to tackle Horrible Hackett, are you?" she said.

"*Expose* him would be more like it."

"And just who's going to do that? You and Dan?"

"That's right."

"And who else?"

"The whole of Block B probably. But that won't be necessary. All we need is the facts to lay before Haydon. He probably hasn't the foggiest notion of what in hell is going on around here."

"And couldn't do anything about it if he had. As you've reminded us all so often." As Haydon himself had said that day in his office: "I'm *only* the director. And that's *all* I am."

"We've got to try," Sam said. "Dan's threatening to organize a strike."

"He must be crazy. But that's no reason why *you* should be."

"What I'm proposing isn't crazy. Unless you prefer to go on eating Hackett's garbage."

"If they send you to Fort Washington I won't be eating at all."

"They won't send me to Fort Washington and I'll be home as soon as I can tonight. And pose till I'm rigid. But don't wait up." He kissed her. "And stop worrying."

Outside, the sun was rising, lashing the sky with color, raising long welts of purple and crimson and red and gold until the clouds seemed to be screaming in agony. He stood staring at them in awe, feeling that something extraordinary was demanded of him. But I'm a *sculptor* not a painter, he told himself with relief.

He watched while the sun made its way up over Mt. Hope, lighting it like a candle. Beyond was the horizon, roping him in, shutting out everything but that stump of a mountain, fencing him off from the world of curves and circles and movement and sound. Here there were only straight lines and sharp angles. Here there was no motion except for the wind lifting the snow and the tar paper, and the shapeless figures moving slowly across the fields. Here there was no sound—words froze just beyond the lips—except for the sirens at six and ten, blasting the evacuees out of bed in the morning and knocking them back in again at night. Every day began and ended with a shriek.

His feet slid on the icy ground. He had never felt freezing cold before or seen snow before. He had watched it fall with delight as it snuggled down on fields and roofs, laying white paws on doorsteps and windowsills, rearing up into huge mounds through which the small, slight Japanese struggled in their huge Caucasian army boots and their twenty-pound pea jackets; until the wind came like a giant broom and swept it away, leaving bald spots here and huge lumps there that melted slowly into weird, agonized shapes. Now the camp was a great sheet of ice, crisscrossed by streams of dirty water. The wind rose, stabbing him through the rips and tears in his secondhand army jacket. Battle-torn, he thought, and shuddered. He had displaced a dead soldier.

Up ahead, he saw Mr. Tsuda, the head-counter, bent under the wind in his heavy clothes, feeling his way slowly across the ice with a pointed stick. Sam wondered how he managed that trip, day and night, across the ice to the latrine and the mess hall and the wash house. He wondered what would happen if he ever lost his way like poor Mr. Sato. As he watched, the old man slipped and fell. He lay on his back without moving, his eyes closed and his body straight, and the sky to cover his face.

Sam picked him up and carried him to the latrine. He opened his eyes and smiled. "So sorry," he said. He was not hurt, he insisted. "My legs are perfectly all right, you know. It's my eyes. My glasses were broken and I can't seem to get new ones. In fact, I'm afraid my eyes are getting much worse. For it seems to me that it is always dusk here."

"It seems that way to me too," Sam said. "How are your sons?"

Mr. Tsuda shook his head. Nick, the elder, was in jail again for gambling and Yoshi was still in Roperville, canning beets now that the harvesting season was over.

"When's Yoshi coming home?" Sam said.

Mr. Tsuda shook his head again. "Not till the camp starts paying wages. That's what he said when he left. But he never writes anymore. Just sends those ugly green checks. He is worried about what will happen to us if we are ever released from here with no money and no jobs and no homes. He thinks the Japanese will never get jobs in this country again." He shook his head for the third time. He had taught Japanese poetry before the war. He did not think Americans would be interested in Japanese poetry anymore.

Sam thought of the rumors about Roperville that had been floating around the camp for months: that the evacuees were cheated and robbed and even attacked there. Most of the men had quit long ago.

"Sometimes I'm afraid he will never come home," Mr. Tsuda said. His sons were all he had. "I am most grateful to you," he told Sam. "Though I was rather curious to see if she was right about it."

"Who was right about what?"

"Your poet, Miss Dickinson. About freezing."

"Do you like American poetry?" Sam said.

"I like *hers*. So sharp, so intense, so vivid. So much feeling in so few words. Like the Japanese."

He refused to let Sam wait to take him back to the stable. "I must manage for myself," he said. "Even without glasses." He thanked Sam profusely, gave him a deep bow, and turned slowly into the dark doorway of the latrine.

Sam walked on, past the Issei wash house and the Issei shrine built with boards stolen from the building sites. Stealing was a necessity here. The administration set guards around the construction areas, but the guards stole the wood too, to keep their fires going in the bitter cold. Everyone stole: wood for furniture, wiring and bulbs for lights, scraps of metal for tools. Most evacuees had come with little or no money and—without wages—even the most timid and law-abiding stole. Sam had stolen whatever he could to make the stall livable.

Mrs. Oshima stole shoes from the camp store for her little girl; Mrs. Noguchi stole soap from the hospital for her husband. Teenagers, no longer able to forage for food from the mess halls, stole candy and cookies and chewing gum and Cokes from the canteen. With only a few hours of school, no planned activities, no family life, they ran wild. A fire had started mysteriously in one of the warehouses. The Japanese, Sam thought, were becoming acculturated.

Only five men were still working on the pipe-laying project, including Sam. The others, all Issei over fifty, had drifted away as the weather grew colder, as they missed more and more meals because they worked so far from their mess halls, as they received no pay. Wages were finally being paid in the camp—but not to them.

The director himself had organized the project, had promised them $12.00 a month instead of the usual $8.00 for manual labor, had stressed how important the work was. "A real public service," he had said. "We, in the administration, will be very grateful." He had chosen Mr. Watanabe, skinny, scared Mr. Watanabe, as foreman, the only Japanese foreman in the entire camp. Mr. Watanabe's head popped up and his eyes popped open. He had been many things in his life but never a foreman. He had worked for many Caucasians before opening his tiny grocery store, but never for anyone like Mr. Haydon. The others—bosses of work gangs and captains of fishing boats—were harsh men who cheated and abused and beat their workers. One drunken captain had actually tossed a sailor overboard just for getting in his way on deck. But Mr. Haydon was different. Mr. Watanabe trusted Mr. Haydon. Yet after three months on the project, there was still no pay. And the weather had turned very cold.

The other men insisted that Mr. Watanabe must do something. "You must go to see Haydon," O'Donnell, the lawyer, said, citing the Geneva Convention. He had been appointed by Haydon to work out a grievance procedure for the evacuees. When the Authority vetoed it, he joined the pipe-laying project. "Something the Authority won't veto," he said. Besides, he believed, like Sam, that the Nisei should do some of the hard manual work of the camp. He put down his shovel and patted Mr. Watanabe on the back. "You're our foreman," he said. "You must tell the director. He probably has no idea that we're not being paid."

But Mr. Watanabe refused to do anything that might indicate a lack of trust in Mr. Haydon, who had trusted him.

"Then you must see the comptroller," Sam said.

Mr. Watanabe trusted Sam. He went to see the comptroller.

Mr. Watanabe stood shivering outside Rigsbee's office in the overheated administration building but could not bring himself to knock on the door. He was about to leave when he heard heavy footsteps approaching from the other end of the long hall. He knocked in sheer panic, to get out of their way.

Rigsbee looked up at him from behind his desk, over several layers of shaggy sweaters. "The men on that project are volunteers," Mr. Rigsbee said. "And volunteers work for nothing."

"No," Mr. Watanabe said. "Not for nothing. For Mr. Haydon. For twelve dollars a month."

"Then where are your work cards?"

"Work cards?"

"Yeah. Everyone's got to have work cards."

"Mr. Haydon say nothing about work cards."

"Well, I can't pay wages without I have work cards." Mr. Rigsbee sneezed into an enormous handkerchief that covered his face like a surgical mask.

"Put the men to work right away," Mr. Haydon had said. Nothing at all about work cards. "You ask Mr. Haydon," Mr. Watanabe said. "He fix everything."

Mr. Rigsbee shook his head and said through his handkerchief, "In this department, Mr. Schweiker's the boss. In this department we've got rules. Rules 'n' reg'lations. Like Mr. Schweiker says. An' the rule is, no work cards, no pay." He wiped his nose. "An' I don't go against the rules. No sir. Never have. Never will. Good Lord, no. Mr. Schweiker wouldn't like that. No, sir. He wouldn't like that at all."

Mr. Watanabe saw the tufts of hair sticking out of Rigsbee's ears and eyebrows and nose, shielding him from hearing or seeing or smelling any need for compassion. Even the wool on his sweaters hung out in long strands as if it were still growing, protecting him from feeling too.

Mr. Watanabe went back to work. The director, he thought, had simply forgotten about them. It was a big camp. He had many other people to direct. He had seen Mr. Haydon walking around it sometimes, but he always stayed on the edges, keeping his distance, staring intently over the fields and barracks, observing it all at once, like a landscape painting. Sooner or later, Mr. Watanabe thought, he would remember them.

At the work place, the men looked up as he came back. When he told his story, there was a howl of rage. Several men dropped their shovels and walked off, muttering as they went. *"Inu,"* Mr. Watanabe heard them say. *"Inu. Inu."*

He watched them go. All his life he had been afraid of Caucasians. He thought of the drunken captain who beat his men regularly and tossed a seaman overboard just for getting in his way. He thought of the gang who had wrecked his shop, squashing fruit, smashing cans, overturning bins, while the Watanabes sat terrified and helpless, waiting to be squashed and smashed and overturned too. Yes, Mr. Watanabe had always been afraid of Caucasians—until he met Haydon. But now, he thought, looking after the disappearing Issei, he was afraid of the Japanese too.

FIFTEEN

THE night Dr. Noguchi arrived from prison, his family met him at the gate. They stood lined up according to age and greeted him formally as they always had whenever he returned home, bowing quietly from the waist with lowered eyes. But now they greeted him in English. At home they had always spoken Japanese as soon as they crossed the threshold.

Dr. Noguchi frowned. They looked grotesque, he thought, shapeless as puppets with their Japanese faces sticking up out of bits of American army gear. His wife, he was pleased to see, was wearing her elegant purple kimono with a brocade obi and smelled, very delicately, of musk. But she had lost most of her hair, he thought, staring at her in horror.

In the stall, he took off his three-piece suit, dusty and wrinkled, exuding the slightly sour smell of the prison locker, and put on a crested black silk kimono. It was one of several his wife had brought with her, along with his special towels. She brushed his suit and hung it on the hanger she had packed for the purpose and then on the nail that Ray, the oldest son, had hammered into the wall for the purpose. Underneath was Dr. Noguchi's white dentist's jacket, which she had washed and pressed as soon as she learned he might be coming home.

Dr. Noguchi sat in the enormous armchair made by his two middle sons. Like a parody of a dental chair, he thought. The entire stall had been completely rearranged to make room for it and the homemade table covered with his personal belongings: his china tea set, his special pipe with the silver bowl and the bamboo stem, his embroidered silk tobacco pouch, and the miniature Western chess set given to him by a grateful Caucasian patient. But what he saw was his family living in a horse stall.

"How could you allow it?" he asked his wife.

"How could I stop it?" she said.

He looked at her in amazement. She had spoken back to him for the first time since he had known her.

"It's better than prison, Papa-san," Toyo said in English. "At least we're all together."

He frowned. "Surely you are not telling *me* what is better? And in *English*." He stood up and said in his most commanding voice: "From now on you will address me in Japanese only. As always."

There were bursts of applause from both ends of the stable. Dr. Noguchi wiped his lips. His hands were trembling. He drew himself up to his full height, bowed to the right and the left, raised his voice and said, first in English and then in Japanese: "Forgive me, please, ladies and gentlemen, for disturbing you with my loud voice. Because we live in a stable is no reason to behave like a stable boy."

He had been a leader at home in the small but prosperous Japanese community and was proud of his position there. In camp, he stayed in the stall, except to go to the latrine and the wash house. He would have avoided them too, Ray said, if his wife could have performed those functions for him. He refused to work, since the only jobs available to him as an Issei involved crude manual labor, which he considered beneath him and which might damage his hands. After one visit, he refused to eat in the mess hall on backless benches with the noise and the smells and the food dumped like garbage into tin plates and eaten with primitive tin forks; food that slid between the teeth like slop. The evacuees would be toothless, if they did not die of scurvy first. His wife brought his meals to him—and sometimes specialties from the canteen—and served them on the wisteria-china plates from home, set out on a lacquered tray. It never occurred to him to wonder how she had managed to bring so much so far, and all unbroken.

She brought him water from the wash house and warmed it on the space heater for his tea and his hands, which he washed frequently between one activity and another—working out chess problems, smoking his pipe, drinking his tea, scolding his children—and between one memory and another. Like a dentist between patients, she thought.

Before serving him, she always put on her purple kimono. At home she had always worn kimonos in the house except for Western guests—and the FBI. The doctor refused to look at her in trousers. In a kimono, she looked slender, elegant, graceful, as a woman *should* look. In trousers she would look like the women he could not always avoid seeing on his way back and forth to the latrine and the wash house; round and squat as a *hibachi.*

"I wear trousers because they are warmer and more comfortable and more practical," she said. "I cannot scrub floors in a kimono."

She should not scrub floors at all, he thought. She ate in the mess hall with strange men and worked in the hospital washing diseased bodies—men and women alike—and emptying bedpans. Her voice, in English, sounded coarse, and her hair, cut like a boy's, made her look too young, too bold.

"Everything is different here," she told him softly one morning on her way to work, standing behind him so he would not see her in trousers. "Here we must all work and we must eat in the mess hall. And we must speak English." She did not tell him that she actually preferred it, that when the Caucasians took him away that evening they had left the door unlocked behind him. She could not live behind a locked door again. "You should work too," she said. "They need dentists at the hospital. It will make your life here a little more bearable."

He saw the toothmarks on the wall as if the horse had tried to bite his way out. Or was that simply the Caucasians' idea of a joke, sneering at his lost profession? Behind him, his wife left silently, taking little Kazi, in trousers too, with her. Even her Shirley Temple doll, he noticed, was wearing khaki trousers.

Now he was all alone in a monogrammed black funeral kimono—in mourning for his life—holding a porcelain tea-cup in a filthy horse stall. The other children had gone long ago. They were always out—day and night, coming and going as they pleased; visiting friends, roaming through the camp, watching movies or listening to jazz, even dancing in that vulgar, uncivilized, Western style. He thought of his large, well-ordered house in California, of his children decorously dressed and well-mannered, seated around him at dinner, waiting for him to serve, to lift his chopsticks, to give them the signals that ruled their lives. Even the little silver horse in the centerpiece carrying a few hibiscus blossoms on its back, seemed to be waiting, with one leg raised, for Dr. Noguchi's command.

He thought of his own father, a stern man who had kept him at his studies for fifteen hours a day in Japan and took him on long, strenuous pilgrimages every summer. Dressed in white with cone-shaped hats, and bells at their waists, and staves in their hands, they had done the Shikoku pilgrimages—eighty-eight temples—on foot, four times, pieced together during school holidays. They had climbed any number of mountains and looked down on smooth, still seas. In Japan, the landscape soared, reaching constantly for the sky. Here there was only Mt. Hope, like an old humped camel, mangy and full of wind.

He stared into his teacup and saw the painting of the dragon looking up at him from the bottom. It had been his favorite cup for years, with the dragon rearing up toward him, his neck curved, his tail flying. But now he looked as if he had been drowned by too much tea taken in solitude and sordid surroundings; like his own spirit, Dr. Noguchi thought, laid low in the bottom of a teacup. He raised his eyes and saw his chessmen waiting, set out on their own table, which took up precious space and was never used. At home he might have ordered one of his sons to play with him. But his sons were not his to order anymore. At home he would have had dozens of friends eager to be invited to sit down with Dr. Noguchi. Here there was no one. He could not imagine playing with any of his neighbors—Mr. Oshima, the gardener, or Mr. Watanabe, the grocer, or that shameful Americanized toady, Sam Curry.

He sat alone all day. Toward evening the Oshimas, two stalls down, erupted in a mixture of English and Japanese and a cosmic anger that marked all their quarrels.

"You stay away from the Noguchis," Mr. Oshima was shouting.

"But why, Papa?" a girl's voice said.

"Because I say so. And because Mr. Noguchi cannot keep his sons in order."

"*Dr.* Noguchi," Jack said.

"He's not a *real* doctor," the youngest boy said. "Only a dentist."

"He spent three months in Fort Washington," the middle boy said. He clearly regarded it as a heroic achievement.

"And he's very distinguished-looking," Josie said. "Except that his hair is too long. Toyo says he won't let a Caucasian barber near him. Why don't *you* cut it for him, Papa?"

"Because I am a gardener, not a barber."

"You should see their stall," Josie went on. "They have such lovely things."

"How do you know?" Mr. Oshima shouted. "Have you been there? Visiting the sons the way your brothers visit the daughters?"

"Oh, Papa. I go to visit *Toyo*. She's my friend. But we never stay. She's terrified of her father and so am I. I just go to pick her up on my way to work or to the mess hall."

"And her brothers? You pick up one of those too? I forbid you to do any more picking up at the Noguchis'. Understand?"

"Oh, Papa, you're impossible." There was a moment's silence and then the door slammed.

"She talks to me like that?" Mr. Oshima said. "And then she leaves, goes out, in the night. Like a woman of the street, she comes and goes as she pleases. That is what she is learning from the fancy dentist's children?"

Dr. Noguchi, sitting beside his heater, shivered. He had seen Mr. Oshima occasionally on his trips to and from the latrine, seen him sitting in the doorway of his stall, staring at a world that had stopped turning. From now on, Dr. Noguchi would make a long detour to avoid him.

He got up and poured out some of the water from the kettle, which was still warm, into a bowl and washed his hands. There was a small sliver left of the soap his wife had brought for him from the hospital. No one else ever used it. He washed carefully, soaping twice, rinsing twice, as he had done between patients. He missed his patients, sitting so trustingly with their mouths wide open, helpless as the fish in the bowl in his waiting room. He missed the feeling of competence, even mastery, he felt when he stood over those open mouths, explorer in hand, with his nurse, alert and reverent, beside him. He missed his neatly tailored shirts and trousers and the white jacket that buttoned to the neck, so crisp, so efficient, so professional. It was hanging, unseen and unused now, on a hook behind the door. He reached for a towel. He could not go on washing his hands all day.

He poured himself more tea, using a plain cup this time. There was nothing for him to do but drink tea. He could not even read during those periods when the stable was quiet. Japanese literature was not allowed in the camp and he refused to read English except when absolutely necessary and certainly never for pleasure. The sight of his wife's English books left over from her university days enraged him: George Eliot and Dickens and Tennyson and Wordsworth. What a docile schoolgirl she had been, he thought with contempt. And now she was a docile evacuee. It did not occur to him that she had also been a docile wife.

But he made his own rules, went his own way. He had been a busy man, rushing in and out while his family watched with admiration, holding his coat, handing him his hat, wishing him hello and good-bye. Here his family rushed by *him,* racing in and out, leaving him alone, shutting the door in his face.

He sat staring into the bottom of his cup, but it told him nothing. It was his wife who could read the tea leaves.

Toyo came home early. She nodded silently to her father and hurried to her cot in the far corner, closing the sheet carefully behind her. The other corner, where the boys slept, was empty. It was always empty, with the sheet drawn back. The older children were never home. Was Toyo sick, he wondered. If so, he knew she would not tell him. His children hardly spoke to him anymore since he still insisted on Japanese, except for a formal good morning and good night. They had never really spoken to him at home either, he realized; merely answered his questions. But here in the camp, he had no questions. Here in the camp, he was afraid to hear their answers.

He sat drinking tea, wondering about Toyo, so still behind that sheet stretched out between them at four in the afternoon. He knew nothing about her except that she worked in the cafeteria, serving food to the Caucasian jailers. He knew nothing else, only how she looked from the front coming in and the back going out.

Yet she had been his first-born and he had been filled with awe and pride and delight when he saw her wrapped up in the nurse's arms, a tiny pearl removed, intact, from its shell. To his surprise, he found that it did not matter in the least that she was a girl. He noticed only that she had come forth whole with all her parts fully articulated. He felt proud, as if he had performed the extraction himself, and waited, fascinated, for her first tooth. But after a while the other children came. She was no longer a miracle, merely a fact. There were other, more pressing facts.

But now she was a mystery again, an unknown fact. He went on staring at that sheet which hung so white and so impenetrable between them. It had always been there, he realized. Only now, in the camp, it was visible.

The others returned, his wife with his dinner from the mess hall, the children to greet him formally before going out again. His wife glanced at the sheet and hurried behind it. The others stared at it silently. Dr. Noguchi stared into his teacup.

"I think Toyo is not well," Mrs. Noguchi said, reappearing with a worried expression.

Dr. Noguchi looked up. "Of course she is not well. No one is well in this place."

"I think she should see the doctor," Mrs. Noguchi persisted.

Dr. Noguchi frowned. "What is wrong with her?"

"I do not know. She will not talk about it. But she is quite often sick to her stomach and she refuses to eat and . . ."

"Of course she is sick to her stomach. Of course she refuses to eat. Because the food here is not edible. That is a wise, even healthy reaction. But it is no reason to hand her over to the crude, hairy hands of a Caucasian doctor with his crude, even dangerous methods." He returned to the chessboard. Mrs. Noguchi set the bowl with his dinner in front of him.

"No vegetables?" he said. "No rice?"

"I'm sorry," she said. "It is what they served."

"It is a scandal," he said, staring at the dish: bread and potatoes and canned beans. "And no sugar for the tea?"

"No," his wife said patiently. "There is *never* any sugar."

"Because of the war," his oldest son, Ray, said.

"Yes, Papa-san," the second son said. "There are lots of shortages all over the country. They're rationing sugar and meat and butter. . . ."

"So?" the doctor said. "And how do you know so much about the rest of the country?"

"We get letters," the third son said.

"Letters? From where? From whom?"

"From California. From our friends."

"From Caucasians!"

"And sometimes they get packages too," Kazi, the youngest, said.

"Packages?" He raised his voice. "What kind of packages?"

"Food packages," Ray said. "They're allowed now. I guess they decided they might as well let our friends feed us after all."

"You take presents from the Caucasians?" His voice was loud and cold with anger. He glared at his wife. "Why wasn't I told?"

"I thought you knew," she said. "You have had many things we never get in the camp. The green tea you have been drinking all week, the sugar, the rice cakes—they were all from the packages."

He stood up. His hands were shaking. He lifted the cup and poured the tea on the floor. He had been tricked, deceived, shamed by his own family. He was no longer its head. He was less than the fish in his office at home which were fed and cared for and which gave nothing in return except the primitive pleasure one might feel in watching them. His family was watching him now as he twisted and turned in the bowl; but without pleasure. He walked to the door in his silk kimono, flung it open, and plunged into the night. "Papa!" they screamed, but he slammed the door behind him.

He rushed out, head down, through the darkness. He had no idea where he was going, only that he must get away from those faces staring at him, distorted now like faces seen through the curved glass of a bowl. The wind followed him, slicing at his ears, ripping the skin from his face and the kimono from his back. Suddenly he saw a light beside him.

"Dr. Noguchi?" It was the Caucasian woman from next door. He bent his head still lower.

"Come," she said, taking his arm.

He was trembling with cold and his mouth was frozen shut. He was too cold to argue.

In her stall, she made him sit down in the chair nearest the space heater while she poured his tea. He looked around him with curiosity colored by contempt. It was a tiny triangle, a mere corner of a stall, really, for the Watanabes had the larger share. He saw bookshelves and two crude chairs and a table made out of orange crates and determination. The walls were covered with drawings and a tiny British flag. Though cramped, the place looked comfortable, even cozy. For a moment he forgot he was sitting in a stable, which he could never do in his own, far larger, more elegantly furnished place.

"I'm sorry my husband isn't here," Nina said, handing him a fat, ugly, broad-hipped cup. It was enormous. Like an old shaving mug, he thought with revulsion. He was glad Sam Curry was not there. He had never met Sam Curry, but he had heard all about him, a cringing, craven Nisei who did the Caucasians' dirty work for them; dug their ditches and served on their puppet "council" and defended their abominable practices. Dr. Noguchi had heard him too, often, far too often, during discussions in the Currys' stall. "It's early days yet," Sam kept saying. "Give them a chance." "It's not Haydon's fault. It's just the usual bureaucratic snafu in Washington." "This is just a *temporary* camp, remember."

Dr. Noguchi imagined him as a grotesque-looking man, small and round and slightly squashed, the perfect shape for a toady. But one day he saw Sam going into his stall. To Dr. Noguchi's great surprise, he was a slim, rather tall, good-looking young man who could, in fact, be taken for one of Dr. Noguchi's own sons.

"Sam will be very sorry that he missed you," Nina went on. "He's at a meeting tonight." Still another meeting, she thought. She had hardly seen him, except in glimpses, for days, making her the only evacuee in the whole camp who virtually lived alone. "He's at meetings most nights," she said.

To advise the Caucasians on how to put me to work, Dr. Noguchi thought. He buried his nose in his cup, grateful for the steam that rose to warm his face. When it cleared, he saw her sitting opposite him holding a pad and a piece of charcoal. She looked very young, like Toyo, he thought, with her hair cut short. Like his wife's, he realized. She had undoubtedly corrupted them all, a young woman in trousers entertaining a strange man at night all alone in her stall.

She had always wanted to do a drawing of him, she was saying boldly, in her high, girlish voice, but had not wanted to intrude. "But now that you're here . . ."

Now that *I* have intruded, you mean, Dr. Noguchi thought, though she had practically dragged him in. He did not wish to be copied by a Caucasian woman, to be added to her collection of enemy aliens and hung on the walls of a stable. He did not wish to be taken sitting on an orange crate drinking tea from a shaving mug and wearing a black silk funeral kimono, to be ridiculed by the Caucasians. She was waiting quietly for his answer, looking at him like a suppliant, as if she had asked an enormous favor. Above her head, he could see the drawings, line drawings mostly, of the camp; small hunched figures bending into the wind, fighting their way through endless stretches of empty space with that mountain like a sawed-off shotgun ready to explode in their faces. One picture, especially, struck him; that of a small boy standing all alone in the middle of nothing, who seemed to have been displaced from the planet itself. He was looking out forlornly but there was no one—except Dr. Noguchi—to see his anguish. Mrs. Curry was still waiting for his answer. Dr. Noguchi looked at the boy and, in answer to some silent plea, he nodded.

Mrs. Curry began to sketch, chattering like a schoolgirl while she worked. "I think your wife is a *wonderful* woman," she said, nailing down her adjectives for future use. "She's the *best* worker we have in the *whole* hospital. So good with the patients—*all* the patients. Not just the young or the old or the Nisei or the Issei. And, of course, being able to speak both English and Japanese is *such* a help." She paused for a moment, squinting at her sketch.

Is she trying to insult me, Dr. Noguchi thought. Reminding me that my wife scrubs and washes and carries slop like a servant.

"It must have been terrible for her all that time when you were away," Mrs. Curry went on. Her short hair lay in a tangle all over her head. Like one of those ugly rag dolls, Dr. Noguchi thought. A slight yank at one end and the whole thing would unravel. Dr. Noguchi flipped up the sleeves of his elegant funeral kimono, which provided a note of sobriety and dignity and discipline to this disorderly scene. He was feeling warmer, more comfortable. She was still talking.

"With all those children and no money and not knowing *what* was happening to you. And yet there she was, working harder than any of us. First to show up in the morning and she *always* stayed on when she was needed. You must be very proud of her. And yet I don't suppose she ever went out to work before, did she?"

"Of course not!" Dr. Noguchi barked. The woman's tongue flopped like a dying fish. And my wife, he longed to say, should not be working now.

Nina looked up shyly. "Perhaps you would come to work for us, too, Dr. Noguchi," she said. "I've heard that you are a dentist."

"I *was* a dentist. Now I am simply an enemy alien. I am no longer allowed to practice my profession."

"But why not?"

"Because I have been incarcerated. Obviously."

"But that doesn't mean you can't go on being a dentist."

"On the contrary, I thought that was exactly what it meant. Here I am permitted only to scrub latrines and build barracks and dig. . . ."

"But they need dentists desperately," Nina said. "Would you be willing to help out? You would be paid, of course." Sixteen dollars a month. It was hardly worth mentioning. Would they even allow him on the hospital staff, an Issei who had once been a prisoner in Fort Washington?

"Would you do it?" she said. "I'll tell Dr. Landau first thing in the morning and then maybe you can start right away."

Dr. Noguchi thought of his empty white jacket hanging behind the door of his stall. He imagined it stiff with disuse. He would have trouble putting it on. "I don't know. I will have to think it over," he heard himself say with surprise. "What kind of equipment have you? I can't work with shoddy equipment."

"Well," Nina said, "there isn't very much." The only dental equipment she had ever seen was something that looked like the electric chair. "But I'm sure they'll do the best they can for you. Shall I tell Dr. Landau you'll be up tomorrow?"

"Up? Up where?"

"At the hospital."

"Are you telling me that I would have to go to the hospital? Work at the hospital?" He had visions of bloody bandages and nauseating smells and Caucasian doctors ordering him about. "I have taken a vow," he said, "not to put a foot down anywhere outside my stall until I can put it down as a free man again."

"Then you could see patients there," she said quickly. "In your stall."

But the impulse had passed. It was bad enough squeezing his own family into that stall. He did not want patients pushing their way in as well. "No. I'm sorry. Dr. Landau will have to get along without me." He put down the ugly mug and stood up. "Thank you for the tea," he said.

She stood up too. "Must you go? I haven't quite finished your sketch."

He did not want her to finish it. He did not want to hang on the wall with that scared little boy and those pathetic stooped figures, another sample evacuee. "I'm afraid I must go," he said. "My family expects me. Tell your husband I am sorry to have missed him. I hear he is a most cooperative and conscientious evacuee. I am sure the administration is very grateful."

She heard the contempt in his voice. He might have been calling Sam *inu*. Is that what people were thinking, saying? Was Sam in danger from both sides: from the Caucasians like Schweiker and the Issei like Dr. Noguchi?

But Dr. Noguchi was thanking her in his usual calm, measured tones. Then he bowed and left.

He had been vindicated. A Caucasian woman had invited him into her stall to draw his portrait and enlist his services. He could return to his family again. He was still recognized as a professional. His wife demeaned herself by working as a maid in the hospital; his sons and daughter worked side by side with their jailers, helping with their office work, their messages, their mail, their food. There were Japanese who were firemen, even policemen. It was the Japanese who were running the camp. Without them it would have to be closed down. Dr. Noguchi would not collaborate with the enemy.

His stall was empty. He felt deflated, depressed. He remembered the insulting words shouted over the partition by a coarse, illiterate farmer in a turtleneck sweater. It was like being stoned—only noisier. The whole stable had heard it, including the Currys. And they had heard him, the elegant Dr. Noguchi, shouting at his family like . . . like Mr. Oshima. Suddenly he saw himself as a foolish old man who had wandered into the freezing night in sandals and a silk kimono.

Mrs. Curry had taken him in to persuade him to work for the Caucasians by comforting him with tea and flattering him with a portrait. Or—worse—she had taken him in out of pity. Worse still, out of consideration for his wife, that "wonderful woman." It was right, he thought bitterly, that his wife should wear trousers.

He sat down and stared at the sheet still stretched across the stall. As he watched, Toyo came out from behind it and walked quickly toward the door. Her face was blotchy as if she had been crying. Why, he wondered. And where was she going alone, at this time of night? But he said nothing. That was his wife's business. *She* was the head of the family now. Father and daughter merely bowed, slight, swift bows that hardly ruffled the air between them.

He went on staring at the sheet. He had a sudden urge to pull it down, but he did not move. Gradually he realized that the Oshimas' stall was silent too, absolutely silent. Was Oshima there all alone too? Dr. Noguchi shivered and reached for his coat—and saw the dentist's jacket hanging beneath it. It swayed slightly, as if shrugging its shoulders.

Tony lay still in the darkness beneath the grandstand waiting for Toyo. But only the searchlight came, punching him in the eye. It had found him at last.

When Toyo finally arrived, she crept into his arms without a word and began to cry. Between sobs, she talked. He lay still, stroking her hair while her tears wet his cheeks and dissolved his dreams. He had always known he would never get that fellowship, would never go to graduate school with a library big as a church and stuffed with books.

"My father will kill me when he finds out," Toyo said. "Or lock me up in that convent on the other side of the camp and I'll never see you again."

He's more likely to kill *me,* Tony thought.

SIXTEEN

Sam sat in the mess hall waiting for Dan with a copy of the *Handbook* in front of him. He opened it and read: *The food at the Centers will be on a par with Army rations.* Last night they had beans and two thin slices of Spam each. He turned the page. *Special food will be provided for babies, invalids, and those on restricted diets.* In fact, there was nothing at all for them. There was not even milk. Recently infant formula had been available, but after two weeks the mothers refused to use it. It was rumored that it was made with saccharin instead of sugar and that two babies had died as a result.

"It's wartime, remember," Sam had said at the last council meeting. "They're suffering from shortages everywhere."

"Not in the staff cafeteria, they're not," someone said. "They get all the meat and fresh vegetables and salads and fruit and eggs and butter they want up there. Not to mention thick cream and plenty of sugar and real coffee."

"They're not just *saving* money on us," Dan said. "They're *making* it. With what Hackett's giving us in this mess hall, he could be feeding us on *seven* cents a day instead of *thirty-seven*, and pocketing the difference." He had seen invoices that made his head spin: canned chili and tomatoes and carrots and peas listed at three times their normal price; food that never reached the evacuees' plates: canned applesauce and apricots and peaches; fresh apples and bananas and pears. He had seen trucks loaded with meat and sacks of sugar and rice backing out of the kitchen compound. Hackett examined the garbage regularly (though nothing but thoroughly rotten food was ever thrown away) and reduced the rations accordingly. "Trouble is," Dan went on, "it will be hard to make it stick. He has friends, the bastard."

"Impossible," Sam said. "Name one."

"Rigsbee, our congested comptroller. And *he's* Schweiker's pocket companion. But we sure as hell have a case. It's worth a try. We've got to do something."

Sam knew he was right. He could feel the temperature rising all around him. After the constitution was dumped, the Issei had remained holed up in their overstuffed quarters, where they sat up to their knees in boredom, varied only by increased drinking and brawling and spells in prison. The rest of the camp was seething too. He had heard muttering in the mess hall and the wash house and the latrine. There had been a break-in at the canteen and packages of potato chips and nuts and cigarettes and chocolate had been stolen. There had been another death in childbirth, and Dr. Landau was beginning to be known as the Caucasian Killer. Signs with INU in bold black letters appeared outside the mess halls and recreation halls and the administration building. The memory of Mr. Sato, even to those who had not known him, still wandered through the camp. At night the barracks and stables, crowded as the Ark, seemed to rock on a rising flood.

Dan had argued for a strike. "Talk will get us nowhere," he said. Sam proposed a meeting with Haydon instead.

The council members had nodded grimly and appointed Sam and Dan to talk to Haydon and demand to see the books.

Sam stared at the oil slicks in his coffee. He would be happy to sit there drinking it all day if he could escape this morning's meeting. This is only a *temporary* center, he tried to tell himself once again. But after six months the phrase felt prickly to the tongue.

He glanced at his watch and closed the *Handbook*. He did not want to confront the administration, to demand his rights. He wanted to be a loyal American, a good citizen, a cooperative evacuee. He looked up and saw Dan coming out of the kitchen with Hackett right behind him like a man following his own best interests. Sam drained his cup and left with a mouthful of dregs.

Schweiker sat near the door, as usual, staring out the window, absorbing all the light for himself. He looked angry and strangely lopsided, perhaps because Rigsbee was not beside him. Rigsbee was home nursing his cold. Cooking his books, Morrissey thought.

The meeting was held in Haydon's office, with Haydon firmly behind his desk and the swivel chair in an upright position. To signal that for once he was ready to direct? Actually, he had been eager to avoid this meeting altogether, to avoid any confrontation between Schweiker and the evacuees. It was only a matter of weeks before the whole place would be shut down and the evacuees moved to a permanent camp farther east. Until then he wanted peace.

But Morrissey had been adamant. "The way the Authority operates," he said, "it could be months before they move us out. And this place is hot as hell right now and getting worse. There seems to be some new provocation every day. The whole camp could blow up any minute, especially with Schweiker walking around with a live gun on his hip and jittery nerves and jittery fingers. I wish to hell he'd take up knitting."

He was thinking, Haydon knew, of the recent incident at Mallabar when someone fired on an angry crowd—which made the crowd angrier. The Army was called in, three evacuees were killed, half a dozen wounded, and still more transported to Fort Washington. The camp was in an uproar for weeks.

"Absolutely not!" Schweiker was saying. "No one, least of all a couple of evacuees, messes with my books." *He* was probably remembering Sinclair, Haydon thought, where two policemen were beaten up during a contraband raid.

Schweiker glared at Dan, who was sitting up very straight with his head high. He looked handsome and lithe and alert. His cane, propped up beside him, gave him an air of elegance and authority. Schweiker had studied Dan's dossier and liked nothing about it, beginning with "Profession: actor" —it was a profession Schweiker considered to be made up entirely of pansies and parasites.

Dan glared back in fascination at Schweiker's cowboy hat and high-heeled boots and the gun stuck to his hip. Like an extra in a grade-B western, he thought, except for that three-piece suit. Schweiker clearly had his roles confused. Or was he trying to play all the parts himself? And what about that gun? Did Schweiker put it on automatically every morning with his tie? Did he take it off before kissing his wife? Did he need it for balance so that without it he tottered? Would he actually use it? On what occasions? Had he already used it? Was he a murderer sitting there with his hat hiding his eyes and his huge boots, sharply pointed for effective kicking, and his gun as handy as a handkerchief?

Haydon was studying Sam, a man lucky enough to have Nina Curry for a wife and persuasive enough to induce her to live with him in a horse stall. He saw Sam frowning at the lump under Schweiker's jacket. Haydon wished, like Morrissey, it could be a ball of wool instead. Should he risk a revolution by the staff and insist that Schweiker obey regulations and give it up? Was he, Haydon, beginning to see through the eyes of Sam Curry? Haydon gave his chair a slight tilt. "Mr. Curry and Mr. Matsui," he said, "have been delegated by the council to . . ."

"I don't care if they've been delegated by Hirohito himself and all the little Hitos," Schweiker said.

"I would like to point out," Morrissey said, pointing his glasses at Schweiker, "that the council's request is entirely appropriate within the meaning of the directive. The power to recommend assumes the power to . . ."

"And *I* would like to point out," Schweiker broke in, "that I have the power to prevent a couple of evacuees from messing around in my records. Who the deuce do they think they are? Some Senate investigating committee?" He lifted his hat to cool his head.

Time to strike a blow for civil liberties, Morrissey thought, clenching his fists. Thanks to his jogging, he felt ready. He took a deep breath, turned toward Schweiker, and said in a loud voice, "Denying authorized representatives of the council access to your records would be unwarranted, would arouse suspicion, and would constitute a serious blow to the credibility of this administration. Which is already in pretty bad odor in case you haven't noticed. Or have you been catching Rigsbee's colds?"

Haydon turned to Schweiker. "I know how you feel, Caspar," he said. "But isn't it entirely possible that the chef in Block B mess may, with the best intentions in the world, be a bit *too* conscientious about trying to save the government money?"

"No!" Schweiker said. "It is *not* possible. Besides, that's a matter for the chief steward and me." He turned toward Sam and Dan. "In case you've forgotten," he said, "there's a war going on out there. People are getting killed out there. People are making sacrifices out there. Loyal Americans all over this country are going without. That's something you Japs don't know anything about, sitting in here, perfectly safe like you are. Housed and fed like you are without lifting a finger or paying a penny. Thousands of you, sitting around all over this country, letting Uncle Sam take care of you, not doing a blamed thing except turning up regalar for meals and making trouble. Too blasted much trouble."

Sam stared back at him, a sharp black diagonal stretched out across one corner of the room like a barrier. Why wasn't he in the Army, where stiff straight lines were demanded and guns were required and killing "Japs" was the order of the day? Another displaced person, Sam thought, and his fingers stirred in his pockets. Someday he would carve him, booted and armed, with that enormous hat hiding his face. "We'd be glad to change places with your 'loyal Americans,' " Sam said. "In the factories or the farms or the Army."

"You could start by doing some work right here."

"He is," Haydon said. He smiled at Sam. "They both are. *Hard* work. Not just sitting behind a desk."

"Which reminds me," Morrissey said. "Did you ever get Tony Takahashi moved out of the BQ? I see he's still around. Whatever happened to that fellowship?"

"It came this morning. A very good one too. Now we're just waiting for his release. It should come through very soon." Haydon had done nothing about moving Tony. Now, thank God, it would not be necessary. But he must remember to tell him about that fellowship. It should cheer him up. He had seemed terribly subdued lately.

"Well, the Isseis aren't working," Schweiker said. "They sure as blazes aren't working."

"They're old men," Sam said, "and they're not allowed to do anything but the hardest kind of manual labor. Like criminals. You can't expect them to break their backs for you, in this climate, without pay, on camp food. Ever eat in a mess hall, Mr. Schweiker? They're convinced that if they do go to work they'll get sick, very sick. And if they ever get sick here they'll never get well. Just be dumped into that incinerator in Roperville or shipped outside the barbed-wire fence—

maybe even before they're quite ready. Ever see the hospital, Mr. Schweiker?"

"Like to investigate that too, while you're at it? You running for president or something?"

"I'm a member of the council."

"Well, stop acting like you're the chairman of Ways and Means. Because we don't have ways and means in here. We have rules and regalations in here. And all your precious council's got to do is obey them. Like everyone else. Obey them." He turned to Dan. "You a member of the council too?"

"No, I'm a cook."

"And a troublemaker. And before that a prisoner at Fort Washington as a dangerous enemy alien. Right?"

"Wrong." Dan could feel Schweiker's glance raking him up and down, skinning him alive. Bastard, he thought. He had not wanted to come to this meeting. It was Sam's idea. Sam with his Caucasian wife was breaking out in spots, *white* spots. Three months in Fort Washington would have changed that, Dan thought, as it had changed him. He longed to punch Schweiker in the jaw, to knock that idiotic hat off his head and expose what was growing underneath; to rip off that gun and make him walk, disarmed, down those long corridors with Japanese faces peering at him over their desks and Japanese bodies forcing him up against the wall; to yank off his boots and make him walk, two inches shorter, in his stockinged feet.

"What's *he* doing here?" Schweiker asked Haydon.

"He's here because he knows what's been going on in the kitchen," Haydon said, aware of Sam's eyes on him. "And because we want to hear what he has to say."

"The only people we have to listen to," Schweiker said, "are the Army and the WCC and the FBI and the . . ."

"The 'moral climate' in this 'Center,'" Sam said, turning to Haydon, "is bad and getting worse. Anything you can do . . ."

"Of course," Haydon said. "If there's corruption in the kitchen—or anywhere else—I want to know about it."

"The kitchen is under *my* jurisdiction," Schweiker said. "Says so right here in the T.O." He reached into his breast pocket for a document—carried above the heart, Dan thought—and began to read: "From the bottom up: Chief Steward, Comptroller, Chief Executive Officer. With the CEO smack at the top. No doubt about it. There's your T.O. right there. Loud and clear. Time we paid attention to rules and regalations around here."

His face, tightened with anger, seemed to be getting smaller, Haydon thought. Soon it would disappear completely under that huge hat. Haydon could not afford to let his chief executive officer lose face. He leaned a bit farther back in his chair.

Any more and he'll be horizontal, Morrissey thought. All ready for Schweiker to cut up.

"No one's disputing your jurisdiction, Caspar," Haydon said. "All we're asking is that you make sure the steward, and everyone under him, is observing the proper procedures."

"You want me to accuse my chief steward?"

Sam looked at Haydon, and nodded.

Haydon sat up. "I think it would be best," he went on, "if we conducted some sort of investigation. To satisfy *ourselves* as well as the council. I'll appoint a committee and"—he leaned back again—"I'd appreciate it, Caspar, if you'd serve as chairman." He smiled at Schweiker and brought his chair forward to an upright position. He had, he thought, landed safely on middle ground.

The man's a veritable seesaw, Morrissey thought.

"It's audit time," Schweiker said. "*And* inventory time. And I sure as blazes don't have time to waste."

"It won't be wasted," Haydon said. "And I'll see that you get lots of help." He paused. "I'd hate to have to appoint someone else."

Schweiker looked at him sharply, but Haydon was smiling blandly again. "It's appeasement," Schweiker said. "I know what I'll find."

"So do I," Sam said.

"So do we all," Dan said.

Schweiker stood up and stared down at them while his lips moved soundlessly: " 'And besides, they learn to be idle. . . . For some are already turned aside after Satan.' " Then he turned and stalked out.

Sam imagined him racing home, breaking speed limits, skirting fences, scattering dust. At home, he would wash down his car as a cowboy washes down his horse, and polish his gun and brush his hat and his suit and his nails and his teeth, brushing away the dust of Mt. Hope. Then he would close his curtains and lock his door and sit down beside a cold fireplace in his empty house, with his boots and his hat and his gun, waiting to go back to Mt. Hope again; waiting to walk knee-deep in Japs again.

But Schweiker did not go home. Instead he went back to his office, sat down at his desk, opened his Bible, and began to write: "Grace be to you and peace. . . . the powers that be are ordained of God. Whosoever resisteth the power, resisteth the ordinance of God, and they that resist shall receive to themselves damnation." He wrote steadily as he sat among the Gentiles, writing to the faithful far away. When he was finished he put it in an envelope and added it to the pile of unsealed, unstamped letters in his bottom drawer.

Alone in his office, Haydon stared out the window at that crooked mountain that seemed forever lashed by a steady wind. He had, he thought, done the only thing possible to prevent an explosion. He was known as a reasonable, rational man, a peacemaker, which was probably why he had been chosen as director in the first place. It was a reputation he cherished and felt he deserved, for he tried hard, always, to ignore his own bias. He had been embarrassed by the questions about Tony. If only his release would come quickly now so he would not have to move the boy and antagonize Schweiker still further.

He went on staring at the mountain. Was he, also, in danger of bending too far in one direction, leaning over backward to counterbalance his own preferences—and save his reputation as a peacemaker? If Sam Curry had not been at that meeting, would he have leaned even further toward Schweiker?

SEVENTEEN

THE staff residences kept their distance outside the main gate of the camp, surrounded by an armed guard. The Haydon house was the largest, and set somewhat apart from its neighbors. Behind it, the fields stretched out to the horizon, empty as the sea.

Morrissey, walking up the driveway, wondered about Mrs. Haydon, alone all day with that empty land like a tide at her back door. His own wife was never home except when absolutely necessary to satisfy ordinary physical needs, most of which—as she pointed out—could be satisfied just as well, if not better, somewhere else. But here, there was nowhere else. Here, here was all there was. He wondered what his wife, a large woman with bangs and snoods and stoles and long silver earrings that hung like ice picks from her lobes, would have made of it. He imagined her taking tucks in the desert and pinning up the mountain.

At dinner Haydon sat relaxed and genial at the head of a long lace-covered table. Opposite him, Jenni, in a long white dress with her blond hair piled up, smiled shyly and turned her head expectantly from one man to the other. Expecting what? Morrissey wondered.

"This is delicious, Mrs. Haydon," he said, and saw her smile broaden and overflow.

"I certainly am glad you like it, Mr. Morrissey," she said softly. "But you must call me Jenni, please. I just can't seem to get used to being Mrs. Haydon." She laughed.

The rest of the time she was silent, except to offer more food or to toss a soft "Oh hon-ee" at Haydon in surprise or sympathy or mock reproof; but so gently that the flames of the candles remained upright and the conversation flowed on unrippled. Morrissey was grateful that his wife was not there.

"Oh, Mike's an inverted snob," he imagined Mac saying. "Aren't you, darling? Always bragging about growing up in Hell's Kitchen, when he's actually spent most of his life at Harvard. Insisting on this lousy job at the backside of the nation, policing poor, helpless little Japs, when he could be sitting in Washington, D.C., advising generals." Morrissey lifted his wine in a silent farewell to Mac and vowed that he would never go back to New York.

Halfway through dinner the phone rang. Jenni jumped up. "That'll be Mommy," she told Morrissey. "She always calls on Monday after the rates go down."

They could hear her in the living room, shouting into the phone as if she did not trust the wires to carry her voice all the way to Santa Monica, California. "Hello, Mommy. You all right? And Daddy and Ginger and Amanda Sue? She had her kittens yet? Listen, Mommy, don't forget to bring my yearbook when you come, will you? The senior one with the blue cover. It's somewhere in my room, I think. Look in the . . . What? But you promised, Mommy. You've got to come. You promised. Please, Mommy." She was crying. They heard her drop the receiver and rush upstairs.

Haydon excused himself in the middle of a sentence and hurried out. Morrissey sat alone, embarrassed, wishing he could think of some way to leave gracefully. From where he sat, he could see into the living room stuffed with furniture. Sitting there before dinner, he had felt imprisoned by tables and chairs, by the grinning piano and the tight-lipped phonograph; by coy koalas and Jenni's friends and relations smiling down at him.

Haydon came back alone. "Sorry," he said. "Jenni's a bit upset. She usually gets upset when her mother phones. It's natural, I suppose. But this time it's worse. This time her mother told her that she's postponing her visit." Which probably means canceling, he thought. "Poor Jenni was expecting her for Christmas. She's been looking forward to it for months, so it came as something of a shock. She's gone to bed with a migraine. She gets them quite often. Like her mother." Or was it Haydon's unkind thoughts that made her head ache? "She asked me to make her apologies."

Morrissey waved a hand. "Please. Tell her I'm sorry. Hope she's better soon. Thank her for the wonderful dinner." He paused. "I suppose she's terribly homesick."

"Oh, yes." Haydon sat down and stared at the little silver swans floating serenely on the tablecloth with the salt and pepper piled high on their backs. "This is no place for her. I've been trying to get her to go home, at least for a visit, for months now. But she won't go." He smiled a tiny, tart smile that made his mouth pucker. "She thinks she has to stay here to take care of me." Feed me, she means, he thought. Stuff me. "She feels terribly sorry for you, you know, eating three meals a day in the cafeteria." He smiled that strange, slightly bitter smile again.

But, of course, Morrissey thought with a shock. He's living under a kind of house arrest, imprisoned by too much food and too much furniture and the peculiar pathos of his wife. Poor bastard.

*　*　*

"I think," Mrs. Noguchi said timidly, "we must take Toyo to the hospital. She is very sick."

"Again?" Dr. Noguchi frowned.

"Still, I think. I believe it is the same sickness."

"What's the matter with her?"

Mrs. Noguchi hesitated. "She is still so tired and weak and she still does not eat."

"That is hardly sick," he said. "That is wise. And I will *not* have a Caucasian pawing my daughter." His wife had been trying to get Toyo to the hospital for weeks. Working there had evidently unbalanced her on the subject of health. "Besides," Dr. Noguchi said, "it seems that most people who go to your precious hospital do not come out well. They come out dead."

He went back to staring at the tiny pieces on his chessboard. He liked to look at them and, sometimes, to move them around, playing both sides himself. Sounds and smells from the other stalls wandered up and down the stables: Mr. Oshima's sake and Mrs. Watanabe's medicine and someone's apricot brandy; coughs and sneezes and shouts and laughs and loud insistent jazz leaped and shrieked and tumbled around him. Opposite, his wife sat with a worried look on her face and a *Life of George Washington* in her lap.

"Would you like me to bring a book from the camp library for you?" she had asked him soon after he arrived. "They have more books now and they are much better. It is very interesting to read what the Americans write about themselves."

"No, thank you. I do not read rubbish. And certainly not in English. And I am not interested in reading their lies."

"Their lies can be very interesting too," she had said calmly.

But she was not reading now. She was staring at Toyo's white sheet, staring hard enough to see right through it. The boys' side of the stall was quiet, their sheet pulled back. They were out. They were always out. Only little Kazi was ever home at night, in the cot beside Toyo's. But tonight Toyo was there too.

Dr. Noguchi went on sitting stiffly in his huge armchair made of orange crates, with a cushion at his back and his hands on his knees, shivering beside the heater in his silk kimono. For the wind blew through the knotholes and around the window and swung the single forty-five-watt bulb that hung like a fading hope above their heads. Not only would his wife go soft in the brain from reading rubbish, she would go blind as well.

Suddenly Mr. Oshima began to shout above the other sounds in the stable. "Where is your daughter, old woman? You tell me. You know. The whole camp knows. Even *I* know." All the other noises in the stable stopped. "She is with that Noguchi boy again. You think I do not know what is going on here? You think I do not know?"

Dr. Noguchi shuddered. His name was traveling up and down the stable like the belches and the farts and the assorted obscenities.

"Her own mother," Mr. Oshima was screaming, "she says nothing, does nothing. Maybe even encourages her. Maybe even *copies* her. In the kitchen, in the mess hall." There was a slight pause. "You say nothing?" he roared. "Because there is nothing for you to say. But you will answer me, do you hear? You will answer me." There was another short silence and then a strangled female cry as if Mr. Oshima had his wife by the throat. Dr. Noguchi could almost hear her teeth rattle. He heard the door open and close and a young man's voice shout, in Japanese, "Stop, Papa! Stop! You're choking her!"

"You shut up," the old man shouted. "You don't tell *me* what to do."

The answer was quiet but very firm. "Stop it, Papa. Let her go. *Now.*"

There was a low moan and a howl of rage and the sound of a strong tradition broken. Dr. Noguchi heard footsteps and the door opening and closing. Then silence, except for a woman sobbing softly. "You keep him away from here," Oshima said between clenched teeth. "Away from me."

"Don't worry," his wife said in a hoarse whisper. "He will not come back. He will never come back."

Mrs. Noguchi looked at her husband. "Perhaps I should go to see Mrs. Oshima," she said. "Poor woman. Perhaps she needs some help. I have learned something about nursing in the hospital."

Dr. Noguchi looked at her angrily. "It would be much better for you to go to look for your son," he said, "who has caused our name to be shamed up and down the whole stable." Which son? he wondered. But it hardly mattered. They were none of them his sons anymore. He owed them nothing. His daughters, thank God, his oldest and youngest children, were properly at home, asleep behind that white sheet. He stared at the chessboard with the miniature chessmen, symbols of power and nobility and a rigid order, waiting for his touch. At least, he thought, he had not been attacked by his own son or shamed by his daughter. He felt sorry for Mr. Oshima.

It was perfectly still in the stables now. He heard Mr. Oshima, his steps dragging, let himself out. A little later, he heard the voice of the Caucasian woman talking to Mrs. Oshima. A nosy, interfering woman, he thought. He would never give her a chance to interfere in his life again. He went on sitting in his enormous chair like a homemade throne, ready to pass judgment.

Toward midnight he dozed off and was awakened by Toyo calling, "Mama." His wife hurried to her while he went on sitting there, staring at the chessmen, trying not to hear the sounds of moaning and sobbing behind the sheet. Finally he picked up the white king and sat clutching it until his palm began to throb, while the sounds grew louder and faster, becoming half-repressed shrieks. Little Kazi, looking frightened in nightgown and bare feet, rushed out and onto her mother's cot, pulling the blankets over her head. His wife appeared and announced that she was taking Toyo to the hospital. "We have waited too long already," she said.

Dr. Noguchi put his coat on over his kimono and, still wearing his sandals, carried his daughter across the camp to the hospital while Mrs. Noguchi hurried on behind him.

At the hospital he stood inside the door and looked down at the girl in his arms. She lay with her eyes closed and her face blank, without pain or blame or fear or hope, merely blank—as an empty dish.

Mrs. Curry appeared and Dr. Noguchi's arms tightened around his daughter. He did not want to give her up to a Caucasian, to reveal her shame and his own guilt—to a Caucasian. Criminal negligence, he imagined her telling the others. Shocking in a doctor—and a father. But Mrs. Curry merely greeted the Noguchis quietly, stroked Toyo's forehead and said very gently, "Put her over there, please. I'll get the doctor." Nothing more.

The doctor came quickly, a tall, gaunt man with a face like an old sock. "We'll do everything possible," he said. Nothing more.

Dr. Noguchi and his wife spent most of the night at the hospital, sitting side by side on wooden boxes. When they finally left, Doctor Noguchi's arms were empty. He put one around his wife, who cried quietly into his sleeve. They walked home in silence, side by side through the winter darkness, a darkness that even the huge searchlight could not penetrate.

For the rest of the night Dr. Noguchi sat and stared at the sheet still hanging across the corner of the room where his daughters had slept. There was no one behind it now. His youngest child was still on the narrow cot beside her mother, who was still sobbing softly. His sons' sheet was drawn. They had, presumably, come in very late and were now sound asleep. But he never looked behind the children's sheets, any more than he peered into their private lives. He sat alone confronting those white sheets from his huge, thronelike chair.

Yet he had failed in the only act of authority he had been allowed for months. And no one had reproached him; not the Caucasian nurse or the Caucasian doctor, who would now be accused of still another death; or even his wife, though she might go on sobbing quietly night after night for weeks. Next to him the chessboard lay open with all the pieces in their proper places except, he realized suddenly, the white king.

The stable was deathly still. Even the Oshimas' stall was quiet. He wondered if Oshima could possibly be sleeping, a man who had suffered such shame, who had been attacked by his own son in his own house with all the neighbors listening. Dr. Noguchi, staring at his elegant, orderly chessmen, felt his eyelids begin to droop. He could sleep. He had lost a daughter but he had not, he assured himself, lost face.

His eyelids closed, but now something strange was happening to the chessmen. The missing king was still gone. Only the black king was there, all alone at one end of the board. As he watched, the others began to move toward the opposite end, getting bigger and bigger until they were life-size. When they were all gathered together, they turned and rushed toward the king—who was still only the size of a chessman—churning up the squares as they came. In a second the king would be trampled to death. Just then he turned, revealing the agonized face of Dr. Noguchi.

He awoke with a start to find the board in perfect order with all the pieces in their correct positions—except the kings, who were lying facedown beneath the table. He picked them up and put the game away. It took up too much room, he decided. Besides, it presented an order he could no longer use. He went on sitting there while the hours passed and the searchlight, at regular intervals, came round to stab him in the back.

Tony Takahashi, sitting at his desk, was worried. Toyo had not appeared with his coffee at nine or his lunch at twelve.

He sat staring out the window, worrying about Toyo who had bound him to her by the strands of her long black hair. But he did not want to think about Toyo.

He preferred to think of the Lawsons, wondering how they were managing without him. For they were poor, in spite of the shelves and shelves of leather-bound books and the portraits of pompous ancestors. The garage beneath his apartment was full of an ancient Hudson which he drove once a week to the grocery store with Mrs. Lawson beside him; a car so old that he drove it very slowly, even tenderly, as if it had sore feet. Who was driving it now? he wondered. And who was trimming their shaggy garden and cooking their meals? For they could no longer afford a cook, and Mrs. Lawson was too arthritic even to open a can herself. He would never see them again. They could never afford to come all the way to Mt. Hope and they could never stand the cold. They might even be dead by now, he thought, for they would age faster and faster without him.

He remembered the day he was evacuated. The Lawsons had seen him off with gifts of fruit and books and a camera and a tiny pocket tape recorder. "The tools of your trade," they said. But they were all confiscated the moment he reached the camp.

He could never be an anthropologist now. Even if his fellowship did come through, he could never use it now. He would have to stay here and take care of Toyo—unless her father had him locked up. In any case, he would never be an anthropologist.

But where was she? Perhaps her father had already found out and had shut her up in their stall. He imagined her lonely and frightened, twisting the ends of her beautiful hair. Perhaps Dr. Noguchi was torturing her right this minute, pulling her teeth out one by one to make her reveal his name, practicing his trade at last.

At 12:40 Schweiker stopped at Tony's desk. Tony looked up, expecting Schweiker to tell him to produce Toyo immediately or be shipped off to Fort Washington. But Schweiker just stood there, chewing his gum slowly, thoroughly, silently. Finally he pushed back his hat, exposing tangled eyebrows and a strip of forehead. He took a nickel from his pocket and told Tony to get him a bottle of Coke and a straw. He had forgotten, Tony realized, to mention the napkins.

"Where's Toyo?" Tony asked the cashier in the cafeteria.

"Don't you know?"

That night, Tony walked round and round the racetrack for hours. It was a wild, dark night with the wind knocking the stars about like billiard balls. He walked with his head high, willing the wind to knock that about too; to knock it into a far pocket.

EIGHTEEN

Six men were still working on the pipe-laying project. The holes in their GI clothes had grown bigger and their shoes were in tatters. Some of the men had tied them up with sacking. Mr. Watanabe felt his bones shaking inside his skinny frame. Sam and O'Donnell built a fire and the others huddled around it.

"You must go to see Mr. Haydon," O'Donnell told Watanabe.

"Yes," Sam said. "He probably still doesn't know a damn thing about what's going on down here. You must tell him, Mr. Watanabe."

"No!" Mr. Watanabe backed away from him and O'Donnell and the feeble little fire that could barely hold up its head. Not even to thaw out would he go back to that terrible building with those long corridors that turned and turned and would not let him go; where mysterious sounds filled the air like clacking teeth and huge Caucasians filled the doorways; where giant soldiers with shoes like sleeping dogs watched and waited for him, coming and going. Mr. Watanabe might get in their way and be tossed out of a window as that sailor had been tossed out of the ship. It would be a long drop for a small, skinny, elderly Japanese. Not even to get his pay, to get *everyone's* pay, would he go back to that fierce man with the hair growing all over him and all of it bristling at Mr. Watanabe. He looked up and saw two soldiers walking toward him with drawn guns. He did not have to go to the administration building after all. *They* had come to him. They had come *for* him.

They were both very young and very tall. But their uniforms looked too big, as though the men inside had shrunk. Because they were guarding unarmed civilians instead of fighting enemy soldiers? "Hands up," the corporal said in a low voice that sounded more like a plea than a command. "Who built that fire?"

"I did," Sam and O'Donnell said simultaneously.

"Well, stamp it out. On the double. But keep your hands up."

"As you can see, Corporal," Sam said with his hands up and his feet stamping, "some of these men are suffering severely from the cold." He looked at the shoes of his fellow workers.

The corporal looked at them too and turned very red in the face. From the cold or the fire or the nature of his employment? Sam wondered.

"Fires," the corporal said, "are strictly against regulations. We got orders to see that it's stamped out immediately."

"Why?" O'Donnell said. He had often seen the Caucasian police and the soldiers at the gate warming themselves around campfires.

The corporal turned slightly redder. "They got to be careful about espionage, don't they?"

"Espionage?" Sam said. "Where? When? How?"

"Smoke signals," the corporal said, glancing toward the tower. His face was flaming.

It would be extremely painful to the touch, Sam thought. He could light a cigarette on his chin.

"Do you wish to arrest me?" Mr. Watanabe said.

"Or me?" O'Donnell said.

"Or me?" Sam said. And cut the work force by half right there, he thought.

The corporal looked down at the dead fire and the frozen feet of the men. Any further embarrassment, Sam thought, and he would make an eloquent smoke signal himself.

"No," the corporal said in a low voice. "Not this time." He glanced up at the tower again and raised his voice. "But there better not be a next time," he shouted—and saved his own face.

"I'll go to see Haydon, if you like," Sam told Watanabe. Poor Haydon, so restless and ill-at-ease inside that well-cut jacket, forever tipping back and forth in his chair, forever searching for a comfortable position.

Haydon greeted him warmly, moving quickly out from behind his desk. "Of course there's some mistake," he said. "We'll go to see Rigsbee about it right now." He walked quickly down the hall, greeting the evacuees right and left with a smile and a name and a title: Mrs. or Mr. or Miss.

In the comptroller's office, he called Rigsbee Ronald and introduced Sam as Mr. Curry. Rigsbee did not get up but remained barricaded behind his desk, with his pen in his hand and his books open before him. He was chewing.

Paper clips, Sam thought, washed down with a little red ink.

Rigsbee pushed back his inkstand, took a paper clip out of his mouth, and sneezed.

"There seems to be some misunderstanding, Ronald," Haydon said.

"Misunderstanding, Mr. Haydon?" Rigsbee's nose was becoming clogged at an alarming rate. He pulled a huge handkerchief out of his pocket and held it open like a safety net beneath his nose.

"Yes, *my* misunderstanding, I'm afraid," Haydon said. "I completely forgot to tell the men they needed work cards."

"Too bad, Mr. Haydon," Rigsbee said. " 'Cause they do. They sure as hell do. Though don't quote me to Mr. Schweiker, will you? He don't like cussing. And he don't like changes in the rules or people making up their own. Likes everything nice and legal. A very pertikkler individual, Mr. Schweiker. Most pertikkler I ever worked for. But that's the way it is and that's the way it's gotta be. Ask Prewett next door, ask Smart across the hall."

Haydon had never heard him say so much at one time before. He was breathing heavily and his nose sounded increasingly congested. He might have been breathing through the eye of a needle. "All right," Haydon said. "May we have the cards now, please?"

Rigsbee spread his handkerchief carefully across his desk—spreading his germs in lieu of wages, Sam thought—and opened a drawer. "Payment begins next week," he said. "*If* they fill the forms out. Correct. *And* return 'em. Fast."

"We've been working for three months," Sam said.

"Yes," Haydon said. "We owe them three months' back pay."

"Can't help that," Rigsbee said, burying his face in his handkerchief again.

"You can pay it," Haydon said. "I'll be responsible."

"I'm sorry, Mr. Haydon," Rigsbee said, and sneezed. "I really am. But in *this* office *I'm* responsible. And I can't give out wages without work cards. That's reg'lations and I can't go against reg'lations. No, sir. I'm having enough trouble breathing as it is."

Keeping his nasal passages clogged up against the air of Mt. Hope, Haydon thought. He nodded and hurried Sam away before Rigsbee's nostrils closed up completely. "Son of a bitch," he muttered. "I *promised* those men."

"Those men are used to broken promises," Sam said.

"Not from me."

"Don't worry," Sam said. "I'll tell them it's not *your* fault."

Haydon looked at him sharply, but Sam had his head down, revealing nothing. Or did Haydon detect a slight contempt in the set of his shoulders? "Tell them they'll get their money," Haydon said. "Somehow."

"I'll tell them, Mr. Haydon," Sam said.

"It's outrageous," Haydon said. "But let's hope things will be better at the permanent camp. Or to give it its correct title"—he smiled slightly—"the Relocation Center."

"*Permanent* camp?"

"Yes. You knew, of course, that this place was only temporary."

"You mean we're going from here to *another* camp? A *permanent* camp?"

Haydon nodded. "It should have happened months ago. This was only supposed to be an *assembly* center." He was looking at Sam uncomfortably, eager to get back to his swivel chair and tilt himself into a more congenial position.

"How long is permanent?" Sam asked.

Now Haydon looked positively pained. "Nobody knows," he said.

At the work project, the men greeted Sam hopefully, certain that Sam Curry, with his Caucasian wife and his record as Defender of the Faith—in the administration—would be successful. Sam shook his head. O'Donnell gave a low whistle and Watanabe's face fell as he bent to retie the rags around his feet. The others merely stared. For a moment they seemed frozen to the spot. Soon they began to mutter. The administration had lied to them again, had cheated them again. They threw down their shovels and walked away. As they passed Sam they spat. *"Inu,"* they muttered. *"Inu."*

Sam lay in bed with his face to the wall. He did not go to work the next day or the next, or to any meetings at night.

He stayed home, in bed, examining the wall. He did not eat or speak or, Nina suspected, sleep. It was worse than after the destruction of his studio. Then at least he had sat up at the kitchen table while his fingers went on working, though with paper instead of stone, folding and creasing instead of chipping and chiseling.

Now he lay still on his thin, lumpy mattress, frowning at the tooth marks on the wall, while the springs pressed weird designs on his back and sides, like print on a blank page. But he had never been blank, he thought. He had, from the first, had "pro-administration" writ large all over him. He had excused when he should have protested, defended when he should have attacked. He had been wrong about everything. *Inu*, he told himself. *Inu*. He closed his eyes.

He saw himself as a grown man sitting, Sunday after Sunday, on Terminal Island, speaking a language his father could not understand. He saw himself as a small boy riding the bus back to school, Monday after Monday, the bus that detached him regularly from the Japanese island and took him to the Caucasian mainland.

He remembered one morning in particular when the bus was full of big, surly, frightening Caucasians in funny hats— American Legion hats, he learned later. That morning the bus made an unusual stop outside a small shoe factory at the edge of town. The men in the hats, carrying clubs and pipes and truncheons, got out and waited silently in front of the factory. The bus and its passengers waited too. The workers, all Japanese, arrived singly or in groups of twos and threes. They looked tiny beside the Caucasians who walked to meet them, massive as upended mattresses, and beat them up, silently, swiftly, efficiently, while the bus and its passengers watched in silence. When the last worker lay in a heap on the sidewalk, the bus, with the Legionnaires back inside, drove away. Sam, crouched behind the seat, felt himself choking with outrage and pity and frustration and tears—and a great lump of shame.

He felt himself choking again, as he turned from the wall. *Inu*, he told himself. *Inu*. He opened his eyes and saw Nina sketching the laundry that hung dejectedly across the stall. "You never should have come here," he shouted at her. "Why in hell did you come?"

"I thought we settled that a long time ago," she said. "Why discuss it all over again now?"

He could not bring himself to tell her. She would find out soon enough, find out that he had been living the worst kind of pipedream and had tried to force her to live it with him.

He thought of her waiting on the street corner that day in the rain, a Persephone waiting in terror to be abducted. He had in fact abducted her, not saved her. If only he had left her there, someone else would certainly have picked her up and dried her off and carried her home; some Caucasian surely, someone like Channing Haydon, far more suitable than Sam Curry, born Sami Kurihara. Then she would be sitting in a studio gazing at an easel instead of in a stable squinting at his socks.

Why was he bringing this up now? Nina wondered. And why was he so depressed? Because with the pipe project and the constitution and the mess hall investigation all abandoned, there was nothing he could throw himself into with enthusiasm? Doing nothing always depressed him. Doing nothing in one-third of a horse stall with a Caucasian wife might easily disgust him. She remembered what she had read in the public library about the Japanese perceptions of Caucasians. Was Sam finally beginning to see her that way too? Her hand, clutching a tiny piece of charcoal, looked enormous. Her arm, held up to the light, showed fine pale hairs to the elbow. She had never noticed them before. Could he smell her too, a woman who was not only a Caucasian but a German and a *Jew* as well, a woman triply cursed? Sam had never wanted her to come in the first place. No wonder he had thrown himself into the activities of the camp so energetically, getting up so early, coming to bed so late. Or had he been spending his time with someone who was not a Caucasian and not a German and not a Jew? He had taken to his cot with his face to the wall so he would not have to see her or hear her or speak to her—or smell her. Now, probably, for the first time since coming to Mt. Hope, he felt like a prisoner.

She left for work very early the next morning and came back very late. Walking home through the night with the giant searchlight intermittently ramming and releasing her, she felt bruised and blinded by the light and the darkness. Near the gate she heard the sound of singing from the Army barracks, accompanied by guitars and banjos and harmonicas; loud, deep, ragged sounds that lay warm and rough on the skin, so different from the sharp, high-pitched lament of Japanese music. She remembered how young the soldiers were, mere boys really, far from home, set down in a barren landscape to stare for hours over the nose of a gun. She remembered when a ball had gone over the fence during a children's baseball game. "Get it, kid," the guards had shouted. "Go get it!" They watched and cheered as one small boy wiggled his way through the barbed wire. But one of those "mere boys" had shot and killed an old man on his way to the latrine. Had he been punished, disgraced, shipped out? Or was he still there, still free, maybe even looking down at her at this very minute? How did he feel when he shot Mr. Sato? Would it be harder or easier for him to shoot again?

In the stall, Mr. Tsuda was taking the head count and flying an enormous smile. "Ah," he said when he saw her, "all the Currys present now. Then may I tell you my good news, please? Mr. Ishii is not interested. Mr. Watanabe is asleep. So will you allow me to tell *you*, please?"

"But of course," Sam said. He was sitting on his cot looking as if he'd just emerged from the bottom of a trunk, blinking at the prospect of good news.

"My second son, Yoshi, is coming home from Roperville at last," Mr. Tsuda said.

"Wonderful!" Nina said.

"When?" Sam said.

But Mr. Ishii did not know. The letter simply said "soon."

How long was soon, Sam wondered, as he had wondered how long was permanent. Words at Mt. Hope were flexible. "Let's hope it's *very* soon," he said as Mr. Tsuda smiled and bowed and backed out beneath the sheet. "Before . . ." He stopped abruptly.

"Before what?" Nina said.

He stared at her for a second. "Before we're moved."

"Moved? Moved where?"

"To a *permanent* camp." He paused. "And this time you're *not* going with me."

She stood frowning, framed by the laundry still stretched across the stall, dangling down behind her. He had a sudden vision of the legs of his long johns winding themselves around her neck in a stranglehold. She turned and began to pull clothes off the line. "Of course I am," she said.

He sat on his cot and watched as she yanked down oversize khaki shirts and trousers and underwear full of patches and huge darned socks. How much longer, he wondered, would she have to go on wearing secondhand GI clothes? She had matured twenty years in seven months at Mt. Hope. Another seven months and she'd be an old woman. And the war might go on for years.

She was folding the clothes neatly, carefully.

"You don't have to go," he burst out as she rolled up a pair of army socks big as hand towels.

"Of course I do," she said quietly. "And I'm going. For two reasons. Because I *want* to and because I *have* to."

"But you *don't* have to." He jumped up, confronting her across the cots. "You're a big girl now. It's time you lived a life of your own instead of trying to squeeze into mine."

She stopped rolling the socks and looked at him. "But I *am* living a life of my own," she said.

"No you're not! You're a Caucasian trying to . . ."

". . . live the life *I* chose," she finished firmly. She kept staring at him as her fingers began to unroll the socks.

"No! It was chosen *for* you. By the Imperial Japanese Navy and the U.S. Government and a damned fool Nisei named Sam Curry . . ."

"Who keeps on talking about equality but refuses to practice it."

"Equal rights to a concentration camp? You want to spend the rest of your life wearing oversize army socks?"

She dropped her head and began to roll up the socks again. "Please, Sam. We've been through all this before. Besides, it's much too late. I'm an evacuee now."

That terrible word, Sam thought, applied to Nina, who was already a refugee. Thanks to him, she was both.

"I'm an evacuee," she was saying quietly. "The colonel said so himself. Don't you remember? 'Subject to all the rules and regulations governing all other evacuees.' I'm a true-blue, one-hundred-percent, paid-up evacuee like everyone else here. It's much too late." She was unrolling the socks again.

He stared at her in dismay. She had become not only independent but stubborn. He had expected to shape her, he realized, like one of his statues, but she had been far more resistant than any stone. Hadn't she come to Mt. Hope in spite of him, even written weeks ahead for permission without a word to him? Hadn't she refused to take up art at his urging, only to do it, at last, in her own good time? And hadn't she persisted in working long hours in that miserable hospital, which was surely emotionally and psychologically and even physically harder than picking up rubbish or laying down pipes? Beneath that soft, timid, girlish manner there had always been a granite determination. And now he had hit bedrock.

She had deceived him throughout. She did not really need him at all, had perhaps never needed him. On the contrary, she seemed to believe that *he* needed *her*. Or perhaps, as a victim so often, she had come to crave the role, had developed a taste for martyrdom. But not at *his* expense, he thought fiercely.

"All right," he said at last. "But if you go, you go on your own, in your own right, because you love concentration camps. Not because you're my wife. I refuse to be responsible."

"You won't be. You never were."

"Or even *feel* responsible."

"Good." She lifted her head and stared at him, gripping the ball of socks with both hands. "Because I'm going. Whether you want me or not; as your wife or not. I'm going." She was not pleading with him anymore. She was defying him.

The bus from Roperville pulled into the camp toward dusk. Mr. Tsuda was waiting at the gate, waiting to greet his younger son, as he had all day every day since he first received the note inside the familiar green check saying that Yoshi would be home "soon."

Mr. Tsuda watched with growing horror while the men inside the bus climbed down, slowly, silently, painfully, with torn clothes and bloody heads. A few were carried out by the soldiers and dropped on the side of the road. They were the last of the evacuees still working at the beet canneries. Some of them looked as if they had been put through the assembly line themselves but were not worth canning. Mr. Tsuda could not see his son.

Soon a large crowd, mostly Issei from the BQ, had gathered. There were no ambulances at Mt. Hope. The wounded lay bleeding in the dirt. Mr. Tsuda could not get close enough to recognize his son. The Issei began to mutter.

Finally a few jeeps arrived and the wounded were loaded on to them and driven away. Mr. Tsuda, peering through the dim light without his glasses, could not distinguish their features. He saw merely a blur of thin, pale faces differentiated only by the patterns of blood. He pushed his way closer and saw one man with his eyes closed and a long red stripe down one side of his head. Was that his son? He stood watching that head roll from side to side as the jeep drove off.

"Fools," one of the Issei shouted after the jeeps. "Working for the *hakujin*. Serves them right."

"Inu," someone muttered. *"Inu."* The cry was taken up. The muttering became a roar.

Mr. Tsuda stood looking after the jeeps long after they had disappeared. He still did not know what had happened to his son. But he knew that he did not want to count heads for the *hakujin* anymore.

NINETEEN

IN his living room, Haydon read: "The sense of shame, the fear of being publicly exposed or ridiculed in any way is a dominant feature of Japanese culture." He was learning about shame, and not just from books. He thought of that scene in his office over the food in Block B and in Rigsbee's office over the work cards. He had felt humiliated both times by his own staff and both times in front of Sam Curry, a man who managed to go his own way in spite of barbed wire and armed guards; a man who refused to sit behind a desk or draw pictures or paint signs; the man Nina Curry had married and followed to Mt. Hope.

"Not my medium," he had said curtly, even insultingly, humiliating Haydon at their very first meeting. "Those men are used to broken promises," he had said after the meeting with Rigsbee; as if Haydon's word were no better than the others'; as if Haydon himself were no better than the others—

the Schweikers and the Collinses and the Rigsbees and the Hacketts. Sam was right, Haydon thought, for he had allowed not only broken promises but broken heads into the camp, had permitted violence to be bused in from the neighboring town.

It was eleven P.M. He reached for his pipe. Opposite him, Jenni, in enormous round horn-rimmed glasses, was writing a letter home. Ever since her mother's Christmas visit had been canceled, she had taken to wearing glasses and writing letters, long letters to family and friends and acquaintances of all kinds, including the mailman and the vet and the salesladies at The Designing Woman, with footnotes to Amanda Sue and her new kittens. What in the world, Haydon wondered irritably, did she find to write about—her boring, bad-tempered husband?

He opened Montaigne. "Unhappy is the man, in my opinion, who has no spot at home where he can be at home to himself—to court himself, to hide away." He felt caged. He thought of the evacuees, squeezed into cubicles, packed into mess halls, stuck back to front in endless queues.

Jenni looked up, frowning through her glasses. Like two huge portholes, Haydon thought, with poor Jenni staring out at a stormy sea.

"How come you never bring your friend, Whatsis Morrissey, home for dinner anymore?" she said. "I'll bet he'd like a change from those terrible camp meals."

It was natural, Haydon thought, that she would want another mouth to eat her food and praise her cooking. Especially since her husband agreed with Montaigne that "a man should consider less what he eats than with whom. No sauce is so pleasant . . . and no dish so gratifying as good company." Besides, it would give her something to write home about. "I'm sure Michael would love it," he said. "But he's in Washington."

"Someone's got to go," Morrissey had said. "Before we have an explosion around here. To persuade the Army and the WCCA and the War Department and all those other damned fouled-up agencies to send supplies and some system and sanity and a touch of humanity to this place. And I'm the logical person." He had found something to do at last. "*You* certainly can't go. That would leave Schweiker in charge. Besides, the last thing that's needed around here is a legal officer."

"How long do you expect to be gone?"

"Long as it takes. I'll bully Congress and the Supreme Court and the president, himself, dammit, if necessary." He picked up his suitcase. "Meantime, try to keep Schweiker muzzled."

"It's what I've been trying to do all along," Haydon said.

"No. Not muzzled. Appeased."

Haydon let him go. It was better than having Morrissey confront him constantly from behind those well-polished glasses. Could he really see better than most?

Jenni was confronting him now with her glasses off and her soft, pleading look securely on. "What about all those other people on your staff?" she said. "When Daddy was a director we had bunches of people to dinner *all* the time. Daddy said it was good for morale."

"Well, it wouldn't be good for *your* morale. The staff's taste in food runs to hamburgers and coconut custard pie. Besides, it's not the staff whose morale needs lifting. It's the evacuees. And I don't see you . . ."

"No. I suppose not." She was gazing into the dining room with its Sèvres china and the swan-shaped pepper and salt holders and the wedding silver anchored on Mommy's old lace tablecloth with only the tiniest patch in one corner. Her neck drooped, then lifted. "We could have just the ones who work in the office," she said. She had seen them the day she took the kirsch for Haydon to open, surprised to find how neat and attractive the young Nisei looked; not at all like the pictures in the newspapers and magazines of "Japs" with huge sticking-out ears and teeth and enormous, sinister eyeglasses.

She remembered one girl, especially, whom she met in the ladies' room, a scared-looking girl. She was washing her hands when Jenni came in, and she glanced up in alarm. She looked very young, even younger than Jenni, and even more timid. She smiled, a timid little smile. She seemed frightened. Of what, Jenni wondered, looking around. But all she saw was her own reflection in the mirror. Of me? No one had ever been afraid of her before, the youngest, and smallest and weakest, who could not sing like Jackie or act like Gerry or design like Junie. It was, she thought, an enormous compliment.

She smiled. "I'm Jenni Haydon," she said. "My husband . . ."

"I know," the girl said. She was staring at Jenni with awe. No one had ever looked at Jenni like *that* before either. She felt slightly embarrassed. "I shouldn't be here," she said. "I don't think Channi likes it."

The girl smiled. "I shouldn't be here either," she said.

"Why not?" Jenni said with surprise. "Why shouldn't *you* be here? You work here, don't you?"

"Oh, yes. I work in the cafeteria."

Jenni's face lit up. "How wonderful. I've always wanted to learn to cook Japanese. Daddy just *loves* Japanese. Would you come and teach me? We've got a huge kitchen and . . ."

"But I'm not a cook," the girl broke in. "I just wait on tables and help clean up. Besides, I wouldn't be allowed out of the camp."

"Not even to my house? It's just across the road."

"Oh, no. We're never allowed out. Except to pick sugar beets in Roperville."

Why would anyone want to do that? Jenni wondered. "Well, I don't think Channi would let me come here," she said. "I really shouldn't be here now."

"Neither should I," the girl said. "Not in the staff ladies' room."

"But why not, if you work here?"

"Because I'm not 'staff.' Only Caucasians are 'staff.'"

Jenni had no idea what "Caucasian" meant but the girl was quite pretty, with her features neatly tucked in and her hair long and shiny down her back. "Don't worry," she said. "I won't tell on you if you don't tell on me."

"Tell on *you?*" The girl stared at her and began to giggle. In a second Jenni was giggling too.

She hadn't giggled since, Jenni thought now, sucking her pen. She looked at Haydon, who was stuffing his pipe while reading, and spilling tobacco all over the floor. "Maybe we could invite just a few of the young evacuees who work on your floor," she said. "Some of them looked awfully nice."

"They are," Haydon said. And they'd be good company for her, he thought. Much better than her husband; or Mrs. Morrissey if she were here or Mrs. Schweiker if she existed. Or Mrs. Collins or Mrs. Rigsbee, who were sure to be large, rather terrifying women in pink cardigans with fat fingers and little rhinestone earrings. Poor Jenni. "I'm sure they'd love to come," he said. "And it's awfully good of you to think of it. But you see, we really can't have just a few and we can't possibly have them all."

Jenni frowned but brightened after a second. "We could send the food down there. Much more convenient for them, really."

"But, Jenni darling, you can't feed the whole camp and we can't send your delicious cooking down to just a few. We'd have a riot on our hands."

"Over my cooking?" She grinned. Then turned sober. "I suppose they'd have to eat it in those horrible mess halls, off tin plates and tin forks, wouldn't they?"

"I'm afraid so." He lit his pipe and reached for Montaigne.

She sat watching him for a second. "Oh, well," she said at last. "They're Japanese, after all. They probably wouldn't really *like* French cooking, would they? But it would be nice to have company once in a while. Wouldn't you like some company, honey? Once in a while?"

He looked up. "Yes. Of course I would. And as soon as Morrissey gets back, we'll have him over. Or anyone else you want. All right?" He paused, and for a moment sat staring into space. Then he put down his book and leaned toward her. "Jenni, what I would really like is that study. I could use the guest room. No one's used it since we arrived. And I don't imagine anyone ever will."

"But honey, you know Mommy will. She promised. As soon as her migraines are gone and the holidays are over and the weather is warmer . . ."

"I'll get out whenever she comes. For as long as she stays."

"But there's no room for a desk in there. I'm planning to put a dressing table for Mommy in there. Besides, you're a married man now. I don't want her to think you're still studying."

She's frightened, poor girl, Haydon thought: of being all alone in the evening as she is all day. He had yanked her up out of a warm, pleasant life, away from family and friends and the pursuit of an illusory career like her sisters; had set her down where the wind blew constantly and winter seemed to have moved in for the duration and the sun, like an absentee landlord, made rare and reluctant visits. She was trying, in the only way she knew, to take root. She was as much a displaced person, he realized suddenly, as anyone at Mt. Hope. And he had displaced her.

Her eyes filled with tears. She leaned over and took his hand. "Please, honey," she said. "You can read perfectly well right where you are, can't you? In that nice big comfortable old lounge chair Mommy sent all the way from Los Angeles. Can't you?"

He patted her hand. "Of course I can. And I will." He leaned over and kissed her. "Now we'll forget all about it, shall we?" She smiled and returned to her letter.

He sat watching her for a moment. Her hair seemed to have become lighter and brighter again recently, perhaps in anticipation of her mother's visit, though he knew she would never come. Poor Jenni. He wished he felt an inclination to stroke that smooth, bowed head that bent so indiscriminately for Mommy and Daddy and Amanda Sue and the recipe for Dijon mustard sauce. Instead he found himself thinking of Nina Curry, whose hair had become short and curly at Mt. Hope, as if she were in a constant froth—as she was that day in his office. He longed to dip his fingers in it. He found himself wondering what it would be like to live in a corner of a horse stall with her. In her sketches, the stalls, despite the overcrowding, looked neat, even cozy. He imagined the Currys sitting together, reading together, lying together on that narrow cot. He did not think he would mind being crowded there. Or would she be bored, too, with a man who spent his evenings cavorting riotously between the pages of a book? He bent his head to Montaigne again and acknowledged that, for the first time in his life, he felt lonely.

Jenni, sucking the end of her pen, looked up and stared at him. It would have been nice to invite that girl from the ladies' room and her friends to dinner. Channi, of course, saw them every day. For the first time, she wondered about his life at the camp, which was where he really lived, rushing there early in the morning and returning so late in the evening that he was often in danger of spoiling her carefully prepared dinners. He works too hard, she thought, as she had thought many times and written home many times. But now she had a new thought, a thought she did not write home. In fact, she did not go on with her letter at all. Instead, she sat staring at her husband and sucking the end of her pen. It had a new, slightly bitter taste.

The phone rang. "That'll be Mommy," she said, jumping up, all smiles. "To tell me she's taking the 4:09." But she returned with her face flat with disappointment.

"Bad news?" Haydon said.

"Well, it's bad for me. It isn't Mommy at all. It's some man for you. Says he's Mayor Somebody-or-other from Some-place-or-other."

"Roperville?"

"Could be."

"Then it's probably bad news for me too."

It was. The mayor spoke rapidly. Tension in the town had been growing with the enemy attack on New Guinea. Two "Japs," it was rumored, had been seen sneaking around the corner near the Western Union office. A mysterious fire had broken out in a boxcar in the railroad yard and several scraps of paper with strange marks—Japanese, people said, though no one in town could read it—had been found along the tracks.

"Hallucinations," Haydon said, meaning lies. "Not a single evacuee is missing from camp. Or ever has been."

"Well, these people don't like imaginary Japanese either," the mayor said. "They keep saying the government promised that . . ."

"I know what the government promised." Haydon broke in irritably. It had been published, it seemed, in every newspaper west of the Mississippi: "Every precaution will be taken to protect the welfare of the surrounding residential areas and to prevent the interned Japanese from contacting or in any way embarrassing or affecting the lives of the Americans living in the areas."

"Not a single evacuee has ever been outside the camp," Haydon said, "let alone 'embarrassing' the Americans of Roperville. Except"—he was laying down his words like paving stones—"when your worthy citizens urged us to send them in to do their dirty work: to harvest beets for the farmers and can them for the factories. For which they received damn little besides bloody heads."

"I know," the mayor said. "One group cheated them and the other beat them up. And now the whole damn town is getting ready to blockade your camp. Which would be simple as Simon. All they have to do is seal off one road. I could call in the National Guard, but that would just escalate the whole situation. I'd rather not do it 'less I absolutely have to. They've called a mass meeting for tomorrow night. You'd better be there."

"I can't possibly leave the camp. But I'll send one of my staff." Who, he wondered suddenly, for Morrissey was still in Washington. Schweiker? Collins? Rigsbee?

"No," the mayor said. "It's gotta be *you*. And you'd better come early. Real early. 'Cause you've got a hell of a lot of preliminary bouts before the main event. Other words, you betta see every damn leader of every damn organization in this damn town *before* the meeting—personally and individually. Try to talk some sense into them. I've set up a whole series of appointments with the whole damn bunch: business, professional, veterans, Elks, PTA, Garden, Badminton, Pinochle and Parcheesi, Sewing, Cooking and Crafts, and the Rita Hayworth Fan Club. Plus the Monday Morning Club and the Wednesday Afternoon Club and the Thursday Evening Club. A small town like this and we've got 'em all. Plus a cozy little fascist organization calls itself Citizens United."

"United for what?"

"Against. Everything and everyone they don't like. It's a long list and your camp is right at the top. I'll expect you first thing in the morning." He hung up.

Haydon sat staring at the phone. He would have to go. Which would leave Schweiker in charge.

TWENTY

HAYDON left the camp early the next morning. At noon Dan stood behind the counter in the mess hall, serving spaghetti, watching the evacuees pour in and the food run out. The meeting with Haydon had made no difference except that Hackett watched him more carefully than ever. "He hopes he'll catch me pinching a paper napkin," Dan told Emmy.

"Hear you've been complainin' to the top brass," Hackett had said the day after the meeting, sticking his face into Dan's. Close up, Hackett's face looked bumpy as a waffle. "Don't like the food here, huh? Well"—he poked a dirty finger between Dan's eyes—"there's things aroun' here *I* don't like, neither. Like dirty yellow scum tellin' lies to the administration. From now on *I* do the talkin'. Unnerstan'? An' what's more, I can tell 'em everything they need to know. Like who's responsible for the waste aroun' here. I found half a dozen loaves in the garbage last night. Untouched. Not even sliced. An' twenty people still on the chow line."

"Unsliced? Hell, all you had to do was blow on them. That wasn't bread. That was a heap of mold. Even the ants wouldn't touch it."

"I *tole* you. *I* decide what gets thrown out aroun' here. An' nuthin', but nuthin', gets thrown out without I say so. Unnerstan'?"

Dan watched as the line kept moving and the food kept dwindling. Soon there would be nothing left but slabs of stale white bread known as bullet bread. Biting it was like biting the bullet. The spaghetti was disappearing fast. Hackett was standing in the doorway as always. Adding to the garbage, Dan thought. At the end of the line he saw Mr. Ishii, carrying his grandson in a blanket. He might have been some allegorical character in a medieval morality play: Death with Sleep in his arms.

Sam was sitting in a corner of the hall with Ray Noguchi, O'Donnell, and the Tsudas. Nick Tsuda was out of jail and Yoshi was out of the hospital. Sam was back at work again, hard work, digging wells in the wilderness. The new camp, with the beautiful name of Lake Emerald, was certain to be much better, he told himself. But this time he told no one else. It might be months, even years, before they were moved. They might all, old, young, and unborn, live out their lives at Mt. Hope. And if they ever were released, where would they go? What would they do? Their homes, their jobs, their money were all gone. And nobody anywhere wanted them back. Why had he never thought of that before?

He worked hard, no longer from a sense of loyalty and cooperation but, simply, for the camp: for Nina and the Matsuis and Noguchis and Tsudas and all the others. Besides, what else was there for him to do? He needed to bend his back, to gouge out earth as he had once gouged out stone, carving a landscape as he had once carved a statue. And he needed to be out of the stall. Though he had resigned from the council and the block committee and his position as the administration's chief defender, he was out every night anyway: helping Dan with his productions, playing chess with one of the Tsudas, even wandering into the BQ to listen to Mr. Wada's flute and to hear Japanese again. Though he needn't have bothered. Nina was out most of the time; it was especially busy at the hospital because of an epidemic of flu. He had not spoken to her for days. It was becoming a habit, a habit he was cultivating assiduously. It might, he hoped, persuade her to leave.

O'Donnell was frowning at the spaghetti sauce, which had separated back into its component parts on his plate. "Christ, I'm looking forward to Lake Emerald," he said. "To decent food and decent housing and enough hot water at one time to . . ."

Ray Noguchi was shaking his head.

"Lake Emerald is a beautiful name," O'Donnell said.

"So is Mt. Hope." Ray pulled a letter out of his pocket and began to read aloud.

It was from Jack Oshima, who had asked to be transferred from Mt. Hope right after the fight with his father and had been sent with evacuees from other camps to Lake Emerald. They had spent four days on the train, an ancient, rickety train that coughed and wheezed, spitting blood all over the tracks. It had a wood stove, gaslights, and broken seats. By the third day, the food and water had disappeared—along with the heat and the light. "We were sure we were supposed to die on the way—and be buried at Lake Emerald," Ray wrote.

They had survived the trip—except for an old woman and a young child—though they barely survived the sight of Lake Emerald, the perfect spot for a mass grave: cold and completely empty, for nothing but tombstones could possibly grow there, not even barracks. The few that stood tottering in the wind seemed hardly enough to house the blasts blowing from all directions at once. There was no lake and certainly no hint of emerald. Instead of one raggedy mountain, they were surrounded by a whole jawful of jagged peaks.

Sam thought of Mt. Hope, so "improved" by the evacuees, with irrigation ditches and wells and miles of pipes; with gardens and lawns and cellars against the heat in summer and caulking against the winds of winter, that it was considered too good for horses. It would be used as an officers' training school by the Army after the war.

"So," Jack's letter went on, "we're digging ditches and building barracks and laying pipes all over again. Some people are convinced that the Authority will go on moving us from one site to another so we can 'improve' all the barren areas of the country for them. Until there are no more left. Then they'll just dump us in some terrible spot, someplace not worth improving, someplace no one's ever heard of, to die."

"My God," Sam said. He had been wrong again. He was glad that for once he had kept his mouth shut.

There was a long pause.

"They may find themselves with a riot on their hands," Yoshi Tsuda said. He had a red wound down one side of his face. "Maybe that's what they're hoping for. Then they could just shoot us down right here. Spare them the trouble of moving us around."

"Maybe we should give them what they want," Nick Tsuda said.

"Wonder why we haven't," O'Donnell said. He pointed to the letter. "After this."

"Because no one knows about it yet, I suppose," Ray said. "The letter only came this morning."

Sam tried not to think of Nina, who would insist on going to Lake Emerald, whatever the conditions, doing penance for being Caucasian—which made him feel guilty for being Japanese. It also made him furious. He did not want to think about Nina.

He looked around and spotted Mr. Ishii at the end of the line, thinner than ever, looking as if his skinny arms might break under the weight of that small boy. Late again, Sam thought. He wondered why.

Mr. Ishii was always late, though he did nothing all day but sit with his grandson on his lap or play *goh* or drink *sake* with his stallmates, the Tsudas. But most of the time he was alone with Ken-chan, reading or staring into the small pocket mirror he always carried, staring into the depths of his soul, at his "self without shame"; that part of him which had developed in his earliest years, the "eternal purity" the mirror reflected. He looked at it more often now, to make sure it was still there.

Sam stared at him with irritation. Why did he always come to the mess hall so late, when the food was sure to be gone? Was he trying to avoid questions and curious stares, afraid that the very breath or glance of a stranger might infect the boy?

"He's so jealous of his grandson," Nina said once, "that I sometimes think he's trying to make the rest of us forget he even exists, burying him deeper and deeper in his arms." She dreamed once that Mr. Ishii had died but they could not release the living child from the dead man's hold.

Maybe that's what he's afraid of, Sam thought, one of them surviving the other. Maybe he's trying to make sure they go together—by simultaneous starvation—with a lot of assistance from Chief Chef Hackett. Sam still had some spaghetti on his plate. He got up and offered it to Mr. Ishii. "For your grandson," he said. "I'm afraid that's all you'll get. They've run out again."

The old man looked bewildered, as if he'd been standing on line for something entirely different. Maybe that's why he's always so late, Sam thought. He's forever waiting on the wrong line.

"Come," Sam said, leading him to his table. He passed the end of the chow line, where seven or eight elderly Issei were waiting patiently. They had been fixing the roof of one of the barracks. They looked cold and tired and hungry. And angry, Sam thought. He nodded to Mr. Watanabe. "How is it on the roof?" Sam said.

Mr. Watanabe bowed. "Cold and windy and wet. But"— he smiled broadly, a smile that threatened to slip off his thin face—"we have work cards at last. How is it down the wells?"

"The same. But we have work cards too."

"Much may it prosper you," Mr. Watanabe said in Japanese.

"And you," Sam answered in Japanese.

The two men smiled and bowed.

The others, advancing toward the serving counter, scowled at the empty serving dishes and the slabs of stale bread. Soon the scowls turned to mutters. Suddenly Mr. Tsuda stood up and, carrying his plate with nothing on it but a block of bread, walked toward Hackett, lounging in the doorway. Mr. Tsuda walked slowly, with great dignity, carrying his plate with both hands, his arms outstretched as if bearing an offering. When he reached Hackett, he made a slight bow. "Mr. Chief Chef," he said in a loud, clear voice, "my friends and I, we wish to share our lunch with you." There were snickers all around the hall.

"Yeah?" Hackett said. "Well, I already had my lunch."

"*Your* lunch," Mr. Tsuda said. "But you did not have *our* lunch, Mr. Chief Chef, *this* lunch."

"What *did* you have?" someone shouted.

"Steak and fresh vegetables and salad and . . . ?"

"We would like you to have some of *our* lunch as well," Mr. Tsuda said, still holding out his plate.

"You must," someone shouted.

"Specialty of the house."

"Specially aged for evacuees."

A group of young men at the back began to throw large hunks of bread and banged on the tables with spoons and forks, shouting,

> "We can't eat this rotten bread
> Feed it to the chef instead."

Suddenly, spontaneously, men from all over the room got up and started toward Hackett. In the back of the hall, Mr. Ishii pulled the blanket over his grandson's head and hurried out. The chef disappeared into the kitchen, and the men started after him. Dan rushed to block the door, followed by Sam.

"Don't be damn fools," Dan said, filling the doorway with his cane like a bar across it. "That bastard would just love an excuse to get the Army and the FBI in here. Like Pine Gap and Mallabar. Remember?" Of course they remembered. "Innocent people killed and wounded," Dan went on, "and arrests and deportations. The Army occupied the camps for weeks. Well, we don't want that here. So let's break this up now. Okay?"

"He's right," someone said.

"Of course he's right."

They all knew and liked Dan; knew him from his performances in camp shows and behind the serving counter, cheerful and friendly, serving up the muck with a joke. "Cheer up, mates. It's rice instead of potatoes today. And *meat!*" he would announce, holding up a small black hamburger the size of a doughnut hole. They all knew he had been to see the director about Hackett's meals. They grew quiet and stood staring at him.

"Such food is an insult," Mr. Tsuda said. "Not only to the body but to the mind and the soul."

"And the sight. Just looking at it causes severe gastric disorders."

"Yeah. We oughtta do something about it. Quick."

"Let's talk about it first," Sam said.

"No more talk. Talk makes nothing. Only more talk."

"No. He's right," Ray Noguchi said. "Let's talk first. Then act."

"We can talk in my stall," Dan said. "Tonight."

"And invite representatives from the other mess halls," Sam said.

Later, when Dan was sweeping up the lumps of stale bread,

Hackett appeared. "I've just told Personnel," he said. "I don't want troublemakers in my kitchen."

"That's fine with me," Dan said, dropping the broom.

"Or in this camp," Hackett shouted after him.

The next morning the FBI appeared, asking questions. People were picked up on the streets, at work, in the barracks for "interrogation." To be followed by arrest and deportation? More INU signs appeared, in red and black, on doors and windows and walls.

That evening everyone was ordered to the barracks immediately after dinner. All doors were locked while the search for contraband went on. One old woman who was in the latrine when the search began was locked in there all night.

The police removed nails, tweezers, hammers, rulers, pliers. "Dangerous weapons," they said.

"Necessary tools," Mr. Watanabe said.

They took all the electrical appliances, including hot plates which had finally been permitted for infants and invalids. "Is allowed," Mrs. Oshima said. "For my husband. My husband is sick." She produced the wrinkled paper she always carried in her pocket. "See?" she said. "From the director. Is allowed." They took it anyway. They even took the tea canister where Mr. Oshima kept the meager wages that his wife and children had finally been paid. He did not trust the camp bank.

"That's not *confiscating*," Josie Oshima said. "That's *stealing*."

Dr. Noguchi stood in the doorway of his stall. "What do you want?" he said.

"Never mind," they said, pushing past him. "We'll find it." They took his lacquered chopsticks and his chess set and his silver-bowled pipe. They ripped up Mrs. Noguchi's Whitman's Sampler box and took all her poems.

* * *

Emmy Matsui waited in the middle of her stall with Miko by the hand while the police frowned over Dan's drama scripts. "Where's my husband?" she said.

"Your husband?"

"Yes. Daniel Matsui."

The men looked at each other. The older man put on his glasses and consulted a list. " 'Daniel Matsui, Emiko Matsui, Emiko Matsui.' " He looked up. "She's right. We have two Emikos and no Daniel. So where's Daniel?"

"That's exactly what *I'd* like to know," Emmy said. "Why isn't he here? Where is he?"

"I wonder," the younger man said. He was sleek and well-groomed and carried his billy like a swagger stick. "Could be," he said, looking around the stall with raised eyebrows, "he's busy somewhere else. Or"—he lowered his brows—"could be the FBI's got him."

"Why would the FBI have him?"

He waved Dan's scripts at her. "Because of these, maybe. Look damn peculiar. Could be some kind of code. We'll just take them along to be sure."

"Then you'd better take me along too," Emmy said. "I typed them."

"That won't be necessary," the older man said. He was slower and heavier and kept his billy in his pocket.

"I insist," Emmy said. "*And* my five-year-old daughter. She watched me do it."

In their stall, the Currys watched the search in silence. There was not much left to be confiscated, but the police examined everything scrupulously, rummaging through papers, turning out pockets, shaking out clothing piece by piece, scattering everything all over the floor. They were about to leave when the blond policeman stopped suddenly and pulled a book from the shelf. "Well, well, well," he said. "What have we here?"

The bald policeman put on his glasses. *"The Sun Also Rises,"* he read slowly.

"Sounds like Jap propaganda to me," the younger one said. "Arrogant bastard, leaving it right out in the open like that." He turned to Sam. "Thought we were too stupid to spot it, huh?"

"Wait a minute," the bald man said. "Sounds familiar somehow. Seems to me my wife's been reading something like that."

"Yeah?" The blond one grinned. "Maybe we should take her in too." He slipped the book into his pocket.

"Like having your belongings pawed over?" Sam said as soon as they were gone. "And removed? Soon there won't be a damned thing left. Then they'll start pawing *you*." He paused. "You might as well know now," he went on. "I've just learned all about Lake Emerald, our *permanent* residence. It's going to be worse than here, much worse. I doubt if they'll want an 'Authorized Artist' there. Because they'll need all hands to build their miserable camp—in freezing weather."

Nina stared at him in silence. Her eyes looked darker than ever now. He would never be able to see through them. What would he do, he wondered suddenly, if she *did* leave.

"So?" she said.

"So why not go home."

"I *am* home."

"No! You're in a concentration camp, for God's sake. It's time you realized that. And you might also realize that you don't belong here. Might not even be wanted here."

"Then where *do* I belong? Where *is* my home? Where *am* I wanted? Where do you want me to go? Back to the Waverley School for Girls? Back to bombed-out London? Back to Nazi Germany?" She began to cry, soundlessly, with her eyes wide open and her face perfectly still, as if, he thought, the tears were being pumped out of her mechanically; as if the stone head of his Persephone, broken off at the neck, had suddenly begun to weep. He reached out and took that weeping head into his arms.

* * *

Tony Takahashi found the word INU in big red letters scrawled on a scrap of paper on his pillow. He picked it up, stuffed it into his pocket, and started out again. He knew he could not spend another night in the BQ. But as he reached the door, half a dozen policemen arrived and forced him back inside.

The men were ordered to stand beside their beds. Judo, who had just finished a *mogusa* treatment, was still lying down. The police circled the barracks, ripping off sheets and blankets and lifting mattresses. They found bits of money tied up in socks and stuffed into slippers. It disappeared into the policemen's pockets. "Robbers," the Issei began to mutter. "Thieves."

When the police came to Judo, they lifted him bodily from his bed and dumped him on the floor. Then they ransacked the bedclothes and found his samurai sword under the mattress. "Well, well, *well*," one policeman said, lifting it up. "The FBI will be mighty interested in this. *And* you." They took Judo and his sword away.

The men watched in silence until they were gone. Then they turned to Tony, still standing beside his bed. *"Inu,"* Mr. Wada muttered in his soft, low voice. And spat. *"Inu, inu,"* the others snarled as they began to move slowly toward him.

INU had been printed in large block letters on the door of Mr. Ishii's stall. He stood staring at it, an Issei who had come to the internment camp in the uniform of his jailers; who had refused to live in the BQ; who had remained aloof from his fellows. It never occurred to him that the word might have been meant for Mr. Tsuda or Yoshi. He stood absolutely still for a long time with his grandson in his arms, staring at that short, sinister word. Then he went inside, to his part of the stall, and sat down on his bed. He was ashamed to say anything to the Tsudas.

He was still sitting there with the boy asleep beside him

when the police came. They found nothing but his old World War I uniform rolled up in the bottom of his bag.

"Ashamed of his American uniform," the short policeman said.

"Oh, well, it's a World War *One* uniform, after all."

"It's still disrespectful. I think we oughtta take him in."

The tall policeman stared at Mr. Ishii, who was sitting motionless, watching the boy asleep beside him. "It's a helluva long way back," he said. "Let's leave it till later. He's not going anywhere."

As soon as the raid was over, Mr. Ishii picked up his grandson, who was still fast asleep. He slept most of the time now, as if practicing for death. Mr. Ishii bundled him up, put on his own jacket and cap, and nodded to the Tsudas sitting silently around their heater, the only thing in the stall that was still intact.

It was dark outside, but Mr. Ishii walked firmly, steadily, across the field and around the track, where he could almost hear the sound of horses' hooves galloping up behind him, ready to knock him down. He walked all the way to the other side of the camp, to St. Ursula's Orphanage with its huge cross flashing intermittently in the glare of the searchlight. He stopped on the threshold for a moment and looked down at the boy in his arms. When he came out his arms were empty.

He began to walk again, not back to the stables but toward the edge of the camp. Near the fence, he heard a shout. It sounded very far away. He kept walking with his head cocked toward the barbed wire, listening to a different voice. Finally, as he reached the fence, there was another shout and then a shot. Mr. Ishii fell on his back with his arms flung out and his face to the sky. For a moment, he imagined he could see the mountain, in spite of the darkness. It bent its crooked, headless neck and gave Mr. Ishii a deep, deferential bow.

TWENTY-ONE

WALKING to work, Haydon felt the tension in the camp. He had, as it turned out, spent two whole days in Roperville and talked every minute of the time: to gourmets and gardeners and pinochle players and movie fans—and dozens of others, individually and en masse. It felt more like two months. The blockade had been averted—for the time being. But something new and nasty, he thought, had sneaked into the camp in his absence. The queues looked straighter, the people stiffer. The cold felt solid; he could rap his knuckles on it. People walked with their heads down to avoid the wind and each other's eyes. The word *inu* was not only written but muttered often now, under the camp's cold, collective breath. FBI men stood in pairs on the streets and cluttered up the corridors of the administration building.

There was a stack of papers on his desk. He read two reports on an incident in Block B mess hall. One called it a protest, the other a riot. He read through the list of items confiscated in the camp-wide search the night before. It contained nothing more sinister than some Japanese poetry and a few knitting needles done up in a piece of wool. He felt angry, worried, sick. For once, he longed to talk to Morrissey, who was still in Washington. He would have to talk to Schweiker instead. He reached for the phone.

Schweiker arrived looking furious, his legs wide, trying to balance all that rage on his high heels. "You wanted to see me?" he snarled. He might have been dragged out of bed at three in the morning to tie Haydon's shoelaces.

"Sit down, Caspar," Haydon said genially. But this time he stayed seated behind his desk. "Sorry to interrupt your work, but I've been wondering if you know who ordered this last raid?"

"*I* did." A tiny worm of a smile wiggled at one corner of his mouth.

It was more of a smile than Haydon had ever seen there before. "Why?" he said.

"Looking for contraband, of course."

Such as a Whitman's Sampler and a collection of drama scripts, Haydon thought, and three knitting needles. "And who invited the FBI in?"

"*I* did. As acting director of this camp."

"Why?"

"*Why?*" Schweiker looked at him with contempt. "Didn't you read my report? Because of the riot, of course."

"What riot?"

"The riot," Schweiker said slowly, raising his voice like a man talking to a foreigner or a fool, "in Block B mess hall."

"That was hardly a riot."

"What would *you* call it? Thirty mean-looking Isseis, plus that ex-prisoner."

"What ex-prisoner?"

"That number-one troublemaker from Fort Washington."

"Dan Matsui? I understand he was responsible for *preventing* a riot."

"Don't you believe it. Been making trouble ever since he got here. Complaining about the food, making slanderous charges against the chef. Then he stages a riot in the mess hall along with that other number-one troublemaker who thinks he's special because he's got a white wife. Though she's really a Jew. Only way to prevent a riot is with one of these." He patted the gun on his hip. "Everyone on the staff should have one. It's the only thing everybody—including the Japs—understands."

Two more days as acting director, Haydon thought, and he would have armed the entire staff. For once, Schweiker was sitting upright with his jaw set and his arms crossed. As if he were still in command.

"But I think we've got them all now," Schweiker was saying.

"All what?"

"All the members of that little Axis plot."

"What little Axis plot?"

"Six of them meeting in the chief troublemaker's stall. After curfew, of course. In fact, they're *all* chief trouble-makers, all six of them."

"Which six?"

"Dan Matsui and Sam Curry and that judo instructor from the BQ." He pulled a list out of his pocket. "Someone named O'Donnell and a couple of Isseis named Tsuda and Watanabe. Nice collection, wouldn't you say?"

"I know those men," Haydon said. "What were they meeting about?"

"Well, it sure wasn't Bundles for Britain." He pulled another sheet out of his pocket. It was a petition to Haydon requesting the administration to (1) improve the quality and quantity of food in the camp; (2) look into the matter of back wages; (3) allow a Japanese-language section of the camp newspaper.

"But that's exactly what we've been trying to do for months," Haydon said. "Or, rather, to get the Authority to do. You know yourself these are problems we've discussed in staff meetings almost since the beginning. What's wrong with them?"

"Everything. One: meeting without a permit and without a policeman present."

"But those rules refer to *public* meetings. They hardly apply to six men sitting quietly in someone's stall."

"Two: speaking Japanese, which is strictly against regalations."

"Which also applies only to *public* meetings. It was not intended to dictate what people speak in the privacy of their own barracks."

"Three: circulating a petition. Which is strictly illegal."

"It is? Since when?"

"Yesterday afternoon."

"Then they could hardly have known about it, could they?"

"Ignorance of the law is no excuse."

"Besides, I'm not aware that they circulated any petition."

"But they were planning to, weren't they?"

"Look, we can hardly . . . "

"Never mind. We got them on other counts. Besides, who knows what they're *really* plotting. That petition was probably just a cover."

"A cover for what?"

"Some kinda sabotage, a' course. In case you haven't noticed, this place is boiling for trouble. First, the so-called investigation of the food. Then the mess hall riot. Then this secret meeting. It all adds up. And last night we got Judo for beating up a fellow inmate in the BQ."

"Which 'inmate'?" Haydon said sharply.

"And right after the raid they got an Issei for trying to escape. Heard enough?"

"Escape?" No one had ever tried to escape, not even Mr. Sato. There was no place to escape *to;* only wind and brush and freezing cold. If anyone did make it to town, he would be caught immediately—unless he managed to peel his face off first. "What do you mean 'got an Issei'?" Haydon said.

"Shot him, of course."

"Dead?"

"Dead."

"My God." He looked at Schweiker with loathing. "Who was it?"

"Name of Ishii. Never worked a day the whole time he was here. No, sir. Not a single day."

There was a long pause while Schweiker shifted his hat and fingered his gun. "Who was beaten up in the BQ?" Haydon asked.

"Another Issei, I suppose. They're always beating each other up down there."

"What happened to the others? The men at the meeting?"

"Locked up."

"Locked up?"

"You bet."

"Sam Curry and Dan Matsui and the judo instructor?"

"Like I said."

"My God!" Haydon said again. "They're the most popular men in the camp. You've arrested the leaders of *both* groups— the Nisei, who up to now have been our friends—*and* the Issei. You know what that will do, don't you? Unite the whole camp instantly—something we've never been able to do— *against* us."

"Yeah. Funny, that. I thought they were supposed to hate each other. So how come they're holding secret meetings together?" He stood up and leaned across the desk until the tip of his hat almost brushed Haydon's nose. "I'll tell you how come," he said. "Because they don't hate each other at all. Just pulling the wool over our eyes, that's what. So they could go on making their secret plans. It's *us* they hate. All of them. Like I been saying. Why wouldn't they? They got a nice little pro-Axis plot going on here, right under our nose. Planning to disrupt things, start a riot, organize an uprising. When it comes right down to it, like I been saying right along, a Jap is a Jap. Never mind if he's a Issei or a Nisei or a Kibei or any other kinda ei. They're all Japs, aren't they? And it's time we did something to stop them."

"Stop them from doing *what?*" Haydon's chair snapped

forward so that Schweiker had to step back or have his head bumped. Haydon stood up. "I'm going to see the prisoners," he said.

"You'll have a bit of a trip," Schweiker said. "They're in Roperville."

"Roperville? What the hell are they doing in Roperville?"

"Awaiting trial, of course."

"In *Roperville?* They're supposed to be *here*. This is entirely a matter for the Center. I want them returned *immediately*."

"I reckon it's out of your hands now," Schweiker said. And now the smile wiggled straight across his mouth.

Suddenly there was the sound of shouting outside. A huge crowd was marching toward the administration building.

"Holy smoke," Schweiker said, staring out the window. "We've got a full-scale revolt on our hands." He turned to Haydon with clenched fists. "I *told* you. This is what comes of mollycoddling prisoners."

This is what comes, Haydon thought, of unwarranted searches and seizures and false arrests.

"Get the Army in here," Schweiker demanded. "And fast."

The strikers were camped outside the administration building. They built fires and sang songs and played guitars and banjos and samisen and *shakuhachi*. Issei and Nisei and Kibei mingled indiscriminately around the flames. They installed a public address system and played American jazz and classical Japanese music. In between there were speeches: in English and Japanese, by Issei and Nisei, urging action or patience, retaliation or negotiation. The crowd listened to them all.

In spite of the cold, the demonstration was like a giant picnic. People seemed good-natured, cheerful, happier than ever before in the camp, warmed by the fires they had built and the bodies around them.

Inside, the administration building was silent, almost empty. Most of the Caucasians were afraid to come to work. Haydon had been out to speak to the crowd several times. A man used to addressing colleagues and conferences and classes, he had forced himself to face the cold and the mob and to shout feckless words into the wind; urging everyone to go home, to make a list of all articles confiscated during the raid. If they were not contraband, he promised, they would be returned.

But the crowd was not satisfied. The strike committee was firm. It wanted investigations into the deaths of Mr. Sato and Mr. Ishii, and all prisoners returned to the camp from Roperville immediately. Everyone knew that no Japanese would ever get a fair trial outside the camp. Besides, no charges had been made. In fact, it was not at all clear that any crimes had been committed, except for the murders of two old men, which were being completely ignored. As for the attack on Tony Takahashi, of which Judo was accused, he was already under arrest when the assault occurred. The petition, Haydon acknowledged, simply demanded, in reasonable and appropriate language, the legal rights the committee members had been taught. And regardless of who had actually attacked Tony, he, Haydon, had clearly provided the opportunity, had virtually engineered it.

Sitting at his desk, he stared at the fires standing up boldly in front of the administration building. Children ran constantly from one to another, connecting them, uniting them. Beyond lay the huge fleet of barracks, their tar paper flapping dejectedly. They looked deserted, decayed. The evacuees had moved out of the buildings provided by the Authority to gather around the fires they had built for themselves; warm, bright, lively flames swaying freely in the wind, soaring up to stroke the sky.

Haydon spent most of his time on the phone: to Roperville to talk to the mayor; to the state capital to talk to the governor; to Washington to contact Morrissey and to protest to the FBI and the WCCA and the WRA and the attorney general, demanding that the prisoners be returned. In between he went out to try to persuade the crowd to go home, to disband until the legal officer came back, until he, Haydon, could reach the proper authorities; trying to explain, once again, that his hands were tied. For the mayor was out of town and the governor refused to get involved and Morrissey was never in his hotel room. The authorities in Washington were adamant. "This is war," they said. "Those men are enemy aliens," they said. "They stay locked up," they said. "Right where they are." There was nothing Haydon could do. The crowd listened politely and stayed where it was too, right outside his office window.

The rest of the time, he was forced to contemplate Schweiker, sitting motionless in Haydon's office, staring at the crowd with his hat over his eyes, maintaining his precarious balance with his hands clenched in his pockets and his lips moving inaudibly: " 'The night is far spent, the day is at hand: let us therefore cast off the works of darkness, and let us put on the armor of light.' " Every now and then he roused himself to say in a strangled voice, "Call in the Army, for Pete's sake."

They sat there steadily for two days. They did not go home at all. By then they were the only people left in the building. Haydon moved merely between the crowd and the telephone. Schweiker moved nothing but his jaws. Had he been chewing the same piece of Dentyne for two days? Haydon wondered why he stayed. Haydon stayed because it was his job to be there and because there was no reason for him to go home. Jenni had phoned on the morning of the second day. She was going back to California until the strike was over. She was leaving a refrigerator full of roasts and casseroles and *gâteaux* and *glacés*. "But I don't suppose you'll come home to eat them," she said sadly. "You'll just stay down in that horrible camp the whole time. Like you always wanted to." She burst into tears.

Dr. Noguchi sat alone in his empty stall, in the empty stables. Everyone else had gone to join the strike. He felt abandoned. He found himself listening for, longing for, aching for sounds, any sounds: radios, records, guitars, even drums; for the sound of human voices screaming, cursing, coughing, belching. He would have been happy for *any* company: Mr. Watanabe, the grocer, Sam Curry, the toady, even Mr. Oshima, the gardener, shouting insults about Dr. Noguchi above the partitions.

Mrs. Noguchi still brought her husband food and drink from the mess hall, but she merely rushed in and out again. "You are not ashamed to be part of a mob?" Dr. Noguchi asked. "To take part in a riot?"

"We are not a mob and it is not a riot," she said. "It is an orderly protest in defense of our basic human rights. We must all stand together, firmly, steadily, loyally against injustice. Otherwise it *will* be a riot." She might have been talking through a megaphone.

She stood in front of him in her trousers. Had she forgotten she was wearing them? Or was she too busy to bother to change and too rushed to hide behind his back so he would not see them? Or, more likely, she no longer cared. He stared at her. Actually, she looked quite nice in trousers, he thought with surprise; not spreading in all directions like the others but slim and elegant as always. Her face and hands and feet still looked dainty and she still moved as smoothly and gracefully as she had in a kimono. But of course she looked perfectly appropriate in trousers, he thought, a woman who went out to work every day and brought back food and drink for her husband every day and was actively engaged in a strike.

She rushed out again, leaving him alone again, to drink tea again and wonder about his wife and children, who were willing to meet the world—whatever piece of it was offered. But he had locked himself out of the world and into an empty stable.

He thought of himself as he used to be, in a white jacket, leaning over submissive patients who opened and closed and emptied at his command. His fingers began to twitch. He thought of his white jacket hanging on the hook beneath his kimonos. It buttoned right up to the chin. Like Mr.

Oshima's turtleneck sweater, it might help him to hold up his head.

The crowd outside the administration building grew larger, the fires higher. A stage had been erected for movies and plays and skits and concerts of all kinds. There were strike songs—in Japanese and English—sung to American and Japanese instruments, and a bamboo flute with a subtle and melancholy tone that turned the sharp air tender. People joined the strike who knew nothing at all about the issues. They came for the entertainment, the liveliness, the comradeship, the fun; a release from the grim, gray routine of the camp. People who lived at opposite ends of the camp saw each other for the first time. People who lived side by side spoke to each other for the first time. Mrs. Noguchi, the elegant doctor's wife, and Mrs. Oshima, the gardener's wife, bowed and smiled and introduced their youngest daughters, who were exactly the same age. Mrs. Sawada's daughters-in-law appeared for the first time without Mrs. Sawada and without her barrel. They wore woolen slacks and pea jackets for the first time and smiled and spoke English for the first time to the young men around them, laughing and swinging their arms, free at last from the tyranny of Mrs. Sawada and those wide, awkward sleeves.

For Mrs. Sawada's claims had been recognized at last and she had been transferred to a luxury hotel in the East reserved for the internment of the rich and influential. She had left her barrel (she would have an enamel bathtub and constant hot water where she was going) and her daughters-in-law (there would be maids and cooks and porters where she was going) behind. The young women blessed the U.S. Government, danced happily around the campfires, and donated her barrel for a trash bin.

Inside, Haydon and Schweiker watched and waited. Haydon stared at the crowd outside his window and at Schweiker beside the door, that conscientious man who came early and stayed late and now refused to leave at all. He sat motionless in his black hat and black suit and black boots, a rigid man who moved nothing now—not even his jaws to chew his gum—only his lips to say words Haydon could not hear. Occasionally he raised his head and said in a strained voice as if now even his throat had become constricted, "Get the troops in here fast. Before it's too late." Otherwise he was merely a long, lean stripe of a man, still and silent as a shadow. Yet substantial enough, Haydon thought. The room was beginning to tilt beneath his weight.

Haydon found himself longing for Morrissey, round restless Morrissey, forever in motion: wiping his lenses, adjusting his glasses, his pink face flooded with feeling. Haydon needed Morrissey's legal advice, his moral passion, his very presence as a counterweight to that long, black, silent figure who sat, hour after hour, beside his office door.

Schweiker roused himself and said in a harsh dull whisper, barely moving his lips, "Better call in the Army. Crowd's getting big. Could get ugly any minute now."

Was he right? Haydon wondered, and remembered Tony lying immobilized in the hospital.

Haydon had gone to see him as soon as he heard the news. The hospital looked flimsier than ever without the crematorium. Haydon had finally had it moved to a site outside the camp. His only accomplishment, he thought grimly. But without it, the hospital seemed about to topple over in the wind.

Tony lay on his back completely wrapped in bandages. Even his face was covered except for five tiny holes. No one would ever know now that he was Japanese.

Nina was standing beside his bed. "Poor boy," she said. "If he dies, it will be murder. Not only by the men who beat him up but by the men who put him there, in that terrible BQ."

And the man who left him there, Haydon thought. "*Will* he die?" he said.

"I don't think we know yet. We'll send him to the hospital

in Roperville as soon as he can be moved. If it's not all filled up—with evacuees—by then." She glanced at her watch and hurried away.

Haydon sat down beside the bed and told Tony, at last, about his fellowship. But the figure on the bed remained absolutely still. Haydon could not tell whether the eyes behind the holes were open or closed, whether any breath came and went. He sat there for a long time, watching for a ripple beneath those bandages. But they remained still and stiff as concrete.

And now he was confronted by another study in concrete, he thought, observing Schweiker staring intently out the window, so rigid he might have been hypnotized by the crowd. Or was the crowd hypnotized by Schweiker? Haydon had the strange feeling that as long as Schweiker sat there, staring at them, the strikers would not, *could* not disperse. He had fixed them there by sheer force of will, in order to bring humiliation to Haydon and the Army into the camp. "Crowd's getting restless," Schweiker said.

Was it? Haydon wondered. Sooner or later, he knew, it would.

That evening he took a walk around the camp for the first time since the strike began. It looked different with the fires leaping up to singe the stars and turn the searchlights pale. Some people smiled at him, some stared, some glared, some turned their backs. Most were strangers, but he recognized quite a few whom he knew to be friendly, conscientious, cooperative; young Nisei who worked in the administration building like the Noguchis and the Oshimas and Yoshi Tsuda; older women who did the hard, heavy work of the camp like Mrs. Noguchi and Mrs. Oshima. He thought of others who, though supporters of the administration, would certainly be here with the strikers if they could: Sam Curry and Dan Matsui and O'Donnell and Tsuda and Watanabe. He had, he realized, quite a few friends in the camp. But they had all been driven to strike, those who were not locked up in prison. He was alone with Caspar Schweiker.

Nina Curry appeared suddenly out of the darkness. "What are they doing to Sam and the others?" she demanded.

"Just keeping them in jail. Which, I grant you, is bad enough."

"You've got to get them back," she said. "Get them back soon. Before something terrible happens." She was crying.

He thought of the cannery workers who had come back from Roperville with torn clothes and bloody heads. He thought of the blockade he had so narrowly averted. He could still see the faces of the crowd and hear the shouts of "Jap-lover" and the chants of "Out. Out. Get the dirty Japs out."

"I want them back as much as you do," he said. But she was gone.

He stood staring after her, thinking how much she had changed from the pale, scared girl he had first seen being "processed," with her back against the wall: like one of her line drawings grown into a full-scale oil painting. From living in this harsh place or living with Sam Curry or practicing her art? He, on the other hand, the wrong man in the wrong job with the wrong wife, had dwindled into a caricature. He had abandoned not only his profession but his identity. He was living with his head inside another man's hat. It had given him a stiff neck.

He walked on. And now he saw hostile faces and heard low muttering as he passed. There had been outbreaks in other camps, he reminded himself, when the crowd had hurled stones and bottles, destroyed property, even attacked policemen. And it occurred to him, again, how well the strike had been organized: not a spontaneous outburst at all, but a carefully planned strategy. Work crews kept the mess halls and the kitchens and the hospital and the fire department operating. Bells rang regularly, for meetings and announcements and changes in shifts. There was, obviously, no intention of destroying property or causing bloodshed or giving aid and comfort to the enemy. Yet someone, he reminded himself, had beaten poor little Tony—possibly to death.

TWENTY-TWO

THE demonstration stayed outside and Schweiker and Haydon stayed inside. Haydon began to feel that he was imprisoned, not by the crowd but by that still, black shape across the room; that his only hope of escape was to be rescued by the strikers. Otherwise he would be trapped here until the whole camp was moved to permanent quarters—with a new director.

For he would not be the director again. He would go, too, but as a social psychologist this time, to *study* evacuees—*and* their jailers—not to govern them. He would be his own man again, doing his own work again, in his own way again, with no Schweiker to cast a permanent shadow across his office floor. And he would live alone again, working where and when he pleased, with a desk in every room in the house if he pleased, eating as little as he pleased. Jenni, he was certain, would never come back. "You'll just stay down in that horrible camp the whole time. Like you always wanted to," she had said. When, he wondered, had she realized that?

Across the room, Schweiker stirred. "What are you waiting for?" His voice sounded bent and rusty. "That crowd could turn nasty any minute. And then it'll be too late. Because there won't be any warning. They're sly, sneaky bastards. You won't know what they're gonna do till you feel that bullet in your back. You don't call the Army in now, you're gonna have one helluva massacre on your hands."

Haydon noted the swear word with satisfaction. "And we'll certainly have a massacre if I do," he said. The soldiers sent to guard the camps were young, unseasoned, nervous. They had killed two harmless, innocent people already. Yet staring at Schweiker, Haydon had visions of evacuees running wild, shouting, looting, burning, hurling rocks, perhaps even attacking the staff and their families just outside the gate. He was responsible for them too.

Outside, the crowd was singing. Inside, Haydon was stifling, as if the two men had used up all the air. He might have to call the troops in just to keep from suffocating. Actually, though he could not decide to call them in—his instincts were all against that—he could not decide *not* to call them in, either. The only time in his life when he had followed his instincts wholeheartedly, he had married Jenni. If he called in the troops, he risked violence *against* the evacuees. If he didn't call them in, he risked violence *by* them. He would be a bloody fascist on the one hand and a bloody fool on the other. He swiveled his chair restlessly right and left, back and forth. Across the room Schweiker sat as still and rigid as a stone. Haydon could almost feel his desk and the chair beneath him begin to slide in Schweiker's direction.

He longed for Morrissey to come back, to tilt the room the other way, bringing it into balance, allowing Haydon to take his usual stance between them. But this time, he realized, there was no middle ground. This time no compromise was possible. This time, he must choose between two extremes.

This time there were no objective data on which to base a decision and nothing to help predict the outcome either way. This time he could not invoke caution or patience or careful deliberation. Worst of all, this time to do nothing was an act in itself.

He leaned back in his chair as usual, but could achieve no new perspective. And he could not overcome that tilt in the floor.

Mr. Oshima was alone with his toothache. The only human being left in the stable, he thought, abandoned by his family like an old plough not worth the fixing. For the last two nights he had slept with nightmares. The first night he dreamed of horses' hooves outside his stall. Last night the hooves had come closer, had pounded up the stable steps. Tonight, he was certain, they would race right in and trample him to death—displaced horses come back to claim their homes again now that all the people were gone. All but Mr. Oshima.

His wife came regularly to bring him food but refused to stay to hear his complaints and accusations. He missed her. She had fed him and warmed him and listened to him. No one else had bothered. She had even spoken to him when he allowed it. His children had said nothing but "Hi, Pop" and "Bye, Pop" on their way in and out. Only Jack, his oldest child and first son, had continued to talk to him in Japanese; until the night he realized that no words in any language could reach his father—or protect his mother. Mr. Oshima had not seen him since and his name was never mentioned in the stall. Where was he? In the camp jail? In Fort Washington? Had he been shipped out to work on some farm hundreds of miles away with miserable pay and miserable conditions? The *hakujin,* he knew, were always trying to get the evacuees to do their dirty work, outside as well as inside the camp. Had Jack signed up? If so, would it be for the duration? Had he been attacked like the sugar beet workers, possibly even murdered? Mr. Oshima's tooth throbbed painfully.

Soon he heard sounds, the sounds of small, subtle movements nearby. He was not completely alone. Someone else was in the stable, someone to play *goh* with and drink *sake* with and talk to; someone who would help him forget the pain in his tooth and keep the horses away.

It was someone close by: Sam Curry or Mr. Watanabe or one of the Tsudas three stalls down. Mr. Oshima assumed it was a man. The women were all sheep, like his wife. They would follow anyone. Only a man would have had the courage and sense to resist the mob, to stay home in silence and dignity. He listened again. He was proud of his sharp ears that had once been able to hear the clouds settling on the hills and the chrysanthemums turning in the wind. Now he heard the swish of a kimono and the shuffle of sandals and the sound of two hands rubbing, rubbing, rubbing each other. His heart sank and the pain in his tooth grew worse. It was Noguchi, hero of the stable because he had, for a short time, been locked up in Fort Washington; an elegant man, a doctor who sat in his stall all day in silk kimonos, rubbing his soft white hands, rubbing away the very idea of Mr. Oshima, whose palms were hard and grubby and smelled of earth.

Actually, Mr. Oshima reminded himself, Noguchi was not a real doctor at all, only a dentist, and now not even that; merely a useless old snob whose hair was too long and who had been deserted by his family, too. If the horses ever came, they would gallop right over him as well. Under those hooves, the gardener and the "doctor" would be on a level, side by side in the dust.

His tooth was throbbing again. Noguchi was a dentist, he reminded himself; a dentist who needed a haircut. And he, Oshima, was a barber with a toothache.

He got up slowly, washed his hands, put on a clean shirt and took the barber's shears his wife kept hidden in a pair of long johns. For this, he told himself reassuringly, would be a strictly professional call.

* * *

By the third day, the weather had grown colder. The fires outside the administration building took on a different shape, became thin and pinched and pointed as icicles. The temper of the crowd became thinner too. People stamped their feet, stamping down the cold and their own impatience. The shape of the crowd changed also. Instead of a large, cheerful, undefined mass, it was breaking into two sharply edged groups: the Issei here, the Nisei there; Japanese spoken here, English there, as if the same fires could no longer warm both. The continuous blare from the loudspeakers became maddening as each group tried to drown out the other. Drawings of dogs appeared, on barracks, on the police station, above some of the fires. Banners with red numbers arranged on a white background so as to look, from a distance, like the Japanese flag, were flown in some places, American flags in others. The flags and the dogs were torn down and raised again. Insults were hurled back and forth, sometimes accompanied by stones.

Inside, the two men went on watching. Schweiker sat still as always, a long dark stain that seemed to Haydon to be spreading closer and closer.

"Crowd's getting nastier," Schweiker said.

"Why not go home, Caspar?" Haydon said. Schweiker's devotion surprised and impressed him even while it irritated him. "There's no need for you to stay."

"Except to make sure you don't get us killed. Only I don't see how the hell I'm gonna be able to stop it."

Haydon smiled slightly. Schweiker's language was definitely deteriorating. "All the more reason for you to get out," he said.

Schweiker turned his head from the window. "You crazy? How'm I gonna get out with that mob planted there like they are? They're blocking the whole damned parking lot."

Which is the real reason he's been sitting here immobilized for three days, Haydon thought. He's literally scared stiff. "I'll get some of the guards to escort you," he said.

"No thanks. I don't want some of the guards. I'm staying right here until the whole complete entire force comes in and breaks up that mob."

"You may have a long wait," Haydon said.

The phone rang. It was the mayor of Roperville, just returned from a conference. He was sending the prisoners back. "I told Washington I don't want a multiple lynching on my hands," he said.

"Sanity at last," Haydon said.

"Appeasement again," Schweiker said.

But the crowd refused to leave. They had had too many broken promises, Ray Noguchi, chairman of the strike committee, said. They would stay where they were until all the prisoners were back.

They waited in silence. But when the van from Roperville arrived, Judo and Dan were not there. A great howl went up, not an Issei howl or a Nisei howl but a united, full-blown bellow of disappointment and frustration and rage.

Haydon reached for the phone. Judo, he learned, had been sent to the hospital with strange, unidentified sores all over his body. He would be returned as soon as it was certain that he was not contagious. Dan Matsui had been sent, by order of the FBI, to a special camp for further investigation. His family had been allowed to go with him. Haydon hung up in a rage.

Suddenly he was aware of shouts outside, loud, angry, threatening shouts. The strikers had finally become an angry mob, a mob that would not take kindly to the relocation of the Matsuis or even believe in the ultimate return of Judo. We've united them again—against us, Haydon thought. There was the sound of a stone hitting the building.

Schweiker bolted from his chair. Haydon could feel the whole room lurch with him. "For God's sake," Schweiker shouted, "call in the Army."

He had blasphemed at last, Haydon noted, but he did not move.

Schweiker strode to the desk. "You some kinda traitor? Well, I'm not *asking* you anymore. I'm *ordering* you. Get on that phone, damn you, and get the Army in here. *Quick*." He was standing over Haydon with his gun in his hand, pointed straight into Haydon's face.

Haydon stared at him. Morrissey was right, he thought calmly. "Try to keep Schweiker muzzled," he had said. But Haydon had merely tried to keep him appeased.

"You gonna call them or not?" Schweiker said, leaning closer, so close he might have been trying to get Haydon's head inside his hat. Close up, his face looked small, too small for such a big man, with his tiny eyes crowded up against his nose and his mouth shriveled up in dead center to avoid falling off. Close up, Haydon could see the little man inside looking out, looking scared. He was terrified, Haydon realized, and trying to spread his fear, like his hat, over Haydon. Haydon, on the other hand, felt remarkably calm.

There was another long shout from outside. Another stone hit the building. "Well?" Schweiker said, moving the gun closer. It was almost resting on Haydon's nose.

Haydon tilted back in his chair, away from Schweiker's hat and Schweiker's gun and Schweiker's breath in his face. "No," he said quietly. "I am *not* going to call in the Army." He had decided at last.

"Then get the hell away from that phone, damn you, and *I'll* call them."

He was actually becoming quite profane, Haydon thought. He gave another tilt to his chair, blocking the phone completely. "Oh, no you won't," he said. "That order has to come from *me*."

"I'll tell them you're down with a bad case of fever. *Yellow* fever. A double dose. Too damned scared of the Japs. And too damned fond of them."

Haydon, enjoying the profanity, did not move. The shouting outside settled down to a steady chant.

"Jesus Christ!" Schweiker shouted. "That's the sound they

make before they attack." He leaned forward again, bringing the gun close to Haydon's face again.

"Oh no," Haydon said. "They're 'sly, sneaky bastards.' You said so yourself. 'You won't know what they're gonna do till you feel that bullet in your back.' Only they haven't got any bullets. *You're* the only one with a gun. And there's no reason to call in the Army because so far there hasn't been a single act of violence. Unless, of course"—he looked pointedly at the gun in his face—"*you* commit one."

He snapped his chair back to its upright position and stood up, forcing Schweiker to retreat. To his surprise, he was eye to eye with Schweiker. He had never stood up to Schweiker before. Without his boots and his hat, Haydon thought, Schweiker would actually be the shorter of the two. "If I do call the soldiers in," Haydon went on, "it will be to have you arrested for carrying a gun. 'No weapons shall be worn by any civilian personnel except by explicit permission of the Director.' Article Five, Section One. That's regulation, that is. A lot more important than who uses which latrine. A regulation you've been breaking since the day you arrived. I don't remember ever giving you permission. I don't remember your ever even asking for it."

Outside, the shouting had stopped. A single voice came over the loudspeaker, a calm reasonable voice; the voice of Sam Curry or Ray Noguchi or O'Donnell. Actually, Haydon realized, there were many who might speak just like that, telling the strikers to go home, they had won their point. Now it was up to the director to negotiate. A mob like this would only frighten the Authority, would make them angrier and tougher and the director's job more difficult. After all, it was not Haydon who had ordered the raid and called in the FBI and allowed the prisoners to be transferred.

"That's right," someone shouted. "He wasn't even here."

"It was the chief executive officer."

"Yeah, Chief Executioner Schweiker."

"*He* ordered the raid."

"*He* called in the FBI."

"*He* sent the prisoners to Roperville."

"Right! It was Schweiker."

"Yeah, that's right. Schweiker."

Shouts of "Schweiker!" came from different parts of the crowd. Soon it was taken up by everyone and chanted in unison: "Schweiker, Schweiker, Schweiker."

"Now will you, for Christ sake, call in the Army, you fuckin' bastard?" Schweiker shouted. "Or are you waiting to see me lynched first? Well, I'm not waiting. Get away from that phone."

"You want to watch your language," Haydon said quietly. "They're not going to lynch you. *You're* the one with the gun, remember. The *only* one."

"You *crazy?* They could do it with their bare hands. So move, damn you. Move!" He was sweating heavily now.

"Feeling warm, Caspar?" Haydon said. "Why not take off that heavy hat and give your brains a chance to cool?" He reached out to remove it for him.

"Oh, no you don't, you lousy bastard." Schweiker stiffened and clutched his gun. "You keep your fuckin' hands off me." There was a sudden explosion and Haydon was on the floor, with Schweiker staring down at him.

Haydon lay on his back and stared up. Schweiker looked enormous, so tall Haydon could not see the end of him, could only guess where his head was. If, indeed, he had a head, which Haydon doubted. For Schweiker was, after all, a practical man and would never carry around anything he couldn't use. He had, in the end, even used his gun. And then Haydon remembered Schweiker's hat. Of course he had a head. He needed it for his hat.

"Okay, Caspar," he whispered. "You win. *Now* you can call in the troops. *Now* we have a perfectly valid reason." He smiled slightly at that black blob floating far above him. Too bad he hadn't been able to take off Schweiker's hat. He had, he realized, never seen Schweiker's hair. Maybe he didn't have any. Maybe that was why he wore that hat all the time. Maybe *that* was the trouble with Schweiker. He was totally bald. I must tell Morrissey, Haydon thought.

He could hear the voice outside still going on, that smooth quiet voice, the voice of reason, reminding the crowd that it could disband now. They could trust the director, who had acted in good faith throughout. He had prevented the Roperville blockade, he had brought the prisoners back, and, above all, he had not called in the Army.

Haydon, listening, smiled again, for he knew he had done the right thing for the wrong reason. He had refused to call in the Army not so much out of principle but out of passion— his loathing for Schweiker. But perhaps this time his instincts had been right. And he had indeed done all those other things the voice mentioned. He had even—here his smile twitched a bit—reunited the Currys. Yes, he thought, as he felt a fierce throbbing in his side, he had done more than merely move that crematorium. He had actually, for a little while, been the director. He had even reduced Schweiker, a scared, sweating, *swearing* Schweiker, to life size. He wished Morrissey had been there. He smiled very slightly for the last time and closed his eyes.

Morrissey, back from Washington at last, knocked on the door. When he received no answer, he opened it anyway and saw Haydon stretched out on the floor beside his desk. He hardly noticed Schweiker with his chair pulled up close to the window, staring out as usual. But now he was not slumped down as usual, with his hands in his pockets as usual. Now he was sitting up straight, holding his gun out in front of him with both hands. He sat there rigidly with his gun pointed at that dark empty space outside the window. Only his lips moved, steadily, soundlessly: " 'For which things' sake the wrath of God cometh upon the children of disobedience.' "

On their last day at Mt. Hope, Sam and Nina went to say good-bye to Ken-chan at St. Ursula's. They had been visiting him ever since he was displaced from his grandfather's grip. Stepping across the threshold of a Catholic orphanage was like stepping back into childhood, Nina thought, except that now she and Sam were stepping into it together.

Ken-chan, standing up surrounded by other children, looked much bigger. Released from Mr. Ishii's arms, he looked healthier. He might have been my son, Sam thought, reliving my life in a Catholic orphanage. But Sam, at least, had had parents to go home to at the end of the week. Ken-chan had no one.

When they left, Sam looked back and saw the boy standing all alone in the empty doorway, a tiny figure looking out on a world which, for him, was empty too. Like the small boy in Nina's drawings, Sam thought. Someday he would give that look and the small boy behind it a permanent shape to set beside the monumental figures he would carve again: Ken-chan surrounded by Samson and Joseph and Hecuba and Ruth. But simply to turn the boy into stone was hardly enough. He wanted to do more, to turn the boy into his own son. He turned to Nina. "Let's adopt Ken-chan," he said.

"Oh, Sam, could we?" She was beaming. But in a moment the light had faded. She remembered little Miko at Mt. Hope, forever sick and confused and bored and frightened, with her father constantly disappearing. Conditions at Lake Emerald would be even worse, and Ken-chan's new father was about to disappear too. For the Army had decided that it wanted the Nisei after all, wanted them for the Italian campaign, where casualties were unusually high. All young Nisei were expected to enlist, to move—in one giant step—from concentration camp to army camp; and Sam was prepared to make the jump.

"You're going to fight for your Caucasian jailers?" she had said angrily. "You're going to be a good citizen, a loyal American, an idiotically cooperative evacuee?"

"No," he had said quietly. "I'm going to fight Nazis."

Ken-chan would not have a father again for a long time,

she thought, taking Sam's hand. Indeed, might never. "Let's leave Ken-chan with the nuns for now," she said. "It will be better for him there and the nuns will take good care of him. And as soon as the war is over, we'll go and get him." Or if necessary, she thought, *I* will get him, in a taxi—like the Fräuleins.

At least they were *Japanese* nuns, Sam thought, who would allow Ken-chan to keep his Japanese name and his Japanese tongue and cultivate a taste for shadows.

They walked on, hand in hand, across the camp for the last time, past the barbed-wire fence and the ghosts of Mr. Sato and Mr. Ishii; past the administration building and the memory of Mr. Haydon. A decent, even kind, man, Nina thought, in charge of a concentration camp; another displaced person—in a tweed jacket. Yet he had turned Nina into an Authorized Artist and brought Sam safely home from Roperville. She was sorry she had never been able to thank him for that. A good man and a good director, she thought, even if he did not know about the coffee in the mess halls. Sam had been right after all.

Tomorrow they would all be gone. Tomorrow there would be only Mt. Hope, its hole like a single eye glaring down at the deserted camp with its empty barracks and empty towers and the tar paper flapping in the wind; until the Army moved in and reclaimed the site as its own. Then the dry land would be watered, and solid, comfortable buildings would rise like a new growth. Even the climate would change, with steam heat in winter and air-conditioning in summer. Eventually the mountain itself might crumble, might lay its broken neck in the lap of the land at last.

There would be nothing left at all of the Mt. Hope Assembly Center except in the mind: a hard, undigested lump to be skirted by day and bumped by night. It would be, for decades, a silent memory, unmentioned by Caucasians and Japanese alike, buried in the depths of the past; as the Center itself had been buried in the depths of the country.